THE IMP OF EYE

Kristin Gleeson
and
Moonyeen Blakey

An Tig Beag Press

Published by An Tig Beag Press

Other works by Kristin Gleeson:
Celtic Knot Series
Along the Far Shores
Raven Brought the Light
Selkie Dreams

Non Fiction
Anahareo: A Wilderness Spirit

Other Works by Moonyeen Blakey:
The Assassin's Wife

Sign up to my mailing list and get a
FREE novella
www.kristingleeson.com.

ISBN: 978-0-9931567-5-5

To Moon, with love
1945-2014

.

CHAPTER ONE
Magotscroft, Eye Near Westminster, June 1440
BARNABAS

Mistress Jourdemayne fetches me such a cuff round the head, I almost bites me tongue in two.

'You little imp. Don't try to cheat me again, Barnabas,' she says, kicking the sticks I've collected for the fire. 'I know what the fishmonger asks for broiled carp.'

'It was only a groat's worth of salt herring,' I says. I sits, muttering by the hearth, nursing a bruised knee from the stumble I've taken against the hearth fender.

'Don't I feed you well enough, Master Barnabas?' she asks.

She spits out the words and I shrinks from her shadow as she looms over me. Her hands is on her hips and her feet are planted firm-like. She's in a temper, her hair all sticking out and her face screwed up, but there's still somefink powerful about her.

'Well, have you lost your tongue? Isn't the food here good enough for your fine palate, sir?'

'Aye.' Me answer's low and sulky. 'It weren't much that I took.' I hate being caught out in false dealing.

'A groat's a groat, Barnabas,' she says. Her voice's as hard as a nail. 'So tonight you'll eat nothing at my expense.'

I'm just about to give her a cheeky gobful, when we both hears the sound of horses outside. Then there's shouting and running feet and a fierce knocking at the door. When the kitchen door swings open Petronille, the Flemish lass, appears, pink-faced and all her words tumbling out wrong.

'A lady is comen—with horses, Mistress Jourdemayne, for to see!'

Before I draws me bref, Mistress Jourdemayne has me by me arm and yanks me round, and next moment she's billowing outside into the courtyard to greet the visitors. A horse-drawn litter's arrived wiv servants dressed fine.

'Mistress Marjory Jourdemayne?' asks one of 'em.

Me mistress sinks so low she nearly sits on the ground, all charm and smiles. She greets the woman. 'Lady Stourton.'

I stands to attention like a man-at-arms, watching a lad not much bigger than meself hand down a portly woman in a purple velvet gown dripping wiv gems. I makes a bow likes to a duchess as the heavy woman wheezes and gasps her way to us.

'Welcome, Lady Stourton, welcome,' says Mistress Jourdemayne. 'Let's go into the house at once before you catch a chill. My home is yours.'

What a load of piffle, I finks, following the procession. The fat woman totters on me mistress's arm. Mistress Jordemayne jabbers about the weather and women's ailments, while the servant boy follows so close to his mistress he near steps on her gown. The rest of 'em pick their way through the mud and stones, muttering oaths about the muck and the east wind what's blowing up their arses.

Petronille gawps at the men as they enter and leans forward just enough to give 'em a gander at her paps. Cook takes over and shows the servants into the hot kitchen while Mistress Jourdemayne guides the fat lady into the parlour. She flicks her head for me to follow, and I knows by the glint in her eye, it ain't sensible to disobey. I don't wants to go. I know what'll happen and I'd rather not. Still, I follows 'em into the room, muttering to meself. The lady manages to heave herself onto the settle and I takes me usual place behind it, so me mistress can see me, but the lady can't. Petronille carries in a tray of spiced wine and sweetmeats and gives me a big wink as she leaves.

Me mistress disappears for a moment to fetch the black box from the press in the stillroom what she keeps locked. She sets it down on a small table between her and her guest. It's a showstone what's in the box and all the fine ladies and gentlemen pay her good money to look into it. The joke is she can't see nofink. But you'd never know. The fat lady's mouth goes all of a quiver as the black velvet's drawn off and the ball shaped crystal emerges. In the candle-light it glitters and flashes sparks what bring gasps from the on-lookers. It's really somefink, though it gives me frights so bad sometimes I shakes. Today I feels in me bones is gonna be one those times.

'Now, Lady Stourton, you must clear your mind of everything except your question.' Me mistress' voice goes all deep and dark like, and her words fancier than usual. 'That way, we'll be able to connect to the spirits, and seek their advice.'

She nods to me and I closes the shutters on the windows and snuffs out all the candles save one, so's the chamber's as gloomy as a grave-yard. The fat lady gasps and begins to wheeze like a broken-winded horse. But eventually she folds her sausage fingers and shuts her eyes.

'You think on your question while I prepare the stone.' She nods to me again. I shakes me head. I won't do it. She gives a frown so dark and full of meaning I can't mistake it. I drags meself over and takes up the silk cloth next to the showstone and make like I'm polishing it, but really I'm looking in it, deep down searching for pictures. Sometimes they don't come at all, but this time I barely blinks me eyes and one comes. It ain't good. I can feel the shaking coming all over me again. I frowns and place the showstone back on its little cushion, like it's a hot ember, and step back behind the settle. Me mistress checks the lady who still has her eyes tightly closed and then looks to me. I shakes me head and puts me hands about me throat and sticks out me eyes and tongue like I'm strangling. She frowns and nods. I stands back then and steadies meself while me mistress takes over the show. She'll have plenty to work with, now. I've already told me mistress all that I found out about the Stourton lady from the tongue wagglers at *The Turk's Head* after the last time the lady came.

'You may open your eyes, Lady Stourton.' Me mistress leans forward and lays her hands on the showstone. She rubs it and mutters somefink under her bref. It could be a receipt for a pork pie for all the fat lady knows. A hum starts up and it turns into a little whining noise. I tries not to laugh.

'We are in luck, Lady Stourton. The spirits are with us today.' She does that whiny hum again and waves her hands a little. 'It's clearing, clearing. Yes, now I can see something.'

The fat lady leans forward. Her nose nearly hits the showstone. 'What, what is it?'

'Oh, my lady!' Me mistress looks up and stares at her all wide-eyed and innocent. 'I see a scroll and the seal on it is that of the Royal House of Lancaster! Does Sir John expect a royal appointment, my lady?'

'He has hopes, Mistress Jourdemayne,' the fat lady says. She wheezes deeply, all excited.

Me mistress gives her a wide smile and nods. 'In three months your husband will have the king's favour. I see a purse filled with gold. I see servants unfolding tapestries and carrying in furniture. A tall house and an orchard filled with fruit trees—'She looks back down at the showstone waving her hands over it slowly. 'Hmm. Yes….. something's changing here.'

'What is it, Mistress Jourdemayne?' The fat lady's voice comes out in a squeak what sets her jowls quivering.

'It's—it's like a candle being snuffed out.' She shakes her head, gives a huge sigh. 'Is your husband a gambling man, Lady Stourton?' The purple velvet bosom's heaving. Me mistress puts her hand on the lady's arm. 'Caution would be more prudent at this time,' she says. 'Especially at court. The King can give favours one moment and then take them away the next.' She pauses, her face all solemn. 'Perhaps your husband should reconsider going to court or he might get more than he bargained for.' She says this quietly.

'What are you telling me, Mistress Jourdemayne?' Her voice is high. She ain't happy.

'Ah, Lady Stourton, I cannot change what the spirits tell me. I'm merely advising you to apply caution. You have come here for advice and all I can tell you is that there are dangerous waters ahead and my abilities are giving you the boat with which to manage these waters.'

The fat lady sits back, gulps down her wine and finks about what's been said. I can't say me mistress ain't good at what she does. She is good. Real good. She nods at me and I takes off out the door to tell Petronille to fetch more wine. I won't return. I knows better than to go back in there, but the mistress'll be looking for me soon enough. I makes me escape and runs like the devil through the rowdy kitchen where Cook's cavorting among a group of tipsy servants playing knuckle-bones, and bursts through the door into the yard. Nick is waiting there and grabs me by the arm.

'Whoa there, Barney-boy!' In the greying shadows, Nick's eyes spark like flint. 'Just where do you think you're going?' Nick can be a nasty piece of work. He works in the stable and watches me every move, like I'm going to do somefink personal against him. He don't like that me mistress lets me do fings, but he don't dare bully too much. Just enough so's he feels he's in charge.

'I'm off on an errand. Mistress said Father Thomas needs me.'

Nick scowls down at me. He don't know whether it's a lie or not, so he shoves me down to the ground. Before he can say another word I scrambles up and takes off down the road.

∾

I knows where I'll find a welcome. Off down to the river to me mate Tom, the wherry boatman. We's been mates for a long time and I loves it there with him on the river. Sometimes he lets me row when he's got no people on board. Then I feel like I can go anywhere. Even Spain,

Jerusalem and them places where they had the crusades long ago.

Me luck's wif me. Tom is there in his wherry just about to take off wif two men bound downriver. 'Barney-boy! You're late.'

I'm small and quick, so I jumps onto the boat as light as a feather. I'm good at this and Tom knows it and grins. We shove each other like pals do and I settle in the back. I ain't sposed to be here wifout paying, like, but since we's mates he says it's okay as long as I pretends I'm his boy.

The water in the boat's bottom seeps into me clogs but it don't bother me. Some say the river's stink could stun an ox when it's summer time, but I loves it. I look out to the river and imagine meself on a fine big ship, sailing to places where there's so much sand you can't see nofink else and you feel warm all the time. The tide is with us, so the run is quick, and before you know it I'm at Queenhithe docks helping the two fine gentlemun out.

I decides to stay a while at the docks. Besides the barges, it's full of cayers, cogs and caravels what have come from all over. It's the place to see different kinds of people, like sailors with gold earrings and dark skin and strange clothes, hoisting cargo, coiling up the ropes and shouting all sorts. I tries to talk to 'em. Most times they only speak their own strange lingo, but I do get lucky and find some what can understand me. And that's the best.

Today I'm not so lucky, and I goes wondering for a while, just taking in the sights before I hear a shout and a stout hand grabs me collar. Father Thomas.

'I thought I might find you here, you young cur,' he says with a growl. 'Why didn't you come by yesterday as I instructed?' He starts dragging me along the streets and it's no secret to me where we're heading. His own church,

St Stephen's in Walbrook. Nearly thirteen years ago some jade dumped me in a dung heap on St Barnabas Day and that's where this man found me. Thomas Southwell, Canon of St Stephen's Chapel in the palace of Westminster and rector of St Stephen's Walbrook. And a physician too. All them titles don't satisfy his need for more, though.

We reach the church and make our way to his rooms in the building beside it. After a word to his man we go into his study and he locks the door. Next door is the room I used to sit with the other foundlings and learn me writing, reading and Latin. I loved it, but that learning is little use to me now. There ain't no escaping Father Thomas and what he wants.

A moment later there's a knock on the door and one of his servants brings in two steaming trenchers and sets it on the small table.

'Hungry, Barnabas?' he asks.

Me mouth waters. I sits down on the stool. The steam makes me nose run and I wipes it wif my sleeve. I can see the bone and gristle bobbing about on the surface. Boiled onion and some kind of greenery.

'Eat up, we've much to do,' Father Thomas says.

I takes up the horn spoon and slurp up the contents. I can't say I ain't hungry because ain't I always? Wishing there was more, I lick the last drops on the spoon. I look up, and see his pale eyes watching me.

'I need you to scry for me, Barnabas.'

I groan inwardly. Seeing spirits is what got me in a bother in the first place, and why Margery Jourdemayne took me on in her household. I'd as lief be a gong-farmer's servant than work as a scryer. Never had no choice, though. Once Father Thomas found I could see spirits, he taught me the rest. Conjuring's a burning offence, though. I've smelt them fires at Smithfield in me dreams and actually saw a burning once and I can't forget it. It's the smell of cooking flesh what gets to you, and then there's the screaming. That's another matter.

'I've water ready in the bowl,' says Father Thomas.

I wipes me mouth on the grease-stiff cuff of me sleeve and gives him a sullen nod.

The bowl's heavy; black wiv heat and age. I reckon someone used to cook in it, but Father Thomas keeps it just for scrying now. I watches the liquid wobble against the sides and settle, and then I bends me mind to the task. The water's smooth like the glass Mistress Jourdemayne keeps in her chamber. Her husband bought it as a gift, so she can admire herself. She caught me looking in it once and boxed me ears.

Fierce now, I shut out everyfink else and gets still-like and the quiet settles on me like a warm cloak. It's a feeling I likes and I just let it stay there for a bit before I looks and stares at the inky liquid. In a wink me mind kind of opens up inside, so I'm looking and not looking into the water, if you know what I mean. It's like I see through it and out into a different land. I like that.

A figure pops up and hobbles across me mind's eye.

'It's Limpin' Sam,' I says out loud. 'He's got a partridge under his arm.'

I've seen this spirit before. He dresses in rags like a beggar, and his hands is blue wiv cold, but he has the merriest face. His eyes is the colour of blackbird's eggs, and he's a snub nose, dimples in his cheeks and a wide, curving mouth. Sometimes he sings, sweet as a chorister, but he don't speak. He brings me fings instead. I'm supposed to work out what they mean. I don't know who he is or was, but he likes me and he brings me stuff. This night it's a bird.

'It's a fat partridge,' I says. Father Thomas' bref warms me cheek as he leans in to hear. 'Sign of plenty, I reckon. Someone's got somefink good coming his way.'

'Ah!' Father Thomas sighs wiv satisfaction.

'He's showing me a cooking pot over a fire, now.' I watches Limpin' Sam pointing to the bird and then sticking it whole into the bubbling water, feathers and all.

Wiv a squeal of surprise I jerk back.

'What is it?' asks the priest.

'Forget what I said before. I got it wrong. There's some fellow wiv fine feathers…wealthy, fat, thinks well of hisself…struts about and imagines he's doing real well, but he should take care he don't get into hot water. He ain't very bright, by the look of it. He's in for a rare shock. Somebody's out to teach him a lesson. If you know him, Father, you should warn him to beware them what he's offended.'

'Enough!' The priest's voice is harsh now. He ain't pleased wiv this information. 'Summon Bethor, Barnabas. I want to be sure.'

But I don't like this at all. Bethor's a different kettle of fish from Limpin' Sam. He's a mighty spirit what can grant men priceless treasure, help them create miraculous medicines or be powerful likes a lord or somefink. It's a chancy fing calling these spirits. They doesn't like being told. Father Thomas says Bethor's a good angel and won't harm me. But Bethor comes in a great whirling storm and his face is bright as fire. I'd rather let them as wants to come to me, like Limpin' Sam, than getting a proud angel to do me bidding. But I don't argue.

I says the words what Father Thomas's taught me so carefully, and wait, feeling me skin prickle and hearing the air rushing in me ears. The ritual has to be done right, he says, though I don't understand half the words I have to use. The priest prompts me now and then.

'Speak.'

It's always a shock when Bethor's voice roars in me head and dazzles me eyes with the blaze of his appearance. Flames leap like sun-rays round his head. The light's so blinding I can't make out his features.

'What shall I ask him to do?'

The priest's fingers is talons on me arm and his breath grows moist against me ear. 'Tell him to bring us wealthy patrons,' he whispers.

Me mistress needs customers, he means, and she'll pay him a portion of what she makes from them. I nod anyway and do as I'm bid.

I feels Bethor's desire to be free. He strains against me will and when I tell him what he must do, I knows he thinks we're greedy bastards and he'll make us pay. I lets him know in me thoughts like, not to blame me and that like him, I'm only obeying orders. He laughs. I let him go and he's gone in a whoosh of burning flames.

'What did he say?' Father Thomas grips me arm tight.

'He'll do it.' I says the words to send off the spirit what he taught me then, even though the spirit's already gone.

'Good boy.' Father Thomas pats me shoulder.

But I'm seeing somefink else—a woman in the black water of the scrying bowl, and I can't take me eyes off her. She's dressed in a white linen shift and carrying a heavy candle. The flame of it flickers dangerously and the hot wax drips on cobblestones by her naked feet. What does it mean?

'Enough, boy!'

The priest is shaking me back into consciousness. I smells the draughty chapel and musty old robes, and someone's hammering on the chapel door.

'Who's there?'

Father Thomas is on his feet and snatches up the bowl. The water spills on the floor. His robe swishes as he crosses the floor, the lone candle in his hand, and he disappears through to the larger room.

The hammering continues and then I hears the slide of the bolt and the door creak open and some whispering. Father Thomas comes back in the room and a man follows him. I knows by his long gown and cap that he's one of those learned men what Father Thomas likes to talk wif.

'This is my boy, Barnabas,' Father Thomas says. 'No need to worry. He knows how to keep secrets.'

The man's creepy an all—got a beaky nose and face like a skull. Before I knows it, Father Thomas wraps a musty, old cloak round me shoulders and he puts some wood on the ashes of the little fire. Thin green smoke trickles from it, making the man cough.

'Sleep, Barnabas,' Father Thomas says. There's a note of warning in his voice as I curls up in the cloak.

They whispers away then. It's just loud enough to keep me awake but not enough so's I can understand what they're saying. Eventually, I manages to drift off.

When I wakes I'm stiff wiv cold in the little black room. The fire's out but I can see the dark lump of the priest on his pallet and another dark shape what I takes to be the man, huddled near the hearth. I tries to shut me eyes and crawl back into sleep, but I'm chilled to the bone. Me head frobs and me eyes is full of sand, and though I try shifting this way and that, it's no use, cos me bladder's full now. As soon as the light turns grey, I hauls meself up and creep to the little niche what the priest uses as a privy.

The man groans as I sigh in the relief of making water, even though I'm shivering. There's a bite in the morning air what makes me arms all goose-flesh, and I wriggles me toes to stop 'em from going numb.

There's no sense in lingering. There's nofink to eat here, and soon people will be filling this place. Father Thomas snores steady and deep now, so I rolls up the old cloak, leave it by the door and shoots back the bolts. The man stirs, but he don't wake. I shake like a dog and sneaks out into the day.

CHAPTER TWO
La Pleasaunce, Greenwich, June 1440
ELEANOR

'Humphrey.' She hesitated a moment before putting her hand on his arm. She could see he was engrossed in his letter and his brow was furrowed. There were papers scattered across the table in front of them. It wasn't good news. Perhaps she would be a welcome distraction. She tried again. 'Humphrey.'

She had on a new gown, a deep blue with gold brocade trim on a very low cut bodice that showed her breasts, still milky white and soft, to best advantage. It made her look younger, she knew and deepened the colour of her eyes. Humphrey often remarked on her eyes. She leaned over and plumped her lips into a pouting smile.

He glanced up at her for only a moment, but she could tell that he hadn't really seen her. He was already reading the letter again. There was a time when he would have swept all these papers and books off the table and taken her then and there. It seemed a long time ago, now.

She leaned over and kissed the top of his ear and ran her finger along it.

He looked up again and this time he saw her. He ran a finger along her breasts and she gave a soft mewling sound. He kissed her deeply. Now was the time, she thought. When the kiss was finished she spoke.

'Humphrey, I would talk to you about Antigone's future. I was thinking that one of Edmund Tudor's sons might do for her.'

He looked at her and frowned. 'Not now, woman.' He turned away and picked up his letter once again.

'Damn and blast!' Humphrey threw the letter down on the table. 'Bloody Beaufort has gone too far with Henry.'

Despite the fire in the hearth and the warm summer day she shivered. 'Henry, the King?'

'Yes of course, the King. Who else is so bloody weak-willed to believe Cardinal Beaufort's lies?'

'Beaufort is pressing for peace again?' asked Eleanor. She knew that the young King hated this war that had dragged on for decades.

'Not only is Henry agreeing with Beaufort, he's asking him to negotiate with France. It's infuriating. Does my nephew wish to despoil my brother's memory and all that he and the rest of us gained at Agincourt? You would think he was still a young boy under a regent, and not a twenty year old man.'

Eleanor bit her lip. Lately, it seemed the King was always causing Humphrey to be disgruntled. But at this moment it seemed worse. Now was clearly not the time to bring up Antigone's marriage, but she must. She smoothed her gown and laid her hand again on Humphrey's sleeve. 'My love, you must not get yourself so worked up.' She licked her lips and opened her eyes wide.

Humphrey leaned forward and kissed her softly, his hand reaching for her breast. She smiled inwardly.

'About Antigone,' she said.

Humphrey pulled away and frowned. 'What about her?'

'Isn't it time we thought about her future? I thought Edmund Tudor…' Her words trailed off as his face darkened.

'Edmund Tudor, the King's half-brother? Have I not made you Duchess as well as my wife?' He smiled but there was something in his voice, something dark that made her change tack.

'Well perhaps not one of Edmund Tudor's. Perhaps one of your other cousins?' She thought if she was vague he might be more receptive. Antigone was approaching fifteen and still nothing had been done for her. It also begged the question about their son, Arthur. She dare not bring up the matter of their son's future, though, for fear of the answer.

'We'll talk about it later,' he said and pulled her close. She allowed him to thrust his hand down her bodice once more and rub and pinch her breasts as much as he liked. He hadn't done it much lately, but today, her beauty and power weren't to be denied. She'd talk to him later. And maybe share with him that there was the possibility of news. Her courses were nearly a week late, her breasts seemed full. She was certain that her prayers were finally answered.

There was a knock at the door. Humphrey pulled away again and called 'enter.' A servant appeared and announced that Masters Bolingbroke, Hume and Dr Southwell had come to wait upon the Duke, as requested.

Humphrey gave Eleanor a look of regret. 'Yes, yes. Send them in.'

Eleanor blew him a little kiss and took one of the seats over by the fire, away from the table. On the wall opposite, bound manuscripts and printed books lined the heavy wood shelves. Humphrey was so proud of this collection which attracted so many scholars. She enjoyed the visits of these learned men, as well as the poets and musicians that frequented her husband's home.

Hume entered, a bundle of parchment and books clutched in his arms. Behind him, Bolingbroke and Southwell followed, each carrying their own collection of documents. The three bowed in unison and addressed Humphrey. 'Your Grace.' Bolingbroke spied her first and made another bow. The other two followed suit. She gave them a slight nod and smiled.

'Gentlemen. You have some wonders to share with us today?' She arched her brow and smiled at them coquettishly. Hume reddened and looked away bashfully. Master Bolingbroke returned the smile, a glint in his eye. Southwell eyed her sceptically. Such a toady, that man, thought Eleanor. But cunning with it. Called himself Father Thomas when he was working at St Stephen's, as if that would excuse his dabblings with alchemy and other things. Still, he had his uses.

The men took the indicated chairs at the table. The light from the windows behind cast them in silhouette.

Hume started off first, blustering, his fat face red with the effort. 'I must point out an error Master Bolingbroke has made in one of the passages he has translated in his recent work. It changes the meaning of it entirely.'

'What work is this, Roger?' asked Humphrey. He gave him an encouraging smile.

Eleanor looked at Bolingbroke and noted his reaction. His jaw clenched, making the skin of his face, so tight against his bones, stretch more.

'I think, my lord, Master Hume is talking about my work on geomancy,' said Bolingbroke.

The two men tried not to glare at each other as Bolingbroke untied his bundle and placed one group of pages to one side.

'Ah, the work on geomancy,' said Southwell. 'So interesting, so interesting.'

Humphrey pulled the pages towards him and picked up the first page.

'Doesn't geomancy concern astrology?' asked Eleanor.

'Of a sorts, Your Grace,' said Bolingbroke. 'Like astrology, it speaks of signs and houses.'

'It's an ancient way to cast fortunes and predict the future,' said Hume. The geomancer must cast the future through a series of sixteen dots or points drawn from right to left, while thinking hard on the question he wishes to be answered.'

His explanation droned on and Eleanor only took in the occasional word like 'planet,' 'demon' and 'signs.' Her head felt fuzzy. She shifted in her seat in an effort to be more attentive and felt a pain in her lower back. Now she knew the cause of her fuzzy head. Her heart sank and she nearly wailed aloud. How could she expect any other outcome when Humphrey hardly spent a minute in her bed?

She forced herself to endure the rest of the discussion, hardly taking a word in before the visitors rose to depart.

'We will take this up again soon,' the Duke said, a smile lighting his face. 'In the meantime, I'm afraid duty calls me.'

Eleanor knew that was her dismissal, too, and this time she had no complaint. She needed to get to her apartments quickly.

∽

She heard the laughter before she even opened the doors. When she walked in, she saw her ladies dressed up in their russet velvets and scarlet silks with stiffened hennins and cones topping their heads and jewels everywhere, even on the fingers of Master Jolippe, the musician. They sat clustered around Master Jolippe while he strummed the lute, giggling at his words like harpies. Even the nobly born Lady Margaret and Lady Joan, who should have better manners. At this moment she hated them all.

The group looked up, saw her and froze. Lady Margaret gathered herself first and stood to curtsey. The rest of the women hastily followed her lead. In the corner Eleanor spied Alys, her sewing clasped in one hand.

She nodded to her ladies and motioned to Alys. 'Attend me in my bedchamber, now, please.'

When she was safe in her room behind a closed door, with only Alys for company she allowed the tears to flow.

'My lady, what's wrong?'

'Oh, Alys. My wretched courses have come. I need you to clean me up and fetch some clouts.'

'I'm so sorry, Your Grace,' said Alys, her voice kind. She helped Eleanor to lie on the heavy brocaded coverlet that draped the bed and brought over a large silver bowl. 'The water is cold. Shall I fetch some that's been heated?'

Eleanor waved her hand. 'No, no. Don't bother. I shall bear it, like I've borne everything else.' She could hear the self-pity in her voice and it made her want to weep more. Ten years she'd been trying for a legitimate child. Ten years and nothing, for all of Margery Jourdemayne's tisanes and brews. Eleanor had been so sure when she'd first used the potions. Hadn't it been through Margery's efforts that Eleanor brought Humphrey to her bed while he was still married to that goat-face Jacqueline of Hainault? But now that power had disappeared and no other children had joined her two illegitimate ones.

She tried to relax under Alys' calming ministrations. The cool water sluiced her bloodied thighs, wiping off the traces of her humiliation.

'Next time, Your Grace, I'm sure of it. The summer has quickened and so will your womb. And if not then, soon. You are young yet.'

That was the rub of it. She wasn't young anymore. She was thirty-eight and time was running out. She must have a child for Humphrey. A legitimate son and heir for all that was his, and what would be his. It was clear that with weak and sickly Henry on the throne, her husband would succeed him as King, if not soon, then certainly later. And she must be ready for that.

Alys held out a silver chased cup. 'Drink this, Your Grace. It will help the pain and make sure you rest properly.'

Seeing such fine workmanship soothed Eleanor for a moment. How she loved her fine trappings. She sipped gratefully and then lay back on her bolster. Tomorrow she would visit Mistress Jourdemayne. The time of Alys fetching tinctures and philtres was over. She needed to take action.

∽

Eleanor left her men to wait in the warm kitchen and she and Alys followed Mistress Jourdemayne into the tiny chamber adjoining her stillroom, fragrant with the scents of drying herbs and infusing blooms. Alys, her hands fidgeting with her own skirt, took a place in the corner, near the door, as if she would be comforted by being close to the means of escape. Eleanor sat on the settle, pulled off her hood and rested her beringed hands on her dark velvet skirt. It was not her best dress, it did nothing for her eyes, but there was no need for those wiles today. Today was about business. About the future. She patted her hair nervously and for a moment avoided Mistress Jourdemayne's eye.

'We're old friends, Mistress Jourdemayne,' said Eleanor. Her words contradicted the formal tone she'd adopted to mark the distance between their ranks.

Mistress Jourdemayne gave a wide smile. 'We are indeed, Mistress Cobham—forgive me—Your Grace. We are indeed.' She cleared her throat. 'And what friendly help might you seek that brings you here in person?'

Eleanor wanted to sniff at the cheeky remark alluding to her humbler past, but she refrained. 'I must be clear from the very outset, my present business requires some extra—discretion.' She forced a smile. 'Your remedies have served me well in the past, but now I must ask something greater of you. I am informed that you venture into darker mysteries? That you have a showstone...' Eleanor let her words trail off in the hope she would have to say no more. She held her breath.

Mistress Jourdemayne paled a little. Did she want to risk the stone with someone as exalted as Eleanor?

'I would pay you well.'

Mistress Jourdemayne's eyes narrowed and she nodded.

'If you can look into the future, Mistress Jourdemayne, my gratitude will know no bounds.'

Mistress Jourdemayne rose and went to the door and opened it. 'Barnabas!' she called. A moment later an imp of a lad came in, all skinned knees and shaggy hair.

'The lady wants the showstone. Get it ready.'

The boy stood rooted to the spot. He gave a small shake to his head. Mistress Jourdemayne cuffed him around the ear. 'No more of your impudence, lad, you heard me.'

Barnabas reluctantly disappeared into the stillroom and Mistress Jourdemayne turned to Eleanor. 'I apologize for Barnabas, Your Grace. I do try, but there is only so much a person can do.'

Barnabas returned with a casket which he set on the low table before Eleanor. After a moment he opened it. Inside was a clear globe cushioned in velvet. Barnabas snuffed all the candles but the one beside the showstone. It sparkled in the light. Behind her Alys gasped. Eleanor stared at the impressive stone and felt hopeful.

'Your Grace, you must shut your eyes and think of what you particularly desire. Be specific as you can.'

Eleanor did as she was told for only a moment before she opened her eyes just a little, to see what was happening. She saw Mistress Jourdemayne hand Barnabas a cloth. 'Here, get on with it now,' she whispered.

Barnabas took the cloth, picked up the globe and began rubbing it with the cloth.

'Many seek answers in the stone,' said Mistress Jourdemayne, her voice low. 'And many have had success.'

The showstone shimmered under Barnabas' hand. Carefully, he placed it back in the cushion and took a place behind Eleanor, near Alys. Alys eyed him and lifted her chin. Eleanor glanced back at him and caught him shaking his head at Mistress Jourdemayne. Mistress Jourdemayne pursed her lips until she saw Eleanor's eyes were open and then she gave a smile. The smile didn't reach her eyes.

Mistress Jourdemayne put her hands above the globe, and for a moment they hovered there as if she was warming them. A moment later she started waving them around, muttering words with her eyes closed. The words finished and she opened her eyes and nodded to Eleanor.

'Place your hands upon the showstone now and continue to think upon those questions. I will place my hands on the other side.'

Eleanor leaned in and stared into the globe, her hands embracing it. Desperately, she strained to peer beyond the milky depths, Mistress Jourdemayne's head nearly touching hers. A relentless wheel of questions tumbled round inside her. Will I have a child? Will Humphrey keep me by his side? Will he get the throne? Will her son get the throne? She found she couldn't focus on just one question, no matter how hard she tried. Beside her the candle-flame dwindled and belched smoke. She felt a cold draft snaking up her back, creeping towards her neck and around her throat. She gave a strangled sound and dropped her hands from around the globe.

'You saw something?' Mistress Jourdemayne asked, her tone full of surprise.

'I-I don't know. No. I felt something. Something cold.' Eleanor looked at Mistress Jourdemayne. 'What did you see?'

Mistress Jourdemayne gave her a studied look. 'There were many fleeting images, you understand, and I was trying to get them to slow down, to get a clearer understanding and picture, but since you broke contact…. But that is of no matter. The spirits are being playful tonight. That happens sometimes. We will try again another night.'

'Another night?' Eleanor didn't know if she could bring herself to come again. But it did seem as if they came close to finding the answers this night. Perhaps it was because she had asked too many questions that things went wrong. Next time she would be prepared. Next time she would have her answer.

'Yes of course. We will try again,' said Eleanor. 'I will send a message and let you know.'

'I will await your convenience,' said Mistress Jourdemayne. 'In the meantime I'm sure you will mention my skills to others who might need similar services.'

Eleanor drew herself up to her full regal height. 'We'll see how skilled you prove in this area, in time.' She motioned to Alys and began making her way to the door.

Barnabas jostled in front of Alys and reached for the latch.

'Have a care, boy,' said Alys.

A cheeky grin lit his face and his dark lashed eyes. 'Barnabas. Me name's Barnabas.' His remark earned him a haughty look from Alys. The exchange lasted a moment only, but it gave Eleanor cause to feel a small bit better when she left Mistress Jourdemayne's house. And the Lord knew that there were few times that had happened lately.

CHAPTER THREE
Magotscroft, Eye Near Westminster, June 1440
BARNABAS

Ow! The pain of me ear wakes me out of a lovely sleep. I open me eyes and it's me mistress. She's twisting me ear somfink fearful.

'Up, you scamp,' she whispers loudly. She drags me from me pallet. There's some heat in them embers still and I look longingly at me bed. She pulls me out of the kitchen and down the hall. I know where we're going and I drags me feet a little, though I know we'll get there eventually. There's no stopping her, not after she's gotten a whiff of money and further customers from that duchess lady.

She shoves me into the little room and shuts the door behind her. 'Now Barnabas, you refused to read for me earlier, but I won't let you get away with it.' She points to the stillroom. She don't have to say no more. I knows the drill and that there's no escape tonight.

I've the box on the table, eventually, and the lid open not too quick-like, but not so slow as she'd notice.

There's no need to do all them showy fings wiv hands and questions and stuff. I just blink me eyes a bit then look at the fing until the figures appear. This time is no different than any other.

'I sees a fellow sitting on a chair painted wiv swords. He's wearing a long dark robe and his head is bent like he's reading. A candle's burning on his desk and there's a heavy looking book lying open. There's diagrams and drawings and writing—and there's a doll—not what a little lass might play wiv though—more like a little manikin wiv somefink sticking in its belly. Could be a nail—I can't see very clear—but it's got what looks like a little crown on its head—made out of a scrap of parchment or somefink. I can't see the fellow's face cos he's got a hood pulled over it. It's dark all round him. It's like he's sitting in a big black cloud all swirling round him and there's showers of gold falling—'

Me bref is gone and suddenly it's like someone's strangling me. 'I'm choking.' Me words can hardly come outa me mouf. 'I can't do no more, Mistress Jourdemayne,' I says wiv a croak.

Me mistress gives me a hard look, but I can see she knows me words is true. She nods and covers the showstone. 'What can it mean?' she says. 'What on earth can I say to her?'

I'm shaking away, me legs are that weak from what I seen. I knows she ain't asking me, really, though she said the words, but I has to say somefink cos it bovvers me. 'This ain't good, Mistress. This is dangerous stuff. You should leave it alone.'

She looks up at me and for a moment I finks she minds what I say. Then her eyes go all hard-like and I know what's coming.

'It is not for you to tell me what I should and shouldn't do, boy.' She shuts the lid on the box with a bang. 'Now put this back and take yourself off to bed. And remember, you are to tell no one about this, understand?'

~

I sits next to Tom in the wherry, moving me oar in time wif his. The water is smooth as glass. No trouble at all and that suits me fine. I've not said a dicky bird since I got in earlier and we've been up and down many times, taking on different people. Tom don't mind though. He knows I can be quiet sometimes. He just chats to them what likes a little chin wagging and keeps mum when they don't. At the moment it's a chatty old lot that've gotten on board. Two women and a man, got up in all their finery like some fancy birds. The older woman has swanky clothes but ain't so fancy as the ovver two, somefink I knows from the way she talks.

'What do you think the Cobham woman will be wearing?' she asks the younger woman. I can tell she's excited.

'Something very splendid, you can be sure,' says the younger woman. And they goes on like that for ages, talking about dresses, shoes, hairstyles and all manner of fings to do wif what people wear. Me ears can't help but prick up at the mention of Eleanor Cobham, the Duchess what came to the house weeks ago. Not seen any more of her since and glad I am of it. Though the lass what was wif her had lovely titties, nice and round like apples what you could hold in your hand. Leastways what I saw of 'em tucked nice and plump-like in her bodice.

The man catches Tom's eye and gives a weak smile. 'The ladies do love their fripperies.'

'Is the Duchess in the city today?' asks Tom.

'So we hear. The Duke has just returned from collecting the King in Cirencester. They're at the Guildhall today, meeting with the Mayor, and they should be on their way to Westminster Palace, soon. There should be plenty to see in this procession, especially the King. It's been some years since I've seen the King.'

'Hear that, Barney?' says Tom. 'The King is riding through the city today. Why not take yourself off and have a look-see? Might do you some good.'

He pats me on me head. I gives him a smile but me heart's not in it.

Still, when we comes to Queenhithe, I gets off and wif a nod to Tom makes me way along Bread Street to Chepeside. It's raining now, but still I push to the edge of the crowd what's gathering, waiting for the procession to come.

I don't have to wait long before I hears a blare of trumpets. I ain't never seen the King before and I can feel meself getting excited. I've heard loads about his father, him what was called Henry too. How he was tall, wif muscles that bulged everywhere. A real soldier. Fought loads of battles. Cor, he sounds like someone you want on your side.

I'm finking this when I catches sight of the King. Leastways I fink it was him cos he's got a crown on his head. I thought he'd be wearing finery—like Duke Humphrey—all gold and dazzle and shiny robes. But his servants was better dressed than him. Boy, was I disappointed.

Then Duke Humphrey and that Cobham woman comes next. And any kind of finery you can imagine that woman was wearing. Jewels stuck all over her so's you can hardly see the cloth what holds them. And her neck and hair. You'd've thought her head would ache wif the weight of them jewels. Some people don't like it though. They starts muttering, calling her an 'whore', a 'trumped up farmer's daughter' and worse. It gets a feeling creeping up me spine and it ain't good.

Me jerkin's soaked through, now, so I takes meself off to the Turk's

Head to get warm and dry and also give meself some time to fink about how I might avoid this duchess. Everyfing I find out about her adds to what I knows already—she means danger.

∾

'Did you say you'd seen the king, Barney-Boy?'

Black Jack Hodgekiss, a genial giant wiv a mane of black hair, gives me a wink and slaps a cup of ale in front of me. Caught in the glow of a tallow candle, his eyes is full of mischief and his smile, tucked among a tangle of black whiskers, is wide. 'Quite the hero, our Henry, would you say?' He stands by the board and guffaws.

The reek of the docks blows powerful strong by the door, but the stink of sweat and smoke and foul bref is thicker deeper inside. Today it's hard to make out faces cos the shutters is closed against the driving rain. In the far shadows I catches a glimpse of a skinny drab wiv a feller lolling in her lap, and a cluster of figures huddled over some board game. Near to, in the fire-light, I makes out a ring of faces—labourers and craftsmen by the looks of it—though the high-backed settle's occupied by a stout fellow and his even stouter wife. These two's drinking from a pitcher and guzzling shrimps off a wooden platter. The tipsy rabble of rogues, clustered round the hearth and rolling wiv laughter, moves to make a place for me so's I can sit and dry meself in the heat. Black Jack comes over and stands near, ready for a good old chin wag.

'Did you see the procession?' says a raggy-headed fella.

I tells them what I saw and say how the King was like a wet fart.

'Ah, well, they say he's a religious sort of fellow,' says Black Jack.

'Modest and quiet, inclined to the simple life,' someone beside me says.

'Simple's right!' says Black Jack and everyone loves it, laughing hard and nudging one another. Turns out the King's got no more sense than a flea.

'Yes, but fleas, they knows where to bite, don't forget,' says the raggy-headed fella.

'Let the Council mind that,' says Black Jack. 'And Duke Humphrey.' He glances around and I knows he's looking out for strangers. You never know who might be listening. Even a joke can be called treason if a person's a mind to think it that.

I sneezes then. I want to ask them 'bout the Duchess, but all the sudden me tongue's tied and I can't get the words out.

'Here, you ain't got the sweat, have you?' says Black Jack. 'Your face is pale and you don't look much.'

Shaking me head, I try and give him a cheeky grin. 'Nah, just a cold, I reckon. Nofink catching.'

Nevertheless, I senses a drawing back and a shudder running through the rest of 'em.

'You spend too much time down at Queenhithe, lad,' says Black Jack, heaping more wood on the fire. 'Pick up all sorts of nasty diseases from them sailors down dock.'

A loud squawk cuts off his talk. The drab's customer's rolled off her lap, and almost dragging her wiv him, lands on the rushes wiv a dull thump. Loud cheers go up. The gaming men leaves off their play and turns round to watch the drab pull her skirts from underneath his legs and spit oafs.

Black Jack makes his way to her side. 'Reckon it's time to take him home, Bess,' he says. He shoves the feller into a sitting position.

'That's right, Jack, get him to stand up for her!'

Black Jack tries to haul him to his feet.

'Time to go home, sir,' he says in his ear. 'Give us a hand with him, girl.'

The drab takes the ovver side, and they drags him upright. The feller sways, gives a great belch and smiles up at Jack, slack mouf hanging open, and then turns to fumble at Bess' breasts.

'You owe me a groat,' she says. She steers him towards the door, while the company roars and jeers encouragement.

'Take him back to Grub Street with you, Bess, and he'll give you a shilling!'

The drab pulls a face before the two of 'em leave. A blast of cold air and sleet whips into the room, setting the fire smoking, and we all sits coughing till tears run down our cheeks.

'What's going on, Jack?' Black Jack's wife strides into the room from the back, all elbows and hatchet face. 'Get them drunks out of here before we gets the alderman on our backs.' She glares round, daring anyone to speak.

'No need to worry, Sarah, my love,' says Black Jack. 'Trouble's been sorted.' He circles her waist and gives her a sly nudge from behind. 'Now, what tasty dish have you got for us today?'

She purses her lips so's she can't laugh. She gives him a dig wiv her elbow and wriggles—not too fast though— out of his embrace.

'There's a tasty bit of mutton for them what fancies it,' she says, swiping up empty cups from under our noses. 'Or an hot eel pie.' She gives me a sharp look. 'You look flushed, me lad. What's up?'

Before I can answer I'm struck wiv a fit of sneezing.

'You've got yourself a fine dose of the sniffles. You need a good hot meal to set up.' She turns and orders Black Jack to bring me a pie and I gives her a grateful look.

'I was watching King Henry riding through the street,' I says and gives me nose a swipe wif me sleeve.

'He's not worth getting yourself sick over, me lad.' She gives me head a rub and sets down the pie in front of me. A moment later and she's set down a cup of spiced wine wif honey and I'm feeling warm and heaps better already.

'Do you know Duke Humphrey's wife?' I asks Sarah when she comes to take away me empty platter.

She gives me a cock-eyed look. 'Well, I've seen her flaunting herself in her fine gowns and jewellery as she rides about the city.' She frowns. 'Why? What do you want to know about her for?'

'Oh, noffink. I saw her today, is all.'

'That priest still got you running errands?' Her voice is sharpish.

'You mean Father Thomas?' I gives a nod. No use denying.

'Why ain't he got you a trade yet, is what I wants to know. You can't stay forever with that Jourdemayne woman. And nor should you. I hears all about her. She's no good for you. Lord only knows what she makes you do, that woman.' Sarah crosses herself. Her eyes narrow. 'Ere, you ain't been pulled into that lark wif her and the Cobham woman, have you?'

I lower me head quick-like and shakes it. All me comfort is gone now and it's all I can do to keep from shaking. If Sarah knows 'bout the Duchess' visits to me mistress then the whole of London knows.

Sarah pats me head. 'There, there, lad. Eat up and finish your wine. You'll feel better then.'

I keeps me head down and stare into me cup of wine. It's then that I sees him out the corner of me eye. Limpin' Sam, beckoning me into an old churchyard wiv toppling headstones and gloomy yew trees. He leads me inside the church itself and crouches near a marble tomb wiv a knight carved on top. Brushing away the dust, he uncovers a circle drawn on the flagstones nearby and signs for me to look close at the queer designs around it.

A pale-faced figure in a crown appears, then falls and rolls—becomes a manikin made of wax what melts in flames—and the flames lick and leap and rise, becoming a raging blaze what burns me eyes, roars and shrieks thunder in me ears and I stretches out an arm…

'Barnabas lad, are you alright?' It's Black Jack standing over me now, his face all concern. 'You ought to be in bed, boy. 'Ere, go off into the back, there's a blanket on the chair. Tuck yourself up there for the night. Them Jourdemaynes can do without you 'til the morrow.'

I nods me head, all grateful, though I knows it will take more than a night in the warmth of *The Turk's Head* to feel better.

CHAPTER FOUR
Westminster Palace, July 1440
ELEANOR

Eleanor smoothed her gown once more and tried to find the pleasure in its luxurious colour and cut as she did when she first put it on. The ermine that edged the neckline of her dress was still as expensive, the ruby that nestled at her cleavage was polished to perfection. Her looking glass had assured her that her hair was still the same lustrous gold that it ever was and shone bright under the sheer veil that covered the hennin hat.

She glanced around at the groups of people who meandered around the palace hall, chatting away with smiles plastered on their faces. Sheep. That's all they were. Two-faced sheep, ready to follow anyone who made promise of greener pastures. And clearly now her husband's pastures were not green enough.

She gave a small nod to the man in the puce silk jerkin with trailing sleeves and hose of a startling red hue. 'My Lord Suffolk,' she said.

The man gave a quick bow and mumbled a greeting before hurrying off to a small group of Cardinal Beaufort's men. Cardinal Beaufort, Bishop of Winchester, stood at the centre of the group, his round belly prominent through his long dark velvet robe. There was nothing ascetic or monk-like about this man. He exuded power and confidence, belying his age. Though Beaufort was half uncle to Humphrey, and great uncle to the King, his ruthless ambition and his family's made all the Beauforts easy enemies of Humphrey.

She scowled and turned to Lady Margaret who stood behind her. 'That jumped-up prig Suffolk has no sense of who got him here in the first place.' The remark slipped out of her mouth before she could recall it. Humphrey would be annoyed that she even mentioned this. She bit her lip.

Lady Margaret raised an eyebrow for only moment, but Eleanor saw it nonetheless. Out of the corner of her eye Eleanor spied Lady Alice, the Earl of Salisbury's wife, and made her way over to her, nodding at the few groups of men along the way. Some gave her a polite smile, one or two nodded and of course there were those among the older men who dared to give her a saucy wink. They deserved only the most civil of nods.

'Lady Alice,' said Eleanor, forcing all the resentment and anger from her voice. She was proud of her voice. Its melodious quality had earned praise not just from Master Jolippe but from the other court musicians that often frequented the La Pleasaunce. Eleanor's glanced over Lady Alice's trim figure and noted that it filled her fur trimmed satin gown to perfection. Eleanor tried to convince herself her own figure was nearly as trim and the gown she had on now that was barely a year old was not too tight in the bust.

Lady Alice gave her a neutral smile and nodded. 'Eleanor.'

'Countess.' She used the title to remind the woman that she was still, 'Your Grace,' wife of a royal duke. 'You have returned to Westminster from your estate recently? I have not seen you since the autumn.'

Lady Alice raised her brow. 'Ah, we have been at our residence here since spring and then up to see the King from time to time. It appears that our paths have just not crossed.'

'It seems not.' Eleanor glanced at the women gathered around Lady Anne. Her young daughter, Joan, was there, her dark ringlets escaping from her simple veil. How old was the maid now? She could see the hint of rounded breasts peeping out from her dress. Old enough for marriage. But surely not a marriage so exalted as to that of the King. She turned back to Lady Alice who was putting a question to her.

'Your children. Are they well? Let me see, is it one or two? Two, I rather think. You must forgive me if I cannot remember their names.'

Eleanor's smile froze on her face. 'I have two. Antigone and Arthur.' She could detect the veiled hinting at their bastardy. Born before her marriage to Humphrey. She hardly knew what she said after that. The words just tumbled from her mouth. 'Antigone is fifteen nearly and Arthur is twelve. He is a good lad, tall like his father.'

'Of course, I'm sure His Grace takes much joy from the little lad. When he can spare the time.'

Eleanor nodded stiffly. Why didn't Alice Montecue like her? Her husband was one of Humphrey's allies. She could hear Lady Margaret whispering behind her to one of her other women. With a careful expression on her face she excused herself. 'I must seek out my husband for a moment. I am suddenly reminded that he mentioned he would have me attend him to speak with the King on the matter of my children.'

She moved away from the group, her head held high. There, she thought, let them stew on that piece of information. Briefly she caught sight of Katherine Neville, the Duke of Norfolk's widow, now married to the old knight, Strangeways. Katherine gave her a warm smile and Eleanor took heart from it. Katherine was Alice's sister-in-law and knew what a snob she could be.

Eleanor located her husband with his usual cronies, the earls of Salisbury, Kent and Essex, near the King's chamber door. His face was clouded and dark, and though he spoke low, his voice was angry. She arranged her face in a charming expression. 'Come, all of you,' she said in a sprightly tone. 'No need to be so gloomy. Is not the day warm and sunny and the garden just begging for admiration? Husband, let us see what fresh blooms we might find and lovely scents to inhale. I am told the lavender is particularly fine at the moment.'

Her husband looked up at her and his face held such impatience she had to fight to hold back the tears that suddenly appeared. He was quick tempered at the best of times and she knew she must not rouse him to anger right now. She blinked a few times and laid a hand on his arm. 'It does no good to seem like such a thundercloud here, in view of everyone. Especially those who would not be favourable to you and your cause,' she said softly.

His expression softened, and for a fleeting moment she could see the look that used to be always in his face when he regarded her. She gave him a genuine smile. 'Or perhaps we could greet the King together? Speak only of light things. Perhaps I could charm him with fond memories of the boat rides we used to take on the

Thames? Something that would make him well disposed towards us. Towards you.' There, she could make it no more plain than that. Antigone and Arthur were always on the boat rides and the King, a boy himself, would play with them.

Humphrey seemed to find the idea appealing for he nodded and offered his arm. 'Yes, perhaps that would be an approach the King would welcome.'

He led her away and eventually, they found the King in conversation with Cardinal Beaufort, and Southwell, who was Canon of the chapel here at the palace in addition to his duties as vicar at the church in Walbrook.

Eleanor made her curtsey to the King and nodded to the other men. 'Such a fine day, gentlemen, it seems more of a penance to remain inside.'

She smiled over at the King. His face was pale and his black velvet jerkin and hose hung loosely on him. Dark hollows around his eyes made them look larger than they were. He regarded her carefully.

The King frowned at her. 'Weather such as this can carry ill humours,' he said. 'We prefer to remain indoors.'

'Ah, but Your Highness used to enjoy the trips we made on the Thames, when you were young.'

'I was a boy then and ignorant of the dangers that beset us.'

Her heart sank. She felt Humphrey's restraining hand on her arm. She would not let it go, though. She must not let it go. She tried again. 'Have you seen your brother Edmund of late? Such a dear boy.'

'Enough,' Humphrey said in a low voice in her ear.

The King gave her a dark look. 'I think, Madam, you would do best to look for answers in prayer, rather than in my brother.'

Eleanor caught a quizzical look from Thomas Southwell before she lowered her head in embarrassment. 'I do pray, Your Highness. I have prayed for years,' she said softly.

'Not hard enough,' he said in a sharp tone. 'Either that or you do not come to your Lord with a pure heart.' He turned from her, nodded to Humphrey and strode off.

Humphrey glared at her and followed in the King's wake. Southwell leaned over and spoke to her in a low voice. 'There are other means, Your Grace, that are more effective. And I am happy to instruct Mistress Jourdemayne in them, should you wish. I know you will be suitably grateful.'

He gave her a brief nod and walked off in the direction the King took. Eleanor stood, alone, too stunned to move out of sight of all the people she knew must be looking at her.

✦

She relaxed slowly under Alys' soothing ministrations. With the weight of the hennin headdress removed and her hair loosed from its braids, the ache in her temples eased. Alys had such a light touch, deft with her fingers, and she never made tangles with the comb. It was all done so skilfully. Alys had been a wonderful find, scooped from the kitchens in a hasty moment to help her with a broken leather of her wooden patten. She'd been eager to learn then and still was now. Her speech had improved immensely since that time. Despite any talk among the ladies who attended her, Alys would remain as her valued serving maid.

She surveyed Alys now as she loosened Eleanor's gown. Now fourteen, Alys had grown very comely in the last year, her hair deepening from its brighter red to a lovely russet. Her skin was milky and unblemished and Eleanor could almost envy her youthfulness. There wasn't a trace of the kitchen on her now.

'Will you go back to Mistress Jourdemayne, Your Grace?' asked Alys.

Eleanor stiffened and tried a nonchalant air. She was reluctant to go back to the Jourdemayne woman, especially now that Southwell knew of her situation, but still she was desperate to do something. Everything.

'Oh, I don't know,' Eleanor said. 'Nothing seemed to come from the last time. I'm not sure if it is worth all the risk.' She cast her mind back to the night of the visit. 'I don't remember seeing that lad there before when I was consulting Mistress Jourdemayne for herbs. He was an odd lad.' She looked across at Alys. 'He seemed rather too forward with you. I'm glad you put him in his place.'

Alys reddened. 'Thank you, Your Grace. He was altogether too cheeky for his own good.' Her face softened for a moment. 'Though he has something about him that reminds me of my brother.'

'Brother? You have a brother?' It had never occurred to Eleanor that Alys might have family.

'Yes. He would be about seventeen. I haven't seen him since he was fourteen. He found work on the merchant ships that go back and forth across the channel. I expect he's moved on from that now since I've seen nothing of him since. But I drew a sketch of him. From me memory.'

Eleanor automatically corrected the grammar of Alys' last sentence while Alys drew out a folded bit of cloth from the front of her gown. The cloth was grubby, as though it had been handled many times. Once it was unfolded she could see a faint trace of a face in charcoal.

It was shaped well enough and Eleanor could see that it was a young boy with a perky nose.

'Very nice, dear,' Eleanor said, and yawned. Suddenly she felt really tired. 'Now I need you help me to bed. My husband won't be joining me tonight. He has other things to attend to.' For once she felt glad of that.

It was after she was tucked in bed and just drifting off to sleep that a small kind of plan began to take shape in her mind.

✴

She walked around the library, pulling random books off the shelf, opening them and staring at the page for a few moments before replacing them. Her mind was busy planning what she would say when Bolingbroke arrived. She'd asked him to see her here, where they wouldn't be overheard and no one would remark on it. She told him she wanted to discuss a translation, but that was only a means to her greater concern.

It had been weeks since her humiliation at Westminster and she had been stewing ever since, debating whether to take this step.

The door opened and Bolingbroke entered and bowed. 'Your Grace.'

She tugged at the vivid blue satin dress. Its high waistline concealed her thicker middle and broader hips, but it was still tight under her breasts. Still, beside the accent it gave her blue eyes, she felt it showed their ripe fullness to an advantage and she needed all the help she could get to persuade this man to her bidding.

'Roger,' she said, her voice husky. 'Please have a seat at the table.' She ran her finger lightly across the pearls that bordered the bodice edge, pausing a moment where her breasts met and formed a deep valley. She'd ensured a good pinch had made her cheeks a becoming pink.

He took the seat indicated where she had placed a few random books and manuscripts beside the others that he'd been working on. She took the seat beside him and reached for the nearest one. She glanced at it.

'This is the work of which you spoke some weeks back, is it not?' she asked. She smiled softly.

Bolingbroke nodded and flushed red under his dark scholars cap. He fiddled with the folds of his long robe. 'It's the work on Geomancy,' he said.

'Just so,' she said. 'Fascinating.' She turned the book over in her hands. The script was foreign and she couldn't make head nor tails of it. 'I would like to know more of this topic. Perhaps you might translate it for me.'

'Into English?'

She nodded. 'I know my husband asked you to translate it into Latin, but I would also like to read it.'

'It is complicated, Your Grace. Perhaps I could explain it to you.'

'By all means tell me if you feel that would be a better option.'

'Of course, with pleasure.' Bolingbroke launched into his explanation again and she tried this time to be more attentive, but the words flowed over her until she heard a phrase that caught her attention. Predicting the death of a king.

She held up her hand. 'Wait. Are you saying this method of divination can predict the death of a king? But surely that is treason.'

Bolingbroke paled visibly. 'I speak only in the abstract, Your Grace,' he said hastily. 'The work only explains what is possible by this method, not what should be done.'

Eleanor glanced at the door and suddenly felt ill. 'I think it's best not to mention that possibility any more. Words like that can be misinterpreted.' She took a deep breath and tried to clear away the ill feeling. 'I would ask you to help me in another form of divination. One more familiar to people. The horoscope. Would you mind casting mine?'

Small beads of sweat formed on Bolingbroke's upper lip. He looked down at his hands which still gripped the book she'd given him earlier. 'I—I, well, it is not something to undertake lightly for a person so nobly placed,' he said finally.

She leaned forward and patted his hands the glorious expanse of her bosom on view. 'If you would do this one service for me, I would be forever grateful.' She stared into his grey eyes and she saw the little spark of lust that arose. She forced herself to give a lazy smile and rubbed his thumb with hers.

Bolingbroke took a deep breath and lowered his eyes. 'As Your Grace wishes.'

She squeezed his arm. 'Good. I shall expect it as soon as you can.'

'Th-the calculations take some time. It's important that they be correct.'

'Of course, Roger. And I know you'll begin those calculations as soon as possible.'

He nodded carefully and she gave his arm a pat and allowed herself a triumphant smile. Surely now God would smile on her and she would get what she wanted most.

⌒

'Mistress Jourdemayne—'

The Jourdemayne woman executed a deep curtsey and gave her a wide smile. Behind her, Petronille craned her neck, hoping for a view. Eleanor pulled her dark cloak tighter around her. She had said nothing since entering the house, keeping her face hidden in her hood and letting Alys do all the speaking for her. It seems she'd fooled no one. The maid had escorted her here to the small chamber by the stillroom, as before, giving a little titter before scurrying off to fetch her mistress. She'd waited impatiently while wafts of burning meat found their way to the chamber, making her nose wrinkle in distaste. Alys had provided some distraction by describing a small painting she'd spied in the entrance hall. Something about the unusual cast of the eyes. The girl was forever caught up in those things. But now she clutched Eleanor's arm, the tension palpable. She wasn't happy they'd been recognized.

'You are welcome,' Mistress Jourdemayne said. 'I didn't think I'd see you again, it's been so long.' She shut the door on Petronille and indicated Eleanor seat herself on the settle. 'I presume you require the same service as before.'

Eleanor nodded. She didn't trust her voice. Behind her, Alys coughed discreetly and frowned. Eleanor turned her head slightly and gave a small nod. Yes, she did want her to remain. Alys's beginnings were humble, like her own, and so trustworthy in Eleanor's view.

There was a knock at the door and the flaxen-haired Petronille appeared again carrying a silver goblet. She set the goblet down on the small table and made a hasty curtsey. Mistress Jourdemayne nodded. 'Go now and fetch Barnabas.'

The girl looked stricken. 'Oh Mistress, I know not where he be.'

'Then find him, girl, find him,' Mistress Jourdemayne said, her voice full of anger. 'And be quick about it.' She looked down at Eleanor, her face now assembled into a pleasant expression. 'Have some spiced wine, Your Grace.'

Eleanor took up the goblet and had a sip, a hint of impatience in her manner. She tapped her foot. Would the woman ever get on with it, she wondered. The less time she spent in this room, in this house, the better, as far as she was concerned. It had been over a month since that dreadful scene at the palace and weeks since she'd asked Bolingbroke for the horoscope. She hadn't been able to question him, either, since he'd been hiding away in his rooms in the city. And he wouldn't answer her discreet notes, other than to say he was making progress. She couldn't afford to wait any longer, she needed action now, not hints at 'progress.'

The fire in the small grate hissed and spat, making Eleanor jump. She glanced over at Mistress Jourdemayne, who gave her a reassuring look.

'I apologize for the poor quality of the wood. We use up the poor bits this time a year when the fire is little needed.'

Eleanor nodded. Truth be told it was too hot in here for her liking, especially with the heavy cloak she wore. She sighed and pushed it off her shoulders. She could feel the sweat trickling down her sides. The gown was old and plain, so the stains mattered little. Perhaps she could pass it to Alys after she'd have her remove the fine trim. She clutched her hands together and noted how clammy they felt. The fire spat again and still she jumped, the tension growing inside her.

Mistress Jourdemayne rose from her seat opposite and went into the stillroom and returned with the casket. She placed it on the table beside the goblet of half-drunk wine and flipped open the lid. The globe shone, distorting the light from the fire so that it bent and wrapped in strange directions. Her eyes followed it, and she found she was unable to look away.

A knock sounded on the outer door and Eleanor jumped once more. A moment later the boy Barnabas entered, the stains on his grubby oversized jerkin more pronounced than before. His legs were bare beneath except for the wooden shoes he'd neglected to remove before he entered the house. She shuddered to think of the state of his feet.

Mistress Jourdemayne uttered a few rebukes at his tardiness and took her seat again. 'Barnabas is part of the ritual, you see, Your Grace. The spirits like him and when he is present they are easily summoned.' She pointed at the cloth. Barnabas gave a scowl and picked it up.

'Now, Your Grace,' said Mistress Jourdemayne. 'If you would do as before and close your eyes and think of the particular aspect of the future you would like to know about.'

Eleanor closed her eyes this time and thought of her question. Will she have a son by Humphrey? She thought hard, the words repeating themselves over and over, until Mistress Jourdemayne gave her permission to open her eyes. She placed her hands on the globe, as she did the first time and leaned in. The globe was as milky white as before, except for an occasional orange streak created by the flickers from the fire. Mistress Jourdemayne blocked most of the light as she sat forward, her own fingers nearly touching Eleanor's on the globe.

Mistress Jourdemayne emitted the whining noise, softly first and then growing gradually louder. It grated on Eleanor, set her teeth on edge and she licked her lips to keep from shouting at the woman to stop. A moment later the whining stopped and Mistress Jourdemayne began to invoke the spirits.

'We ask your assistance, Athor, Elmdor and all others who have helped us in the past,' she said, her voice low and throaty. 'Elmmmdoooorrathorrrrrr.' She repeated the words over and over while she stared into the globe. The tone was soothing at first, but then it sent a chill through Eleanor and her hands started to tremble.

'I am seeing something. A thunderstorm… and is that a demon with wings?'

Eleanor shivered. 'A demon?' she whispered.

Mistress Jourdemayne held up her hand for silence. 'Ah, no, it is the King. People cheering him. He reaches up for his crown, but wait….' Mistress Jourdemayne fell silent.

'What—what do you see? Tell me!' Eleanor said. She could hear the high pitch of her voice. She gulped.

Mistress Jourdemayne stared into the globe, concentrating. After a moment she looked up and shook her head. 'No, I'm sorry, it's gone. The spirits have given all they can at the moment.' She sighed. 'I hope it gave you some bit of an answer to your question.' She cocked her head. 'I might be able to see more at another time.'

Eleanor frowned. She had no idea what the meaning was of what she'd just heard. There were several possibilities. But at least she had some information. She just needed time to make better sense of it.

Mistress Jourdemayne motioned to the boy and he left his place beside Alys to pack up the globe. He carried the box back towards the door, stopping for a moment beside Alys and grinning. She gave him a haughty look, her hand clutched across her other arm. Eleanor couldn't help notice that the action showed her breasts just a little bit more. She could only assume that Alys had little idea of the display she'd made and she was certain that sparkle she thought she saw in Alys' eyes for a moment was just a trick of the light. Eleanor would bring her in hand quick enough though, or before she knew it, Alys would be carrying a babe of her own inside her. The thought brought her back to her own troubles. She bit her lip. Would this woman be able to help her anymore? Would Bolingbroke? She had no choice but to seize every opportunity. There was too much at stake.

CHAPTER FIVE
Maggotscroft, Eye By Westminster, August 1440
BARNABAS

'I'm sorry, Mistress, I could tell you nofink more wiv the maid there. She would've seen me.' It's late at night and I'm sitting on a bench in the stillroom, me mistress standing above me.

'No, because you were too busy ogling her. I saw you whispering to her later. Giving her the wink. What do you take me for?'

'No, no, Mistress. Honest. I was only trying to distract her so that she wouldn't see you looking to me.'

Me mistress snorts. I knows she don't believe me, but she's no choice. That Alys is one to look at though. Somefink about her and it aint just her titties. Outside a storm's brewing somefink fierce. The rumbles are getting louder. It'll be a shocker.

'Well, I assume you saw something to do with the King, since I managed to understand that word you mouthed. Did you see anything about a child for the Cobham woman, though?'

I shakes me head and look down. It's true enough, I saw nofink to do with the Duchess, but what I did see I wants to keep to meself.

'Well what did the showstone reveal?'

The candle flickers. I'm hoping it's a draught what came in sudden like wiv the brewing storm, but you never knows so I shakes me head. She grabs me ear and twists. I gives a great howl.

'Shut up, you babby, and tell me what you saw about the King.'

'Tweren't nofink. 'E was just on a horse, riding. And you like you said, they was cheering him.'

'Who? Who was cheering him?'

'People. I don't know.'

'And then what?'

'Nofink.' I keeps me eyes down so she can't see I'm lying. But it's no use. She twists me ear again.

'Tell me,' she says and this time wiv a real edge in her voice.

'His crown falls off and a woman catches it.' I mutter it low and hopes she doesn't hear it all.

'What?' she says. I don't know if she hasn't heard me or she just don't believe it.

A crash sounds. Loud and so close I jumps in me seat and gives a wail. Me mistress looks around her and I can see fear in her eyes. She takes a deep bref and pulls me face close to hers.

'The crown falls off and a woman catches it?' she says in a loud whisper.

I nods and pulls away. She sits up and I can see she's finking hard, wondering what it means. I don't wants to know. I only know that I don't like the fear that's taking hold of me, the terrible dread when I remembers what I seen.

'Mistress, it's dangerous. I feels it deep. Leave it alone.'

This time the candle blows out and I shrieks. I can't help meself.

'By Our Lady, Margery, what are you doing sitting here in the dark?' Me master comes hurrying in the stillroom, a lighted taper in his hand. 'Are you injured? I heard a shriek just after that awful crash. It's set off every cur from here to Chepeside. I reckon there's a tree down.'

He stops, sees me face. 'Is something wrong? Has the lad taken sick again?' His face darkened and he shines the light around the room. 'You haven't been forcing him to look into your showstone again? It's bad enough you use it yourself, I don't want the lad mixed up in this kind of thing.'

His voice is loud and fierce-like, and I almost say somefink 'til I feel her fingers gripping the back of me neck, pinching hard.

'No, the lad just complained of a belly ache and when I touched it to see if it was serious he gave off a howl,' me mistress says. ''Tis nothing, Will.'

Master narrows his eyes and I finks he don't believe her. 'I will not repeat myself on this matter, Margery. I want you to exercise discretion when it comes to your herb skills and such. I will not stand surety for you again. Though it's ten years since they had you imprisoned in Windsor for this sort of thing, people don't forget.'

'Will, I promise you, there will be no trouble. I have people of great influence on my side, needing my services. And paying well for them.'

Me master's face goes all thoughtful and I sees he likes the sound of more money coming in. He can't do without his fine sauces and spiced wines this money pays for. He likes it just too much. He nods to us, satisfied.

'Barnabas!'

Father Thomas looks up at me in surprise. He's holding his fevver pen and his fingers is all inky. The parchment on the table filled wiv numbers, circles, triangles and squiggles lies across his desk, so I knows he's writing up somefink about his experiments.

I knew I'd find him in his workshop, cos of the stink. I reckon the whole of the old church reeks of smoke and melting metal, but in here the fug is thick and somefink's bubbling and puffing out a white vapour that curls around the beams what are blackened by smoke from the furnace. I've no idea what he and his friends is up to.

'Mistress Jourdemayne sent me to see you,' I says.

I weave me way towards him, trying not to knock over anyfink. The floor's littered wiv jars, crucibles, funnels and tongs, and stained dishes full of ash. I manage to squeeze meself down on the end of the bench where he keeps his hour-glass and globe.

'She said to give you this message.' I takes a square of parchment from out me sleeve.

The priest drops his pen in the ink-pot and tweaks the message from me fingers. He frowns at me as he unfolds it.

'Did you read this, Barnabas?' His pale eyes glint.

'Would I do that?' I pretends to be insulted.

He gives me a piercing look. 'Yes.'

I tugs me hair and looks down at me wooden clogs, hoping I doesn't look guilty.

'You've no qualms about eaves-dropping or reading other people's letters, Barnabas, so don't feign innocence.'

Father Thomas scans the message, chewing his lip. Me mistress wants his help interpreting what I seen in the showstone. She's wondering if it's what she finks it is and will he want to do more to bring it about. Course she don't say exactly what she finks, but I knows it's the Duchess. She finks the Duchess is going to be Queen. And that will make me mistress rich. A queen what got there because of me mistress will pay her much at the very least to keep her mouf shut. Even finking somefink like that makes me fearful.

'So you'll know that Mistress Jourdemayne's been having regular visits from an illustrious client—?'

'Illustrious?' It's my turn to frown now.

'A noble lady—'

'Ah, yeah—she gets noble ladies all the time—gents sometimes as well. But you means the Duchess?' I says the last few words in a whisper.

'"You mean" is the correct phrasing Barnabas, not "you means". Remember what I taught you.' He says it like he doesn't really care so much at this moment. It's just habit. I knows he's thinking of the message.

'Did she say anything else to you?' he asks.

I shakes me head. 'No.'

He looks at me and his eyes go narrow. It makes me heart sink. I won't like what's coming next, I can tell.

'Now, think, Barnabas and take your time. What exactly did you see in the showstone?'

Slowly, I tells him. It wouldn't do any good to lie, he'd see it soon enough.

He turns back to his chart then and starts writing as if he's lost interest in me. I sits a little longer, swinging me legs. Then I starts looking round at all the muddle of stuff in the workshop—from the still in the corner wiv its pipes and long necked flasks spewing white smoke, to the stack of round, earthen-ware pots what he sometimes puts on the heat. Craning me neck, I examines the shelves full of queer-shaped objects like serpents, and I wonder if he'll let me help him today. But when I turns the hourglass over and watches the sand trickling through, he raises his head to glare at me.

'Not going down to Queenhithe today, Barnabas? No errands to run for Master Hodgekiss?'

I don't like the way he says 'errands' as if he suspects somefink, so I jumps up quick to distract him from asking any more questions. I know me face is red, as if he can see into me mind what I've got cooking up there to ask Black Jack. 'N-no,' I tells him.

'Good,' Father Thomas says. 'I've something I want you to do for me, instead.' He hands me a folded piece of parchment. 'Take this now to Master Pemberton in Wingwren Lane. It's just off of Turnbase Lane. You must wait there. He will give you something for me.' He fumbles in his purse and hands me a coin. 'You may buy something to eat, Barnabas, but don't linger in the streets too long.'

I'm about to scuttle out the door when his bony fingers pinch me shoulders. His grip makes me wince.

'Keep your ears open for anything useful,' he says.

Grinning, I wriggles out of his grasp and bolts through the door faster than you can blink.

A bright sky meets me, and I sets off towards Wingwren Lane at a fast pace. Me mouth fills wiv juices just thinking of the meat pie I can buy at the bakehouse in the Chepe.

༄

Wingwren Lane has a bunch of apothecary shops what is crammed next to each ovver and you gets a powerful stink of green, sweet herbs and all sorts wafting up your nose. Master Pemberton's shop is plonked there in the middle. He's a skinny, nervous fellow wiv spots round his gob what he keeps itching. From all the bottles and jars what line the shelves in his shop there ain't any doubt he's an apothecary. I says who sent me and he takes the cloth bag and drags me through to a mean little chamber wiv nofink but the glow of a rush-light burning. I can hardly sees me own hands, let alone read the letter what he takes from out the cloth bag I gives him. But he holds it near the feeble light, squinting like a mole, his lips moving as he reads.

I sits on a stool and peers around me, ears flapping for the slightest sound, and sniffing like a dog. Beyond the dusty gloom, I catches the scratch of scraping metal, a rasping whirr what makes me think of a blacksmith's workshop. I can smell a tarry smoke in the air. Maybe somebody's brewing somefink strong for a special customer?

'Wait here, boy,' says Pemberton, startling me sudden. He takes the note to the rush light and sets it afire, watching as it slowly goes to ash. He disappears through another small door and I imagines him sneaking along to some dark place where he stores the dangerous stuff of his trade. Somefink keeps me from moving, and as the stink of smoke thickens, I senses a somefink in shadowy corner beyond the weak light. An icy trickle runs down me back. I waits, frozen to me stool.

A child's voice begins to sing. It's an old rhyme I knows. She keeps singing and slowly a figure takes shape. It builds slow, but bit by bit a little maid appears. A sort of shimmer surrounds her, but I sees her clear then, and she looks straight at me and smiles. I reckon she's about five or six, dressed very fine in a little blue smock wiv embroidered sleeves. Her hair floats about her head in wispy, golden curls and her eyes shine wide and blue. At once the singing stops and she puts a chubby finger to her lips, cocks her head on one side as if she's listening.

'Take this back to Father Thomas as fast as you can, boy,' says Pemberton, appearing sudden at me side.

I jumps so when he enters I nearly drops the cloth bag he hands me.

'What?' Pemberton eyes me funny.

'Who's the little maid?'' I says, staring at where she ain't anymore.

Now it's Pemberton's turn to jump. His eyes go all wide and frightened. He grabs me shoulder.

'What maid?'

'A little lass wiv golden hair—singing she was—'

He gasps and grips me tighter, nails digging deep. 'You saw Maggie? You heard her singing? What kind of an imp are you?'

It's plain he's scared, so I grins and shrugs, cos now the spirit's gone I'm meself again.

'Father Thomas don't like me to talk about spirits,' I says, wriggling out of his clutch and making for the door. 'But you got one here, Master Pemberton. Do you want me to tell him to send her away?'

'Maggie's been part of this place since before the old king's time,' says Permberton wiv a shiver. 'Haven't seen her myself, but I've heard the singing sometimes when I've been working here alone. I suppose Father Thomas would send her away if I asked—'

'She don't do no harm,' I says quick to stop him asking any more questions. Besides me belly's growling, and I'm keen to get to me pie before they're all sold. 'I'd best be getting back to Walbrook now.'

He gives me a sharp look but he don't offer no coin, so wiv the bag slung across me chest, I slips into the street like a hound on the scent.

After that dingy hole it's bright and the air is fresh and warm. I sneaks along Sopar's Lane, past the old hag wiv the wizened face what sells roots and seeds and through the muddle of alleys what leads me closer and closer to the pie shop in Bread Street.

'What's it to be, Barney-Boy?' says the pie shop owner when I gets there. She grins down at me, her wide mouth showing her one yellow fang amidst a crowd of blackened stubs. 'Beef's good today. There's some veal and venison mixed in to make a rich gravy and there's dates and almonds too.'

We both knows beef's the cheapest and only kind I can afford, but the owner always likes a bit of banter, and I plays along wiv it.

'Course I'd rather have peacock,' I says, and gives her a wink. 'But if you says the beef's the best, I guess that's what I'll have.'

I tips me coin into her big hand. As she leans down to get the pie I gets a peek at her huge paps in her tight bodice. When she hands me a hot pie, she gives a belch of a laugh what sets her great belly wobbling, and the fat, hairy wen on her chin jogs up and down.

I takes the pie and burns me fingers it's so hot. Still I takes a bite. The gravy drips and the pastry is sticky. Me stomach growls wiv joy.

'Mind you don't burn yourself,' she says. 'Them pies is only just out the oven!'

Mouth too full for speech, I holds up a sticky hand in farewell and leaves. She's right. The pie is too hot to eat and I finks I might as well have a wander down to the docks while I waits for it to cool. Queenhithe ain't so far away.

⌘

The wind stirs the sailor's black hair, but his mouth twists in a wide, gap-toothed grin as he swivels to face me. 'What can I be doing for you, Barney?'

I points to the small ship behind him. 'Isn't that a Portugee caravel?' I asks him. He nods. I knows me ships. Talk to the sailors and ask away all the time, when they've time. I seen one like her only once before, but I remembers. Father Thomas says I'm quick like that. Too smart for me own good. 'Them sails on her. They're lateen sails, ain't they?' I wipes me sleeve across me mouf and nods towards the mast wiv the three-sided sails.

'Lateen sails, them is,' says the sailor. He narrows his gaze and tilts his chin. 'Let you sail close to the wind. And see the big square ones? Them's for speed. A caravel can sail faster than your cog or your hulk. And see its keel?' He squats on his haunches, yellowed finger-nail pointing low. 'That's for shallow waters—gets you into the coast for moving cargo on and off easy.'

'Have you been to Portugal?'

He shakes his head. 'Been to Spain a time or two. Hot as hell and swarming with flies.' He stands then, sniffing and cracking his swollen knuckles. 'Mostly I serves on board cogs back and forth to the Low Countries.' He flicks a calloused thumb. 'That's my vessel yonder.'

A fat boat like a barge bobs on the black dock water, and I spies a wiry fellow wiv a rag tied round his dark curls perched among its tangle of ropes hanging from the mast.

'There's regular work on board the cogs shipping cargo for the woollen trade. Wool, that's where the money is, my young master.'

I wave back to the lean fellow. 'I'd like to sail to the Indies, or the Afric.'

'Then, you'd better talk to yon Portugee captain,' says the sailor, black eyes dancing with merriment. He indicates the cloaked figure on the caravel's deck what's watching dark-skinned crew-men unload barrels. 'I seen you hanging about Queenhithe regular, and I reckon you've a fancy for the sea-faring life.'

'I like to watch the ships.' I face him square on then, raising me voice above the noisy rolling over the cobbles and the men's raucous shouts. 'But I ain't such a fool as to think that captain would talk to me, even if he could speak English.' I nods to the ship. 'What's it carrying anyway?'

'Spices and silks, and medicines from Moorish physicians. They say them doctors know a cure for every illness known to man.' He gives a hearty laugh. 'Well I've still work to do, lad. Best be going.'

I nods and takes off. No good staying where's you aren't wanted if you wants to come back another time. And I do. Always.

I makes me way back up Bread Street and there's such a crowd I knows it must be some kind of procession just gone or about to come. I hear from someone pushing their way through that it's the Mayor this time, and he's going to the guildhall. I would go and have a good old look at them swells but I knows I've cut meself as much time as I can now and should get back to St Stephen's.

I catches sight of Nick talking to some sneaky looking cove, there by the Mermaid. It's only for a moment though. Someone bumps me from behind and another pushes me up against a fat woman wiv a face as fierce as a mastiff. 'Hey! Watch out!' She curses me, then she sees I'm no higher than a flea and gives a grin. Muttering apologies, I backs off, and it ain't until I'm away from the press that I realizes the cloth bag's gone. The cord's still across me chest mind, but some knave's sliced the bag off and hooked it.

*

Me belly churns when I finks what Father Thomas is going to say. Part of me don't want to go back to Walbrook now, but it's no good hiding at Eye cos he'll find me there in a trice. And there's no one in the city I can go to.

I trot through narrow cuts and reeking alleys, making a miserable journey back to St Stephen's. I can hardly keep me pie down by the time I opens the door to his chamber.

'Barnabas! You're as white as a ghost.'

Father Thomas stares at me wiv such a shocked expression I stands stock-still. Do I look that bad?

'I'd almost given you up,' says Father Thomas. 'Where've you been?'

'I went for a pie after I left Pemberton's,' I mutters. 'I was listening to some of the tongue wagglers—'

I glances at the priest as I run out of words. He watches me wiv a sour face. I sighs.

'Sit down, Barnabas, and have some ale.' The priest shakes his head like he's lost the will to scold me.

A moment later I huddles in me chair, a cup of ale in me hands. I sniff loudly, cough a little. If he finks I'm ill he mighten be so hard on me.

'Don't you have something to give me?' Father Thomas says.

I avoid his eyes and he leans over and lifts the bits of cord what held the bag across me chest. I don't say nofink. He waits. He can be patient, but I can feel he ain't pleased.

I takes a gulp of ale. 'I did, Father.' Shame makes me voice wobbly. I forces tears into me eyes. 'But some cut-purse relieved me of it on Bread Street.'

Father Thomas gives an angry snort. 'I thought you were too smart for that, Barnabas.' He smacks me head. 'Lucky for you, there is no harm in a lump of wax. And now it's nearly curfew, so I can't send you back for more. You'd be questioned by the Watch.'

I sniffs, rubs me eyes and wipes me nose on me sleeve. 'I tells you what I did see. Why I wasn't paying as much mind as I should,' I says. 'I sees Nick—Master Jourdemayne's groom, in Bread Street, near the Mermaid. Now that's odd cos he should be back at Eye, and Master Jourdemayne's been ranting at him about disappearing when he ought to be in the stables—'

'And?' Father Thomas looks down at me wiv a curious expression.

'And he was talking to a dark fella in an old yeller cloak. Face like a weasel. He didn't notice me though cos they had their heads close togevver, as if they was plotting somefink.'

Father Thomas gives a big old laugh. 'Is that your best excuse, Barnabas? You saw one of your fellow servants talking to another man?' he says. 'But I must applaud your observation. No doubt Master Jourdemayne will be grateful to receive information about his missing servant, but—'

'Oh I couldn't tell Master Jourdemayne,' I says. 'Yer don't know what Nick's like.'

He gives me a sharp glance and cocks his head as if waiting for more. Then he smiles down at me in that sneery way he has sometimes.

'I'm sure Master Jourdemayne has the measure of this Nick.' He grabs me shoulder. 'Well, it looks like you'll have to stay here the night. Now take yourself off to bed, lad.'

I finds me usual corner in the chamber, near the hearth, and makes meself comfortable. Closing me eyes, me mind drifts off to pictures of Alys. This time I'm tall enough. I can looks down at her and see the tops of her lovely round titties. I starts to slide me hand up her skirt. 'Gis a kiss,' I says to her. I could swive her from here to Greenwich. This time she don't look at me like I'm dirt when I speaks. This time she closes her eyes, opens her mouf and her legs.

When morning comes and the bells wake me, it's me bones that are the only fing that's stiff. I gets up quietly and sneaks off before I'm spotted. Already folk is waking up. They creep about like conies, pushing carts, or carrying large bundles on their backs, heads and in baskets. Maids and boys on errands weaving their way through the carts. I runs down Bread Street towards Queenhithe, me wooden shoes skidding on the slimy cobbles. Already I smells the garbage that runs free in the gutters. It's the heat. It don't half stink this time of year.

If I'm lucky I can make it back to the Jourdemaynes' in time for some bread and pottage. Me mind so caught up wiv this that I run straight into some jade with a swollen belly and there's a hell of a racket.

"Ere, you! Yeh, you, yer little maggot,' says a voice wiv black murder in it. 'Wot do you fink you're doing with Meg?'

I'm trying to get me balance, ain't I? I don't say it, but I thinks it as I struggles to untangle meself from the woman. Her hair is all dyed like a tom-cat's tails. She sets up a caterwauling and sits down in the muck. I'm about to take to me heels again, when a heavy hand comes down on me shoulder.

'Just a minute, young Jackanapes, says a voice wiv an accent. 'I think you and I have some business to do.'

Looking up, I sees a tall, slim fellow wiv oily black hair like a Spaniard's and a diamond in his ear. He's wearing a fancy satin jerkin the colour of peacock feathers, and his leather boots is finely stitched. There's somefink about him what makes me heart sink, but just now the woman's screeching is giving me the ear-ache, and her fat companion's threatening me wiv hanging, drawing and quartering.

'She ran into me,' I answer, bold as brass, and the fat man's mouth opens in a yawn of surprise. 'She must've slipped.'

'Madam,' says the Spaniard, all smiles and fancy manners, 'I'm afraid this young knave is with me. I must apologise for his behaviour.' He hands her some coins and her puffy little eyes narrow wiv greed. 'See that poor Meg gets something warm and comforting inside her.'

'Someone's already given her that!' says a bawdy on-looker, for we've gathered quite a crowd about us now. I can't help grinning. The raucous laughter stops Meg in mid screech. She struggles to her feet, her grimy face twisted wiv fury.

'Never heed him, Meg,' says the fat man by her side. 'It's a rare thing to find a gennlemun these days.'

Meg gives the Spaniard a smile that shows several brown teeth, before the man drags her away. I thanks the Spaniard and gives him a low sweeping bow.

'Now, young sir,' he says, wiv a wink. 'Just where were you headed so fast and early?'

I nods to the docks. 'Just down there, Sir. I'm taking the wherry back to Eye.'

'To Eye, is it? Now isn't that convenient.' He looks at me like I've said somefink funny. 'My companion and I are on our way there.' He looks behind him and holds up his hand. Out of a doorway a tall blackamoor appears. He's wearing long brown robe kinda like a monk's wiv stitchery and fine trim on it. The man comes up beside us and I can't help but stare. His eyes are dark, but I sees they're kind. I nods to him. He bows low and looks at me. His face is all smiles and his eyes is twinkly. I stares at him. I ain't never seen a blackamoor and fight the urge to reach out and touch his skin. Others around me stares, too.

'My friend, meet my companion, Mustapha al Qali,' says the Spaniard with the earring. 'And I am Juan Jorge de Flores. Captain of the Isabella.'

'The Portugee caravel?' I asks. The captain nods. I'm so excited now I can hardly keep from grinning. A real captain, talking to me. What tales he could tell me. And his friend too.

I sweeps them both a grand bow. 'I am Barnabas of Walbrook. Well that's where they found me when I was a babby. But now I works at Maggotscroft at the Jourdemayne household—'

'You work at the Jourdemayne household?' the captain asks.

I nods and starts to speak again but he cuts across me. 'This is a fortunate encounter indeed, for that is exactly where we are headed.' He gestures in front of us. 'Lead us forth, my good friend Barnabas. We would speak to your mistress, Margery Jourdemayne.'

✺

I'm too happy as we goes to Queenhithe to get the wherry to fink about what business they have wiv me mistress. All that's on me mind are the questions I want to ask them. Me only worry is whether Tom will be at the dock when we gets there.

'Is it true you've brung spices and fine cloths wiv you?' I asks.

Captain Flores nods. 'It is the truth, my friend. And other things as well. We've been trading for many months now.'

'And you've been many places?' I names off the places I can remember from talking to the sailors. 'Like Bruges, Lisbon, Tangier and Venice?'

'Some of those places.' Captain Flores gives me curious look. 'You are well versed in your geography, I think.'

I turns red and nods, but still I've more questions. 'Where else have you gone then?' I looks at the Blackamoor and tries to fink of a place he might be from. 'Tunis?'

Captain Flores catches me looking and gives a hearty laugh. I likes the laugh, it's good and honest. Nofink false about it.

'Very good, Master Barnabas. Yes, we have come from Tunis and Algiers of late.'

'Is that where your friend is from?' I asks. I looks at him again and wonders if he can speak our lingo.

The Blackamoor smiles at me, nice and slow, and his teeth gleam white against his lips. 'I am not from either of those places, young man. I am from a place of which you will have heard nothing. But I have spent some years travelling to the places you have mentioned. And many more.'

Captain Flores put his hand on the Blackamoor's shoulder. 'Mustapha al Qali is a man of learning, my friend. Much learning. He has studied in many of the famous libraries. And now he brings the benefit of that knowledge here.'

We've reached the docks and so I've no time to fink about what's been said cos I've caught sight of Tom and I'm happy for that. I waves hard at him and shouts to hold the wherry. He's just landed his passengers and I don't want him taking on any until I gets me friends aboard.

Tom stares when he catches sight of 'em. But I tells him quickly they're important people what has business wiv me mistress. Tom's a good cove and he keeps his trap shut and helps them on board.

The Blackamoor and the captain talk a little bit in a different lingo. It don't sound like the Portugee what I've heard. It sounds different. Strange. I asks them what it is.

'It is Arabic, Master Barnabas,' says the Blackamoor.

'Is that your lingo, Master al Qali?' I asks.

'Arabic is a language I am quite comfortable with, but alas, it is not my own.'

'Do you speak many languages?'

'Not as many as some men I know. I am more fluent in other languages.'

'Like English?'

'Ah, now English I would have some difficulty with if I were to speak about complex topics like mathematics or astrology.'

'You know about astrology? Father Thomas, the man what found me, he knows about astrology.' I'm so surprised that the words just tumble out of me gob.

'Ah, so he is a man of learning too?'

I nods. 'He is. He knows all sorts and does experiments for his alchemy studies.'

I can tell I've truly surprised the Blackamoor now. But then I finks suddenly about me mistress and what business they have wiv her. And I shuts me trap, tight.

CHAPTER SIX
The Palace At Westminster, September 1440
ELEANOR

Eleanor stabbed the needle in her embroidery impatiently. A moment later she sighed and looked up at the door. It remained solid, large and silent. She tapped her fingers against the large frame that held the embroidered piece firmly in place. It seemed ages since she'd dismissed her women from the solar and sent her chamberlain on some errand she couldn't even recall now. And even longer since she had summoned Masters Bolingbroke and Hume to her side. Finally, when it seemed she might even scream, the knock came and the two men were announced.

Eleanor rose from her chair and greeted the men when they entered. 'Master Bolingbroke, Master Hume, I bid you welcome.' She gestured towards the small table and chairs that had been placed nearer the window. She watched them make their way over and slowly unfurl the documents they carried and arrange them on the table.

She moved quickly to the table and sat in the large chair, mindful still of her deep blue damask gown. 'You have what I requested?' she asked. It was difficult to keep the eagerness from her voice. 'The horoscope?'

She'd said the words almost in a whisper and laid her ringed fingers lightly on the parchment spread before her. She could make out a large circle bisected with various lines and symbols.

'It is the horoscope, Your Grace,' said Bolingbroke.

His eyes met hers but she could read nothing in them. She glanced at Hume. His hands fidgeted and he wouldn't meet her gaze.

'Would you explain it please, then, gentlemen?' She looked at Bolingbroke again. 'Roger?'

He gave her a faint smile. 'I'm sure you know something of horoscopes, Your Grace. But let me just say, each planet's position in the heavens at the time of our birth reveals its influence upon us. And we map the heavens on a chart for that point in time and interpret it.' He pointed to a position on the chart. 'For example, in Your Grace's chart I found the strong influence of Jupiter in this section here. This means good fortune and prosperity.'

She looked at the position he indicated and nodded, though it made no sense to her.

'Yet Venus placed here speaks of marriage and controversy—'

Bolingbroke halted and looked at her. 'I cannot be certain of any of this information, you must understand, because I don't know the exact hour of your birth. To chart where the sun and planets were in the heavens at the time of your birth I must know exactly when it was.'

She looked down at the chart, laid out so neatly before her. She could feel herself reddening. Of course someone with her background would have little idea of the exact time of her birth. She couldn't even be certain of the exact day.

'Not everyone is able to be so specific about their birth. In fact is only a small few, like the King.'

Bolingbroke's tone was soothing, but still it made her fume. If she were born to the nobility, like her husband, or the King, it might have been a different story.

'Well what have you found out then?' Her voice was low and angry. 'Can you not see anything of the future, beyond that I have luck yet controversy in marriage? That's something I know already. What about you, Master Hume, can you not see anything beyond the obvious?'

Hume gave Bolingbroke a furious look. 'I told him, Your Grace. I said that it was better to have mentioned this from the start when you first asked for the horoscope, rather than to try and discover information that wasn't there. As it is, all we can see are vague possibilities.' He pointed to a place on the chart. 'If the sun were in this position at your birth it would indicate there is controversy surrounding you.'

'I know that,' Eleanor snapped. 'There is controversy now. I want to know the future.'

'Well, I would say in the future too,' said Hume.

Eleanor glared at them both. 'I'm afraid, gentlemen, you are no help at all. If you haven't sufficient information to cast my horoscope accurately, then anything you say is suspect.' She shoved the parchment off the table onto the floor. 'Useless. Weeks, I've waited, and it's all useless!'

Both men bowed. 'I beg your pardon most humbly, Your Grace,' said Bolingbroke. He leaned over and picked up the parchment and rolled it up hastily.

Eleanor waved her hand at the two men. 'You may go for now, Master Hume and Master Bolingbroke. At the moment you are no use to me.'

'Your Grace, if I might make a suggestion first?' asked Bolingbroke.

She gave him a curt nod. 'What?'

'If I might suggest that we consult Dr Southwell.'

'The Canon at the chapel at Westminster? Why would I want to consult him?'

'Your pardon, Your Grace, but Dr Southwell is a man of great learning in many areas. Astronomy, astrology, alchemy and... and other areas that might be of use to you. He often works with Mistress Jourdemayne.'

'Dr Southwell, who comes here and participates in the discussions of science with my husband?' Eleanor took a moment to absorb this information and try and place him with the Jourdemayne woman. Was it possible?

'The very same man. As I mentioned, he has a wide range of interests,' said Bolingbroke.

'But I'm not certain these interests are all sound,' said Hume. 'I think my own research has much greater merit than Dr Southwell's, which have led him to some very spurious conclusions on several matters—'

'How do you think Dr Southwell might help us, Master Bolingbroke?'

'He might have more specific ways to find answers to your question. He has an imaginative mind, you might say.'

She studied the two men carefully. Hume was irritated and she wasn't certain if it was because of his vanity or if he had real doubts about using Southwell. Bolingbroke looked reassuring, confident.

'Very well,' said Eleanor. 'Talk to him. See what he suggests.' The man dealt with Jourdemayne. Perhaps she could, with some combined help, come up with some way to make her and her children's future secure. But she would need to be careful. Bolingbroke and Hume were right. Controversy always surrounded her.

∽

Eleanor watched the women on the dance floor with discontent. They swayed gracefully to the music, their jewelled gowns and headdresses sparkling in the candlelight. The men sported their share of glitter too. Multi-part hose, colourful jerkins and some wearing slippers with toes curled so outrageously high they strapped them to their calves. By rights she should be up there too, beside her still handsome husband, his hand clasped in hers, showing off her own finery.

She smoothed her gown of deep purple velvet. The dye alone was worth a king's ransom. Her golden hair dazzled even more brightly against it and made her eyes almost violet. She looked well. The fine lines that had crept around her eyes were invisible in this light and only her fine assets were visible now. She smiled to herself. Nearly all of her assets were visible.

Nearby, she heard the King query something of the Duke of Suffolk. No doubt he was pouring poison about Humphrey in the King's ear. She listened hard to see if she might enter the conversation and direct it towards a subject that would put her husband in a favourable light. A moment later and she realised it would be unseemly to lean over her husband's chair and enter in what was clearly a conversation meant only for the two of them. Earlier she'd thrown out hints to the King about dancing but they'd been ignored. So now, with the chair on her other side vacant as well, she was forced to sit and watch as her husband danced with a beautiful young woman.

Finally, she could stand it no longer. 'Who is that woman dancing with my husband?' she asked the King. 'Has she newly come to court?'

Henry looked over at her and frowned. 'Your pardon, Madam? I'm afraid I was speaking with Suffolk and didn't catch your words.'

She swallowed, tried to give him a pleasant look and then repeated the question.

The King scanned the dancing couples and smiled. 'Ah, that is the Dowager Duchess Bedford. Or should I say, Mistress Woodville.'

'That French woman who married a man in her household?' The words were out of her mouth before she could recall them.

The King's eyes narrowed. 'Exactly, Madam. A royal person who married someone from their household.'

She flushed deeply. The irony wasn't lost on her and she'd known the implication of her words the moment she'd said them. 'Of—of course, I meant no harm by my remark. I was only clarifying your answer.'

Henry gave her an icy stare. 'Of course you were.' He turned away with great deliberation. A clear dismissal.

Miserable, she turned back to examine Jacquetta Woodville. Her own eyes now confirmed all the reports of this woman's beauty. Her skin was smooth, her eyes clear and sparkling under her tall hennin and her figure very fine indeed. And the woman had just borne three children barely in the space of three years. And though she'd married in haste, without the King's permission, it seemed he'd forgiven her now. It was all so unfair.

The dance finished amid scattered applause. Humphrey bowed to the Woodville woman and made his way back to the chair beside Eleanor. The musicians struck up another tune and she half rose.

'Shall we take a turn on the floor, Husband?' she asked.

Humphrey frowned and spoke in a low voice. 'I think not, Eleanor. Perhaps it's better that we retire.'

'Retire? But the night is early yet.' She gave him a coquettish smile. 'Remember when we used to dance all night?'

'Not tonight. I am tired. We'll take leave of the King now and return to our apartments.'

She put on a bright smile. 'Of course, Humphrey. If you wish it.'

Humphrey offered their excuses to the King and made their way back to the large apartments set aside for them in the Palace. Humphrey was silent the whole way despite Eleanor's attempts to make conversation. She'd bade her ladies to remain behind at the entertainments in the hopes that she might interest Humphrey in something more active than sleep. Perhaps a cup of spiced wine might help him see how irresistible she looked this evening and she could then convince him to bed her well. Her time was ripe and she'd taken Jourdemayne's herbs most faithfully this past month.

She entered the apartments, Humphrey close behind her, and was startled to come across Lady Margaret wrapped around a lute and Master Jolippe wrapped around her, his lips on her very bare neck and shoulders. The candlelight glinted against Lady Margaret's dark hair, which was only loosely braided and hanging along her shoulder. There was no sign of her hennin headdress.

'Lady Margaret!' she said, deeply affronted. At that moment Eleanor didn't know if she was upset because Lady Margaret's behaviour might get back to the King and reflect badly on her, or that this handsome minstrel was making love to a woman whose olive skin, thick nose and lips left her bloodline open to question of some Moorish taint and therefore of dubious worth. She might officially be the Earl of March's youngest daughter, but Eleanor questioned whether some Spaniard had crept into the countess' bed while the Earl was fighting on the Welsh borders.

Lady Margaret jumped up, the lute falling from her lap and curtseyed low. Master Jolippe straightened and then executed a deep bow.

'Your Graces, I am sorry if we startled you. I was just teaching Lady Margaret an advanced fingering technique,' he said.

'Fingering, is it?' said Humphrey behind him, his voice raised. 'Well you can take your fancy fingering and find some other fool to use it on. I will not have you interfering with my household.' He raised his arm and pointed at the door. 'Out. Now.'

Master Jolippe bowed deeply again. 'Of course, Your Grace. I meant no offence, I assure you.' He grabbed his lute from the floor and scuttled out the door, his golden locks bouncing with the effort.

'As for you, young lady,' said Eleanor. 'I won't have behaviour like I've just witnessed in my household. Is that clear?'

Lady Margaret raised her dark eyes and Eleanor could see the flash of contempt in them. 'Of course, Your Grace. But I assure you, there was nothing going on. I was merely—'

'I know what you were "merely" doing.' Eleanor felt wretched. The hopeful mood she'd tried to cultivate had vanished. The air was full of tension and she could sense Humphrey's impatience.

'Go. Just go,' she said. 'Tell Alys I won't be needing her tonight. I can see to myself.'

She took a deep breath and waited while Lady Margaret made her exit. When she was gone, Eleanor moved over to the flagon on the small table and poured its contents into the cup beside it. She offered it to Humphrey. He took it without a word and sipped. Eleanor's hope rose a fraction. She moved behind him and began to caress his neck and around his ears.

Humphrey brushed her hand away. 'Don't Eleanor. I've no patience for that tonight.'

Eleanor gave a throaty laugh. 'Since when did my lord need patience for love play?' She kissed his head and put her arms down along his chest.

'I said, no.' Humphrey threw off her arms and rose. 'Do you ever listen, woman?'

Eleanor moved back in surprise. 'What do you mean, Humphrey?'

'I mean that despite my words of caution to you these past months to temper your ways, you have not minded me.'

'I don't understand. How have I not minded you?'

'Eleanor, there is gossip circulating about you. This is not the time for gossip. There are many who seek to do you harm. To do me harm. Cardinal Beaufort, for one, and all the other Beauforts who have a drop of royal blood and fancy their chances for more power or the throne. And right now my position with the King is not as secure as I would like it. He doesn't listen to me as he did as a boy. And when he hears gossip about my own wife, it does me great ill.'

'Gossip? What gossip?' She could hear the tremor in her voice. Humphrey had never behaved like this towards her before.

'Something about a horoscope. Have you been consulting with Bolingbroke behind my back?'

She paled under his hard stare. 'I—I only asked him to make out my chart. What is the harm in that?'

'So it is true. Whatever possessed you to ask for something like that?'

She lifted her chin. 'I wanted to see what the future might bring for me. For us. There can be nothing wrong in that.'

'Nell, are you mad? Do you not see that your future—our future is wrapped up in the King's future? He is my nephew, for God's sake. My flesh and blood. You predict the future that holds the time of the King's death. And that is treason.'

She was so terrified by this information she could take little comfort from his use of his old fond name for her. 'Treason?'

He came over to her and took her by the shoulders. 'You must have a care, woman. Watch your tongue. Guard your actions. Be wary of all who approach you. Even those who surround you on a daily basis. Everyone. The people who would bring me down will stop at nothing.'

She looked down at her hands. 'I'm sorry, my lord. I had no idea. I will, of course, do as you wish.'

He frowned and nodded. 'I shall have to trust you on that. I'm off to France in the morning.'

'To France?' The words came out with a wail. How would she ever conceive if he was in France?

Humphrey's eyes narrowed. 'The King wishes me to check on the Duke of York and to ensure that there are no unplanned skirmishes against the French. So I will have little influence on the King should you decide to cause further trouble.'

He shoved her away and strode to the door.

'Where are you going?' Eleanor managed to say. 'I thought you were tired.'

'Suddenly, I have a taste for some fresh air. I find none in here.' He shut the door behind him with a bang.

Eleanor, too stunned to move, stood staring at the closed door. How had this happened? He was off to France in such a temper, all because of this horoscope. Bolingbroke and Hume had said nothing to her about the danger casting her horoscope would create. And all for nothing. But she would waste no more time with a horoscope. Perhaps appealing to Southwell was a better way anyway. The man was a scholar and a priest, surely he wouldn't be interested in court intrigue and seeking more power. And he was acquainted with Margery Jourdemayne. She'd known the Mistress Jourdemayne for years and the woman had never betrayed her trust. She would work with Southwell and Jourdemayne and try and break with Hume and Bolingbroke. Jourdemayne had just sent word to her. Perhaps a visit was in store.

꩜

There was a knock at the door. She'd no idea how long she'd been sitting in the chair, staring out at the dark night. She smoothed her gown and put a smile on her face and gave permission to enter. Alys appeared through the door and curtseyed. Eleanor sagged against the chair again. As much as she knew deep down that it was unlikely to be Humphrey knocking at the door, she still had hoped.

'Your Grace, I thought you might need some help before you retire for the night. The other ladies have all gone to their beds now.'

Eleanor nodded. 'Yes, thank you Alys.'

Eleanor tried to relax as Alys helped her to remove the hennin headdress, unpin the coiled braids and release her hair to flow free down her shoulders. Alys took up a comb and ran it through Eleanor's hair, careful of any snags.

'Your hair is so lustrous, Your Grace,' she said. "It is just like the woman in the painting in the main hall.' Her tone was earnest and full of admiration. It lifted Eleanor's spirits just a little. 'How did they ever manage to paint such a colour? Do you think it's ochre? I've heard they use that, it's from foreign parts, ground up and mixed with some kind of oil to attain such a shade.'

Eleanor, feeling eased under Alys' ministrations, could almost laugh at the girl's wanderings. She was forever talking about one painting or another and was more often than not to be found scribbling drawings on the bits of parchment that Eleanor gave to her when she remembered. She found the drawings and her ramblings annoying only on occasion. Usually they were a welcome distraction. And now Alys' words helped her make up her mind.

'You are good, my dear,' said Eleanor. She took Alys' hand and brought Alys around to face her. 'I can trust you, can't I?' She peered deep into Alys' guileless brown eyes.

Alys nodded. 'Of course, Your Grace.'

'You've said nothing to anyone about my visits to Mistress Jourdemayne?'

Alys shook her head. 'No, nothing.'

Eleanor patted her hand. 'Good, good. Now I want you to take a message to the woman and tell her that I would like to see into this new showstone she's acquired.'

⁓

Eleanor tugged at her hood and blinked at the lad with the unruly mop of sandy hair. It was the lad from the small chamber, the one who'd polished the showstone and had some cheeky remark for Alys. She looked at him now, standing in the hall behind Mistress Jourdemayne. The sleeves of his jerkin barely left his elbows and it was too short in the waist now. The lad had grown, she could see that. He was nearly Alys' height. And though he still seemed young, there was an ancient quality about his eyes so that when he looked at her, as he did now, he made her uncomfortable.

Mistress Jourdemayne greeted her with the discretion she'd asked for. 'My lady, welcome,' she said. 'I believe all is ready for you in the chamber off my stillroom. If you would like to follow me.'

She walked along the now familiar corridor, noting this time the doors were shut, voices were low and the hour was later than usual. She had done her best to make her way with Alys to this household without any notice being taken of her. They had come on a wherry to Eye and made the rest of the way on foot, with Alys speaking whenever there was need. Mistress Jourdemayne had answered the quiet knock herself and it was only the lad, Barnabas, who had joined them.

Eleanor followed Mistress Jourdemayne, Barnabas and Alys into the chamber next to the stillroom. She could see the fire was lit in the stillroom beyond and something pungent simmered away in the pot on the hook above the fire. Behind her, someone appeared on the threshold of the small chamber. She turned and saw Dr Southwell standing there.

'Greetings, my lady,' he said in a low voice.

Too stunned to speak, she gave a small nod. He stepped into the room and gestured her to take a seat. She could only do as he bid. Had Bolingbroke spoken to Southwell after all? She'd told him not to bother, that she was abandoning the whole project. She reached the settle and sat down with a thump as her legs gave way. He shut the door firmly.

She glanced around her, trying to gather herself, restore her dignity and calm. Alys caught her eye and she could see the panic in the maid's face. On the small table in front of Eleanor was an intricately carved box that gave off a faint whiff of cedarwood. Before she could ask about it, Mistress Jordemayne offered her a cup of wine and one to Southwell and spoke about the cooler weather and chill east wind. She was effusive to the point of irritation, but Eleanor hardly minded. Her eyes and her thoughts had turned to Southwell. He was dressed the part this night, sitting in his chair by the small hearth. A dark skullcap on his head and a long dark robe covering his body, he looked every inch the alchemist and practitioner described by Bolingbroke. Perhaps it was the dim light, but there seemed little trace of the dignified scholar that had argued in her husband's library on a regular basis. Or even the religious cleric who spent some days at St Stephen's in Walbrook.

'Mistress Jourdemayne told me about your particular desire and that it might need means more aggressive than have been used up to now,' Southwell said.

'I thought you would be glad of Dr Southwell's expertise, my lady,' said Mistress Jourdemayne.

She looked at the Jourdemayne woman who hovered over her nervously, the lad Barnabas at her side. He stared at Eleanor blatantly. There was no nervousness, just a wary, steady stare. After a moment he looked away and gave a cheeky grin to Alys, who stood near Eleanor.

Alys lifted her chin a little, but Eleanor caught the flicker of laughter in her eyes.

'I came to try your new showstone, Mistress Jourdemayne,' said Eleanor. 'I don't know that we need Dr Southwell's help just yet.'

'Oh, but Dr Southwell knows all about scrying,' said Mistress Jourdemayne.

Eleanor looked at Southwell in surprise. 'You have knowledge of scrying?'

Southwell bowed to her. 'I do, of course. It's all used for the good. I taught this lad scrying, along with his letters and numbers, isn't that right, Barnabas?'

'Yes, Father Thomas,' said Barnabas. His face gave away nothing.

'The lad can even read some Greek and Latin,' said Southwell. The smile he gave Barnabas didn't reach his eyes. 'He'd make a fine scholar if he weren't so bent on mischief half the time and still spoke like a guttersnipe.'

'I'm sure the lad has many talents,' said Eleanor. She took a sip of the wine and indicated the ornately carved box. 'Is the showstone in there?'

Mistress Jourdemayne nodded. 'If you feel sufficiently refreshed, we can begin.'

'I'm ready,' said Eleanor. She set her cup down and a moment later she took Alys' hand. It provided her with a small amount of comfort and hope.

Mistress Jourdemayne leaned over and slowly opened the box. Nestled in a velvet cushion was a beautiful round stone, so sparkling and faceted it was as if a thousand small fires were inside it. Eleanor gave a little gasp.

'Impressive, is it not?' asked Mistress Jourdemayne. 'I had it brought specially from the East.'

Eleanor nodded and her hopes rose a fraction. 'Please, let us begin, now. Shall I close my eyes? Think of my question?'

'That won't be necessary,' said Southwell. 'Just place your hands on the showstone and Mistress Jourdemayne will search it.'

Mistress Jourdemayne gave Southwell a nervous glance. 'Yes, yes, this is a powerful stone and there is little need for any other preparation.'

Eleanor licked her lips and slowly placed her hands on the showstone. It was cold to her touch despite the fire that refracted in its midst. She stared at its centre and its sparking fire nearly hypnotised her. Moments passed in deep silence. She was conscious of the boy Barnabas standing close to Mistress Jourdemayne.

'Well, Mistress Jourdemayne, do you see anything?' asked Southwell.

'There's something there. It's just not clear, yet,' said Mistress Jourdemayne. Her voice shook slightly and she gave Southwell a nervous look.

Southwell stood up and moved over to her chair. 'Perhaps it would be better if you let Barnabas look.'

'No, just give me a moment,' said Mistress Jourdemayne. She moved her fingers along the stone and stared intently.

Southwell laid her hand on her shoulder. 'You're too tired. I think it's best to give the lad a chance.'

Mistress Jourdemayne looked up at him and, after a moment, nodded. She rose and let Barnabas take a seat.

'Barnabas has spirits that come to him,' he told Eleanor. Behind her, Alys gasped.

Barnabas looked at Alys and straightened. 'Mostly I just sees Limpin' Sam.' There was a note of pride in his voice.

'Who is Limpin' Sam?' asked Eleanor.

'Don't know who he was,' replied Barnabas with a shrug. 'Maybe he was a beggar or somefink. He don't speak, but he makes me understand by showing me fings. Or sometimes he sings. His voice is like an angel's.'

'Have you ever heard an angel, Barnabas?' Alys asked softly.

Barnabas glanced at Southwell. 'Father Thomas asked me to summon one once or twice.'

'And did the angel respond?' Eleanor asked. There was something about this boy that disturbed her. She tried to calm her unease.

'Don't know if it was angel or a demon,' said the lad, his eyes kindling at the memory. 'I didn't like the look of him at all. He was angry and cruel-looking and he wouldn't be commanded.'

Horrified, Eleanor looked at Southwell. What had she got herself entangled in?

'No need for alarm, my lady. That exercise was purely in the pursuit of my alchemy studies,' he said. 'The Church permits such things.'

'I'd rather work wiv Limpin' Sam,' said Barnabas. He glanced at Mistress Jourdemayne, who remained silent, watching the exchange nervously.

'Enough talk, Barnabas. Have a look in the stone,' said Southwell.

Barnabas gave Father Thomas a sour look and sighed. He bent over the showstone and studied it. Eleanor watched him in the dim light in fascination, her fingers falling away from the showstone.

'I sees a castle.' The boy's voice sounded awed. 'There's hills around it and green fields. It has high towers and a drawbridge, and close by there's a village wiv a market and lots of people crowded round a boy what's throwing stones on the ground. There's women wiv baskets asking him questions, and he throws the stones to get an answer. He's telling fortunes.'

'Very good, Barnabas,' said Southwell.

'What has that to do with me?' asked Eleanor. There was a quiver in her voice. She'd hoped for much.

Southwell held up his hand. 'Now look again, Barnabas, and tell me if you see anything else.'

'It's Limpin' Sam,' said Barnabas softly, plainly pleased. 'He's showing me books and scrolls. Now he's trimming a quill as if he's getting ready to write somefink. But he looks puzzled. Wait—he's writing fast but he keeps looking round as if he's scared of somefink. Now he's striking tinder and setting fire to the parchment. It burns fast—the little flames is like a river running along it and then they's eating up all the scrolls and books until it's just a big bonfire.' Barnabas looked up at Southwell who'd come to his side. His voice shook. 'It's danger, Father Thomas. He's telling me there's danger ahead.'

'And is that all? What else?' asked Southwell, an edge to his voice.

Barnabas looked back down into the stone reluctantly. 'Limpin' Sam's showing me a purse full of gold. Then he holds up a wooden box, and he puts some folded parchment inside it. Then he locks it up wiv a little key.' The boy looked up, his impish face grown solemn. 'Someone's dealing in secret matters, Father Thomas. You needs to keep things hidden from others. Limpin' Sam's burying the box in a churchyard. That means people is watching.' He paused. 'Wait a minute, he's singing. Do you know a woman what wears a ruby ring?' Barnabas looked at Southwell. 'He's gone, Father Thomas. Disappeared.'

'Look again, lad,' said Southwell.

Barnabas looked down at the showstone once more. After a few moments he shook his head. 'That's it. There ain't nofink more.'

Southwell patted Barnabas' head. 'You've done well, Barnabas, thank you.' He looked over at Eleanor. 'I'm afraid there is only warning to be had in the messages tonight. We must all have a care in our future steps.'

Eleanor clutched her hands to stop their trembling and quickly turned her heavy ring inwards. The last thing she wanted is for any of them to see the ruby stone set in it. It was better that they didn't read as much into that message as she had.

CHAPTER SEVEN
London, October 1440
BARNABAS

'What's wrong, Barney?'

Black Jack Hodgekiss leans so close I smells the ale and onions on his breath. I looks up from the wobbly bench I'm sharing wiv Master Ruggles, the mangy black and white cat, and gives a shrug.

'Your face's as red as a pig's arse,' says Black Jack, with a grin. 'Has that witch been clouting you again?' He wafts a platter of bread and cheese under me nose, his black eyes dancing wiv mischief.

Someone chokes on the ale he's swilling, and the sweaty knaves playing cards round the hearth jerk up at the word 'witch'. Several pairs of eyes is fixed on me and the alehouse's suddenly gone quiet, except the cat what's purring like a trundling cart.

'Nah,' I says. I grabs a lump of cheese on the platter before he whips it away.

'I've paid for that,' someone says.

Jack laughs. He slams his platter in front of bloke crouched at a table in the inn's dingiest corner. 'Eat and be merry, Master,' he says in his booming voice. 'Know now you've done an act of charity in feeding this poor foundling.'

'Thank you kindly, sir.' I gives the bloke a pitiful look. 'May fortune smile on you.'

The man gives me quick dark look before turning away.

'What's the latest, then, Barney?' Black Sam rubs his nose wiv the back of his hand and sniffs, but his attention's back on me.

I looks over at the bloke what's in the dark corner. There's somefink about him that's familiar. Somefink that ain't right. I motions to Black Jack and he leans in close. 'That bloke in the corner. You knows him?'

'He's been in here once or twice in the last while. Asks questions, he does.' Black Jack narrows his eyes. 'He asked about you, nows I finks about it. You know anyfink about him?'

I shakes me head. Best not say anyfink now, though I'm near as certain as I can be it's the bloke what was following me. I don't like it that he's asked about me neither. But for now I've some business wiv Black Jack.

'Here, can I ask you somefink?' I says.

He shoves the cat off the settle and sits down. 'And what would that be?'

I lowers me voice even more. 'I knows some of the drabs what come in here find themselves in trouble sometimes, or need to prevent this trouble, if you get my meaning. Well I might be able to get me hands on fings what could prevent the trouble.'

Black Jack cocks his head. 'Go on.'

'Well I was finking, that if I gives to you the special packets of herbs and fings what can help the drabs, or anyfing else someone might query about, well, we could both come to an arrangement of sorts that bof of us would like.'

'You'd give me a cut?' asks Black Jack.

I nods. 'That's it. What do you fink?'

Black Jack gives me a steady look and then claps me on the back. 'Right, lad. We'll give it a try. You gives me 'alf of what you earns and see how we gets on.'

'A quarter,' I says. 'After all, I'm taking all the risk.'

Black Jack laughs. 'You're a crafty one, Barney. But remember, wivout me, you got nofink.' He pulls me head close to his. 'I tell you what I'll do. Seeing as it's you, I'll settle for a third.' He shoves out his hand. 'Deal?'

'Deal,' I says and gives his hand a shake. I looks over at the bloke in the dark corner. He's staring at us, and though I knows he hasn't heard what we've said, I still feels uneasy.

Black Jack gets up. 'We'll have a drink on it.' He goes over to the barrels, gets us both a cup of ale and returns. 'Now, I hears that your mistress had some foreign visitors come to her.'

I takes a deep sup of the ale and nods. 'A Portugee and a Blackamoor.'

'And what was their business wiv your mistress, I wonders?'

'They had a new showstone she'd asked for. You should see the box it came in. You'd never find the like of the fancy carving it has anywheres else. The Blackamoor told me it came from the East. A place called Constantinople.'

Black Jack gives me a nod. 'A new showstone, eh. Trying to impress her customers. I hears she been getting some pretty fancy folk coming to her now. Even a royal duchess.'

I makes a face. 'I ain't supposed to say anyfink about that. But I can tells you that me mistress has been keeping some fine old company lately. And if it were up to me, I'd turn the lot of 'em away.'

'Problems?' asks Jack.

I shrugs me shoulders. 'Not so much. I just don't likes any of it, anymore. It all feels wrong.'

'Never mind, Barney, me boy. Wiv the two of us setting out in business we'll soon have you shut of 'em all.'

'I hopes that be true,' I says. 'Though it's from me mistress I'm finking to get me wares.' I taps me finger to me nose. 'On the quiet-like.'

Black Jack grins. 'Well, wherever you gets 'em, you be careful. In facts, be careful anyways. It sounds like someone else has an interest in you.'

I glances over to the corner where the man still sits. I'm certain now it's him. I nods to Black Jack and rises. 'I best be going. I've some errands to do.'

'Well, off you go then,' says Black Jack. 'But mind what I said. Have a care.'

I'm up and out the door in less time than it takes to fart, wiv the mangy cat jigging by me heels.

*

I'm in Bread Street when I sees him. For once, the smell of fresh baked bread don't tempt me. I'm dragging me feet, the heavy feeling in me belly weighing me down, so there's no room for hunger in it. The mangy cat twists round me legs and I stops, squatting down to stroke its moth-eaten fur. Its mew's like a wail of pain and I know it's starving, so I begs some chicken bits from a pieman.

'For your cat, is it?' He nods at the animal mewling and rubbing round me ankles.

I thanks him when he gives me the meat and he watches me hand the bits to the cat. It's when I squats down again that I gets a kind of prickling feeling in me back. I mutters to the cat and turn me 'ead a little and gets a glimpse of the dark looking cove what was in Black Jack's.

'Come on, cat,' I says out loud as I rises slow and careful. I pretend to examine the stalls as I walk along the street, the scraggy black and white cat at me heels. But I slips quick into Old Fish Street and then begins to trot.

Somewheres in the alleys leading towards Walbrook, the cat leaves me, streaking away like an arrow and leaping up and over a roof-top. Me hanger-on's still following, though. I dodges into a narrow lane, pressing meself into the shadows to watch him walk briskly by. I sneaks back, weaving in and out all the stinking lanes and short cuts I know, but by the time I comes out into St Swithin's Lane, the wily knave's back on me tail. I runs fast as an hare, but this bloke is quick and don't give up easy.

⌣

'Father Thomas!'

I slams the iron-studded door behind me and dashes straight into the little chamber what he uses for his writing, almost knocking him over.

'Barnabas?' He drops the scrolls and grabs me wiv both hands. 'What on earth's the matter?'

Me legs turn weak now I'm safe inside, so I holds on to his robe to steady meself.

'He won't dare follow me in here,' I says wiv a squawk. Me own voice won't even behave now.

'Who won't?' The priest looks bewildered.

'The fellow what's been following me all the way from *The Turk's Head*,' I manages to say, before I collapses on a stool, panting for breath.

'What fellow?' Father Thomas hoiks me up off the stool and takes me back through the church to the door. He opens it and peers up and down the lane. A couple of tradesmen pushing a cart stop and nod to him, but there's no one else. He shuts the door and looks at me, his face all thoughtful.

'Well, Barnabas, whoever was following you has plainly disappeared, so perhaps you might tell me all about it. Why do you think he's following you? Is it someone you've seen before?'

'Yes, I seen him in *The Turk's Head* and I seen him talking to Nick—I told you about that—I'm sure it's the same fellow—'

'Ah, yes,' says the priest. He sits down on a stool and looks at me wiv raised eyebrows. 'No doubt he's the one who robbed you when you were taking messages to Master Pemberton for me, too.'

'Nah, I didn't see who did that,' I says. I don't like the way he's making fun of me, so I speaks a bit sharp—what makes him give me an 'ard stare wiv them pale eyes of his.

'But you do seem to be seeing this fellow rather a lot, Barnabas,' he says, his voice tetchy.

'Yes, I do, and I think he's spying on me,' I says, bold as anything. 'And if he's spying on me, then he's spying on you as well, Father.'

I got his attention now. 'Where else have you seen this man?' he says. His voice grows icy now, but somefink like fear rings in it. He's on his guard, like he's somefink to hide.

'I seen him hanging around the docks,' I says. 'And Black Jack says he's been asking questions. He asked about me. And just now he followed me all the way here. I seen him slinking in the shadows, so I gives him the slip and crouched down until he went by. But he picked me up again in St Swithen's Lane.'

Father Thomas gives me sharp look. 'He asked about you at *The Turk's Head*? What exactly did he want to know about you?'

I shrugs. 'Dunno. Black Jack just said he asked about me.'

'I wonder who's so keen to discover who you are and where you go, Barnabas.' He twists his mouth into a nasty smile. 'Perhaps next time you should stop and ask him what he wants.'

His voice is 'ard when he says that and I can tells he don't like the fact that I brought the bloke here. But worse than that, I sees Father Thomas is scared. And that makes me more scared.

∾

It's getting late and I knows I've been too long at me errand, dashing up alley-ways and dodging into shops and out the back to be sure I wasn't followed this time. It was almost a game after a while, and I'm nearly sure that dark bloke hasn't seen me.

'Hey!'

Turning, the limping figure stares straight into me eyes. I'd know that face anywhere, but this time he ain't looking at me from no scrying bowl. He's here in the street, large as life. It don't half give me a turn, I can tells you. He don't look happy neither. But he tips me a nod and then scuttles off down an alley-way like he's too scared to hang around.

What's Limpin' Sam doing here in Cripplegate? I don't stop to think. I follows at a run.

It's a nasty, stinking lane and dark. I don't know its twists and turns, so I stumbles into somefink wet and sloppy what oozes into me shoe. The scabby buildings lean too close and I feels as if I'm in one of them nightmares where you runs and runs but never get nowhere. I strains me eyes and tries to make out the dark shape of Limpin' Sam.

All at once I sees a dark figure stooping over a body.

'Hey!' I shouts wiv out finking. The figure takes off. Only a faint patter of feet tells me this ain't no ghost.

I go to the body what lies limp on the cobbles. Kneeling, I stretches out me hand. The touch of a cold cheekbone sends chills through me. I leans closer and sets me ear against a frozen mouth. A faint groan tells me this fellow's still alive.

'Are you hurt bad, sir?' I asks, fumbling at the body to see how badly injured it is. Panic makes me clumsy and I hears a groan. I takes me hand away and me fingers is sticky.

'The rogue took my purse—' The effort of speaking's too much for the poor sod. The words trail off into painful gasps.

But somefink in the voice is familiar. I looks closer at the face and I sees it clear enough to know it's Captain Flores what's bleeding on the cobbles. His bref is heavy and he winces whenever he draws it.

'Help!' I calls, peering into the gloom. 'Someone! Help!'

An alehouse doorway cracks open, and just beyond this feeble light I sees Limpin' Sam watching me. He nods again and then evaporates like smoke into the grisly dark. What am I supposed to do now?

Flores groans again.

'Where's Master al Qali?' I asks, panicked.

At first I can't make out the jumble of words, so I presses me ear to his lips and hears him whisper 'lodgings'.

'Where? Where's your lodgings?'

An awful silence drives fear deep into me belly. Has he died on me? 'Help! Help! Murder!' I cries.

The alehouse door opens again, only wider, and this time people come out onto the street. I hopes they ain't too drunk to be of 'elp.

'What's happened here?' says one.

'Some Spaniard got himself into a brawl, by the looks of it,' says another, harsher voice.

'He ain't no Spaniard,' I shouts in protest. 'This is Captain Flores!'

'He needs a surgeon, whoever he is.'

'Will you help me get him inside?' I asks in me best voice.

They comes over to me, and wiv light from the alehouse to 'elp, two of 'em lifts up Captain Flores and carries him gently into the alehouse, me dancing after 'em and wincing at every groan. Once inside, they spreads him out on the trestle table and I sees what a sight he is. His face is daubed wiv muck and there's a mess of blood on his side.

'Give him some air!' A stocky woman wiv greyish-black hair straggling over her shoulders pushes the men aside. The alewife. 'Give us them rags and some wine, Jake,' she says to the bald-pated fellow at her shoulder.

Her gob's smeared wiv grease like a drab's, but she speaks like a soldier—all brag and bluster and no patience for fools. Wiv out warning, she rips away the torn fabric of Captain Flores' doublet, and presses a clump of wet rags against the still oozing wound. It's plain she ain't no stranger to blood. Fascinated, I watches in silent admiration as she works quickly, cleaning him up. When she's done she chucks the dirty rags on the floor and grabs a leather bottle and spills spirits over the cleaned wound. Captain Flores is still out of it, pale as anything. The only sound you can hear from him is his noisy ragged breaving.

The alewife looks up at me. 'You was wiv him. What 'appened?' she asks.

'I don't know, exactly,' I says.

She give me an 'ard stare. 'Whattaya mean?'

I tries to fink fast. 'I mean, I knows him. I wasn't wiv him, right then. I was in Hugger's Lane when I—I heard a scuffle—'

Everyone's staring at me now. I flinch under their looks and tries to gaver me wits. I can 'ardly tell them a spirit drew me into this alley-way, can I?

'I saw someone running away—a fellow wiv a knife—all dressed in black. I couldn't see his face, but Captain Flores was lying on the ground. The villain took his purse.'

Me babble don't impress. I can see the sneers on a few of their faces. Some of 'em start muttering.

'And who are you, lad?' The alewife grasps me chin and twists me face towards hers. I sees her eyes are sharp and don't miss a trick.

'Barnabas,' I says. 'Father Thomas of St Stephen's in Walbrook sent me with some papers for a scholar what lives near St Michael's—' Twisting out of her grip, I gesture to the satchel hanging across me chest to demonstrate the truth of me tale. 'He's called Edmund Peke, you can ask him if you want—'

'No need. But what's this man to you?'

'I met him at me mistress' house and knows him for an honest man. He's much travelled—'

'And wealthy by the looks of him,' she says, fingering the rich fabric of the ruined doublet. Some of 'em gathered round laugh at this.

I look at Captain Flores' pale face. 'Will he live?'

'Aye, and no need of a surgeon.' She gives Flores a crafty look. 'Thanks to me.'

'I'm sure he'll be grateful,' I says hastily.

She tilts her head and looks at me. 'Just you be sure to tell him I expects a nice sizeable amount of gratitude.'

They all roars wiv laughter at that.

The alewife looks at me all thoughtful-like. 'And why are you out running errands for a poxy priest after curfew?'

'He does important work and I goes on errands regular for him. He schooled me and all. Taught me to read and write, even in Latin and some Greek. The errand today though, took longer than it was sposed to.' I knows I'm babbling, but I can't help it.

'I ain't never seen you round here before,' the alewife says.

'I keep to the main streets in Cripplegate,' I answer, quailing under her fierce glare, 'but not these little lanes and alley-ways. I wouldn't have come here if it hadn't been for the noise—'

'Well, you'd best get acquainted with the place now,' she says. She takes me by the arm. 'You won't be going nowhere else tonight, Master Barnabas. Your friend here ain't fit to be moved, so we'll find him a bed and you'll stay wiv him. But first of all you can take a wash under the pump. You reek worse than a gong-farmer!'

She points to the mess what lards me wooden shoes, and the customers laugh.

'I need to find Master al Qali,' I say, me voice stubborn.

'Master al Qali? Who the devil's he?'

A thin grey-haired bloke steps forward. 'A Blackamoor.'

Everyone, me included looks at this bloke.

'I've seen the fellow in the Chepe once or twice now,' he says, his voice oily-smooth and educated. 'They say he is a learned man from foreign parts and he comes here selling manuscripts and helping with translations sometimes. He goes to Oxford to the scholars and other places where they value such things. He even has sold some to the Duke of Gloucester.'

The customers, they hangs on his words all goggle-eyed, and I can't help wondering why such an learned bloke's lurking in a low ale-house, but before I can speak, the alewife is taking charge again.

'And where might such a fine fellow as that be lodging?' she asks the grey-haired bloke.

'I suggest you try *The Golden Lion.*'

She nods and then sends one of the men to go there and ask after Master al Qali and then turns to me. 'Your friend there keeps some important company. I finks the amount of gratitude I need from him has increased a lot.'

Night don't bring me no rest. I sits beside Captain Flores. He's lying on a straw pallet thrown down on the floor of a small room wiv fleas aplenty. The captain's 'ardly stirred and the only fing I hears from him is a groan now and then. There's plenty of creaks, snores, rustles and squeaks everywhere else, though.

Just as me eyes begin to droop, a sudden sound wakes me. The moon is shining in the small window. I looks down at the captain. His face is still sweaty but not so white now. I wipe his face wiv the damp rag I have. He twists away, and gets all restless. I have to stop him clawing at his side.

'You'll make it bleed if you scratches,' I says in a fierce whisper. I try to soothe him by pressing the rag to his brow and tells him that Master al Qali will be here soon and how the Watch'll find the villain what robbed him. Suddenly, he grips me wrist. I'm shocked to see his eyes wide open, staring into the room.

'It's me, Barnabas,' I says. When he looks at me, I grin and shakes me head like a fool.

'Barnabas—' He repeats me name, but it ain't sinking in. After a while his eyes close and he dozes off. I'm cramped wiv stooping, so I lies out on the boards beside him.

Bawling voices wakes me up from me great dream of sailing across deep waters to places wiv large showstones and buildings bigger than a cathedral. I'm full of flea bites and bruised by sleeping on rough boards, so it takes me a while to come to me senses. The pale light's coming in the window so's I knows it's morning. Besides me Captain Flores lies wiv one brown arm across his eyes. I wonders how he can sleep so peaceful wiv all the racket what's breaking out below.

It's the smell of food what gets me up in the end. Gritty-eyed and scratching, I stumbles downstairs. Me bare feet slaps on the steps, and me mouth's foul as a tanner's privy.

'If it's food you're looking for, you're in for a disappointment,' says the alewife. 'This pock-marked fool's burned the pottage!'

A skinny little lad squats by the fire. He raises his arms to protect his 'ead for the woman is armed wiv a wooden mallet.

'I came to tell yer that Captain Flores seems much better.'

The alewife tosses her tangled hair, lowers her mallet and turns to look at me. The lad scampers off.

'I dare say he could do with somefink to eat,' I says.

The alewife swipes her face and nods. 'Still no sign of your Master al Qali. But then Godwin never came back last night, neither.'

I picks up me wooden shoes from the hearth where they've been drying. The alewife sets a heel of bread and a tankard of ale on the table.

'This'll have to do for breakfast, lad,' she says. 'If my servant girl can manage to move her fat arse from whatever stew she's slept in, we might get some more bread. In the meantime I'll see what's become of my man.'

I sits at the table and tucks into me bread and ale. It ain't much and it's gone in a trice. I hardly finks on it though cos I'm so worried about what to do next. I'm just finishing the last crumb when the alehouse door opens and Master al Qali appears.

'Master al Qali!' I says. Me relief is so great I rushes to him and gives him a big hug. 'You got the message then.'

Master al Qali pats me on me head and smiles widely. 'First thing this morning, Master Barnabas. And I hear you have been acting the hero and have saved my very dear friend.'

'Tweren't nofink,' I says. 'I was lucky to be nearby.'

'It sounds a lot more than nothing,' says Master al Qali. 'There is a knife wound I understand.' He looks behind me and I points above.

'He's upstairs,' I says.

'He's here. And he will freeze to death if he doesn't get some clothes soon,' says a masculine voice from the stairs. Captain Flores, his face still the colour of ash, stands there wrapped in a mangy blanket and a grin on his face.

The alehouse door opens and the alewife enters. 'You shouldn't be out of bed yet!' She stops and stares at Master al Qali, her mouf gaping. She shuts it quickly and looks over at Captain Flores.

'I assure you, Mistress, I'm quite well—'

'Joan, me name's Joan. And you'd better sit down,' she says.

'If you could but provide me with my clothes,' says Captain Flores.

Master al Qali goes over to him and points upstairs. 'If you would allow me, my friend, to have a look at your wound before you dress.'

Captain Flores waves him off. 'It's only a pin-prick, I assure you.'

'If you don't mind, I should like to look at your pin-prick.'

Captain Flores gives in then and starts going back upstairs and Master al Qali follows him.

I looks at Joan. 'Can I have his clothes? I'll take 'em up to him.'

She gives me a nod, but she ain't pleased and mutters somefink about 'dark foreigners.' A moment later I has 'em in me hands and I'm making me way back upstairs. When I enters the room I sees Master al Qali already has the grubby bandage off and frowning at the cut. It's red and pucker but it ain't bleeding.

'Well, it will do until I can get you back to our rooms,' he says. He takes the clothes from me and helps Captain

Flores into 'em. When the captain's all dressed I tug at Master al Qali's arm.

'Do you have any coins? Joan'll want some paying as fanks for her 'ospitality and kindness.' I says the last words a bit jokey like.

Master al Qali nods and reaches inside his robe and pulls out a bag of coins. He shakes out a few and gives 'em to me. 'Here, you may give the woman these and my thanks. Then if you are able, can you help me get Captain Flores back to the inn?'

I scampers downstairs and makes good wiv Joan and am back before he can think twice. We says little on the way there. I'm concentrating hard trying to keep Captain Flores upright. I sees he's still weak from the stabbing, though he's putting on a brave act.

It's when we's in Captain Flores' room in *The Golden Lion* that Master al Qali finally starts to talk. I sits in a chair, a cup of ale in me one hand, a pie in the ovver, while Captain Flores is dozing in his bed wiv a new bandage on his wound. Master al Qali is on a chair beside him.

'How exactly did you come to find Captain Flores?' Master al Qali says.

I finks a bit and for some reason decides to tell the truf. 'It was Limpin' Sam,' I says, me voice soft. 'He led me there.'

'Limpin' Sam?'

'Me spirit friend.'

Master al Qali looks at me queer and then smiles. 'I see. You have the gift of sight.'

I nods and looks down at me ale.

'And he came to you and showed you where Captain Flores lay wounded?'

'Yeah.'

'Well you must thank Limpin' Sam next time you see him.

'I never knows when that will be. Usually, he comes when I'm scrying for Father Thomas, or looking in the showstone for Mistress Jourdemayne.'

'The showstone, as you call it, is that the one we brought for Mistress Jourdemayne?'

'Yeah. Well and the ovver one before it.'

'And cannot Mistress Jourdemayne look in the showstone herself?'

I shakes me head. 'Nah. She pretends she can. And she hoped this new one would do the trick. But it didn't. So now I still have to do it.'

'I take it from your tone you would rather not.'

'Not really. It didn't used to be so bad, when it was seeing only simple stuff. But now I don't like it at all. I sees terrible stuff. Stuff what makes me afraid.'

'Afraid? How?'

I look at him and tears come to me eyes. I don't want 'em there, but I can't help it. 'Stuff about the King. Bad stuff.'

'And who do you see this for?'

I sniffs and looks away. 'A duchess,' I whispers. 'Wife of a powerful noble lord.'

Master al Qali comes over to me and puts a hand on me shoulder. 'All will be well, Barnabas. You must not worry.'

I tries to take comfort in his words. But I'm still fearful, deep down in me bones.

CHAPTER EIGHT
Greenwich, November 1440
ELEANOR

Eleanor made her way along the corridor, oblivious to the draught that blew in from the ill-fitting windows. Her women were back in her apartments and she'd made excuses to go to the library to talk to the poet, John Capgate. Not one of her ladies expressed a desire to follow and for that she was glad. She needed time with her own thoughts.

Humphrey was still away in France and there was no sign he would be home before Christmas. The King had seen to that. More time gone. Wasted. She'd found a grey hair this morning when she'd looked in the mirror. Alys had pretended it wasn't, but she knew better.

In the months since she'd sought help from Bolingbroke and Jourdemayne about her future, the only thing she'd learned was that there was danger ahead and somehow the King was connected. How could her husband's prudish young nephew be a danger to her? It was true that he disapproved of her. But what could you expect from a young man who spent so much time on his knees praying and only took his hose off when he was donning his nightshirt? He was half afraid of any woman that was as well endowed as she.

'Your Grace.'

Eleanor looked up and realized she was standing outside the library and Southwell was at her side.

He bowed to her. 'Just the person I hoped to see. Could you spare a moment of your time?'

She looked at him closely, but his expression revealed nothing about the matter he wanted to discuss. She could only hope it was some point of literature or poetry, a feeble hope she knew.

He gestured to the door. 'Shall we go inside?'

She gave a resigned nod and waited for him to open the door. Once inside, she felt almost disappointed that John Capgate was no longer there, as she'd suspected. The room was empty, though a fire still burned brightly in the hearth. Not long gone then.

Eleanor took a seat by the hearth. Suddenly, she felt a chill and the need for some warmth was strong. After asking permission, Southwell took the seat opposite and settled himself comfortably.

'I have, I think, a solution that could advance your cause very much,' he said in a low voice.

'My cause?'

He gave a wan smile. 'I think Your Grace wishes to have a child that will secure your position?'

'How can I have a child when my husband is in France?' she snapped.

'I'm sure your husband will return soon. I've heard such.'

'You've heard that?'

Southwell nodded. 'Of course it is a rumour. But behind most rumours is some truth.'

Eleanor allowed herself to believe him, just a little. She felt some of the tension ease and found she could even smile at Southwell. 'So, what is this solution you have?'

Southwell withdrew a small cloth bag that was tied to his waist under cover of his dark robe. He laid it on her lap. Its dark colour stood out against the bright red silk of her gown. She'd chosen the red silk to cheer herself this morning, but against this simple brown cloth it almost looked garish, rather than sumptuous. She untied the bag and withdrew its contents.

'Wax?' she asked. A lump of beeswax, yellowed and of no shape lay in her hand.

'Special wax, Your Grace,' said Southwell. 'It will help shape your future, you might say, if I can play upon the words.'

'What do you mean?' Her voice was sharp again. She glanced at the door.

He saw her glance and patted her hand. 'It is only a harmless lump of wax to any who should enter. But if you feel safer to put it away, do so.'

She stuffed the wax back in the bag. Something about it made her uneasy. 'What am I to do with it?'

'When you are certain that you are alone, I want you to shape it into a figure. A human figure. Think of the fine young son you might have and mould it to that. But lay the wax near the fire first, so that it is soft and pliable.'

'And what should I do with the figure?'

'When you have formed the figure, put it back in the bag and return it to me. I shall take care of the rest.'

'And what is the rest?'

'Ah, that is to do with the mysterious arts. We will place it where it will do most good.'

She looked down at the bag. She didn't want to know anything more than what he'd already told her. At this point it seemed her only hope. Let Southwell take on the danger. She would do well to stay out of the details.

'Very well,' she said. 'I will do as you say.'

Eleanor examined the wax figure. It was still soft enough to change shape under firm pressure, so she handled it with care. She worked at it methodically, fully absorbed in her task. Did it look enough like the fine boy she hoped for? She tried to make the face long like her husband's and the limbs sound and well-muscled, but studying it closely, she thought it seemed too skinny for the boy in her mind. It was the best she could do, though.

Carefully, she wrapped the figure in a linen square for extra protection and then put it back in the cloth bag. She looked anxiously around her room for a safe location for the bag. There were so few places that were private. She opened the chest at the end of her bed and pulled out her casket of letters. They were mostly from Humphrey, sent when he was away on the King's business, but there were one or two from her children. She picked up the bundle and placed it under an old gown and put the cloth bag into the casket and the casket back into the chest. She stared at the closed lid a moment, willing it to be safe.

There was a soft tap at the door and Lady Margaret entered. Eleanor had spoken little to Lady Margaret since the instance with Master Jolippe. Eleanor glanced at the chest. Was it closed firmly? Was there any tell-tale sign that it had been open? She scanned it quickly, looking for some bit of cloth hanging and forced herself to shift her glance to Lady Margaret.

'Yes?' she said.

'I thought I might help you dress for tonight. I hear the King will be there and I thought you would want some extra touch with your hair that Alys wouldn't be able to give.' Lady Margaret gave a little moue of distaste. 'She is, after all, not refined in her taste as someone with noble blood.'

Eleanor flushed deep red and pursed her lips. 'I am perfectly satisfied with Alys' services. Some people, even with noble blood, hardly understand more subtle forms of refinement.' Eleanor looked pointedly at rope of pearls that hung around Lady Margaret's neck and ended trapped between the two large mounds that rose from the top of her gold velvet dress.

Lady Margaret looked down at the pearls and lifted her chin, her eyes flashing. 'As you wish.'

'Would you send Alys to me now, please?' Eleanor said. She gave a small smile of triumph.

Lady Margaret nodded and swept back out of the room. Eleanor's smile widened and she let herself savour the small moment of amusement. A moment later she recalled the woman's actions. She might be stuck with Lady Margaret attending her, but that didn't mean she had to be nice to her. She would make her so unwelcome Lady Margaret would plead with her father to find her another place. Maybe that Jacquetta.

❧

When Alys arrived she was out of breath. 'Is there something amiss, Your Grace?' she asked. Her sleeves were rolled up and the apron she wore was damp.

'I have an errand for you, Alys.'

'For me?' The puzzlement was plain on Alys' innocent face.

'It's a private matter,' said Eleanor. 'One that only someone I trust completely could carry out for me. Can I trust you completely, Alys?'

Alys' large brown eyes widened. 'You can trust me. I promise you.'

Eleanor nodded. She had no doubt of Alys' loyalty, but it was just as well to remind her of it. She removed the bag from the casket in the chest and gave it to Alys.

'I want you to take this to Dr Southwell, at his church in Walbrook. St Stephen's, I think. Can you do that for me?'

She took the bag from Eleanor. 'Right away, Your Grace. I'll fetch my cloak.'

Eleanor put a hand on her arm. 'Take one of my gowns with you as if you're taking it for mending, and hide the bag among its folds. I don't want my ladies knowing you are carrying this bag from my room when you pass through the solar.'

Alys nodded and did as Eleanor said. When Alys had shut the door behind her Eleanor leaned her ear up against it. After a moment she gave a sigh of relief. None of her women had questioned Alys or even spoken to her. All was as it should be. No one would notice Alys going to Southwell at Walbrook, and it was far safer than passing the bag to Southwell here, in La Pleasaunce, now that it was no longer just a harmless lump of wax.

◦◦◦

'Did you deliver the bag safely?' Eleanor asked. She sat in the chair in her nightdress fidgeting with her braid while Alys stooped over the hearth. It wasn't until that night, after Eleanor had dismissed her ladies and Alys had come to bank the fire and snuff the candles, that Eleanor was able to speak privately with the maid.

Alys set the poker aside. 'I did, Your Grace. Dr Southwell wasn't there when I first arrived, but Barnabas let me in and he came a short while later.'

'Barnabas?' Eleanor fought the alarm that rose inside her.

'You remember, from Mistress Jourdemayne's household.'

Eleanor did remember, but for some reason didn't feel reassured. Barnabas knew much of what she was about, but she would rather he knew nothing of this. 'Did he see you give the bag to Dr Southwell?'

'He did, Madam. But you don't need to worry about Barnabas. You can trust him.'

Eleanor studied Alys. Her eyes were alight and her face flushed. 'What makes you think I can trust Barnabas?' Eleanor asked.

Alys gave her an earnest look. 'I admit at first I thought he was no better than a guttersnipe. But there is a real kindliness underneath all the cheek. And Dr Southwell seems to trust him. He uses him to help with his experiments.'

Eleanor nodded but she wasn't reassured. That Southwell vouched for him made her feel less comforted. It was almost better to her that he had only Alys' innocence behind him. But there was no help for it. What was done was done.

'There's something else, Your Grace.' Alys clasped her hands tightly in front of her. Her voice dropped to a whisper. 'A man stopped me when I was out.'

'A man? Who? What did he want?' asked Eleanor.

'A dark man, with a surly manner. I don't know his name. He only said he was in the employ of the King.'

'The King?' The words came out in a shrill whisper.

Alys nodded and the words tumbled out. 'He asked me questions about you. Where you went, who you saw. Did I ever notice anything out of the ordinary. Those kinds of questions. But I told him nothing, Your Grace. Nothing.'

'Where did he stop you? Was it after you delivered the bag?' asked Eleanor in a real panic. Pray God it was afterwards and wasn't anywhere near Southwell's place.

'After I delivered the bag I decided to go down Bread Street and to the docks. It wasn't raining for a change and I thought I would see what ships had come in.'

Bread Street was far enough away from St Stephen's that it might well be safe enough, Eleanor thought.

'I didn't like the look of him,' said Alys. 'And he said I was to keep my eyes open and he would ask me again if I'd seen anything.' She lowered her voice. 'He said that if I didn't tell the truth and report what I'd seen that it would go badly for me.' She gave Eleanor a pleading look. 'Oh have a care, Your Grace. It's clear there are those out there who would do you harm.'

Eleanor swallowed hard. Who had set this fellow on her? And why? What were they hoping to find? She thought of her husband's warnings earlier. There were so many of them out to bring down her husband. And they wouldn't hesitate to use her to do it.

She leaned over and patted Alys' hand, attempting a reassuring smile. 'No need to worry, Alys. All will be well.'

～

'Whore!'

Eleanor heard the word shouted loud, but when she turned to see who dared to say such a thing, she couldn't see them. All she could make out was a sea of hostile faces drenched by rain staring at her silently. Up ahead she saw the Lady Margaret smirk at her companion. The pig-faced harlot. She would make certain the smirk was wiped off her face when they arrived at Westminster Palace.

She lifted her chin and motioned her men to resume the wet dreary journey. She had started out in good spirits that even the weather couldn't dampen. The day before, Humphrey had sent word he was back from France and at the palace reporting to the King. She'd been walking on air since then, rushing around preparing to join her husband. She'd packed her best gowns and headdresses, all her good jewels, certain that the approaching Christmas revels would be the finest yet.

Now she was cold, wet and hungry. Even the heavy cloak she had donned against the foul weather wasn't enough to keep off this drenching rain. But the sullen crowds that lined the roads as the entourage neared the palace were worse because they frightened her. In the past, she could laugh and even take some enjoyment from the crowds, especially if she was with her husband, because there were usually several cheers. The crowds loved Humphrey. Now, she could detect no pleasure or interest in the spectacle of her banners and beautifully turned out horses, or the finely gowned ladies and gentlemen. Resentment was what she saw in their faces and heard in their shouts. And even a face or two was filled with hatred, which made her more uneasy.

She felt some relief when she finally dismounted and made her way inside the palace walls, her ladies trailing after her. For a moment she toyed with ordering Lady Margaret on some errand that would keep her out in the drenching rain, but it fled at the sight of Humphrey standing with a group of other lords in the great hall.

'My lord!' she called, her voice filled with pleasure. She made her way to his side, nodded to the others and gave him a quick curtsey. 'You must excuse me, my lords, but it has been an age since I've seen my husband and I must have a moment at least to give him greeting.' She took his arm and steered him away towards the large hearth where a feeble fire burned.

Humphrey gave her a thunderous look. 'Eleanor, you have interrupted an important conversation.'

She patted his arm. 'Oh come now, you can spare a moment for your wife, can't you?'

He sighed. Eleanor leaned forward and pecked him on the cheek. 'Have you no other words of greeting for me? You've no idea what abuse I've just borne during my journey here.'

'What do you mean?' He looked at her closely.

'The crowd. They were different, Humphrey. Sullen, angry. One even called me a whore.' She choked slightly on the last word. It was still so fresh in her mind.

Humphrey's face clouded again. 'Was that it? Was there anything said about the King? About me, or any of the other lords?'

She gave him a puzzled look. 'No, why?'

His face eased. 'I have heard there is growing discontent among the people. In the city many are paying three times as much for bread than they did this time last year and wages no better. It's three years of poor harvests taking its toll. The countryside isn't much better. So, they have no liking for rich nobles flaunting wealth when they're going hungry.'

'So they'll hurl names at me, call me whore, because they're hungry? How is that my fault?'

Anger flickered across Humphrey's face. 'Eleanor, you have much and they have nothing and showing great displays does nothing but remind them of it.' He studied her face carefully. 'Have you heeded the warning I gave you before I left?'

She felt herself blanche under his gaze. 'Y–yes, Humphrey. I've done all you asked.'

He paused a moment, still examining her face. 'Good. See that you continue to do so.'

He began to move away from her but she restrained him. 'We will spend a warm and loving Christmas here, won't we?' She tried to keep the pleading out of her voice.

He looked down at her hand and then to her face. 'I hope so, Eleanor.'

The words echoed in her head as she made her way to her apartments. The whole day had turned out terribly and she felt wretched. She wanted nothing more than to lie on her bed and forget about all of it. When she reached her apartments and opened the door she was relieved to see that no one was there. She noticed the bedroom door and saw that it was closed. She found that curious since she usually left it open unless she was inside. That way she could see if anyone dared to enter it if her ladies were present with her in the outer room.

She walked quietly over to the door and opened it slowly. There was a small creak from the protesting hinges. Inside she could see Lady Margaret bent over her chest, half the contents on the floor.

'What are you doing?' Eleanor could hear the slight note of hysteria in her voice.

Lady Margaret popped up, guilt written all over her face. 'Your Grace, I thought you were in conversation with your husband.'

'As you can see, I am not. I'm standing here watching you ransack my clothes.'

'N-no, Your Grace. I–I was just searching for a particularly fine gown for you to wear tonight. Something to change into that would show the world that you are not a woman to be insulted.'

Eleanor narrowed her eyes. 'You think me a fool, do you?' She gestured to the door. 'Go. I don't need your help. Not now, not any time.'

Lady Margaret gave her a dark look and walked quickly out of the door. Eleanor could hear her retreating footsteps and the outer door open and shut. When she heard the latch take, she went over to her bed and sank onto it, her thoughts in turmoil. What was going on? Was Lady Margaret spying on her? If she knew she couldn't trust anyone before, this confirmed it. Except Alys. Alys was trustworthy. She had to be.

CHAPTER NINE
London, Early December 1440
BARNABAS

I sits in *The Turk's Head* and watch a pock-marked tradesman in a leather apron burst into the fug of the noisy tavern. His face is as red as a furnace. Already some are making revels as though Christmas is already here. You wouldn't know it's fasting time still.

Black Jack comes over to me and shoves a tankard of ale in front of me. 'I needs a word, Barnabas.'

His wife gives both of us a sharp look as she gathers up cups, goblets and pitchers, but she don't say nofink. A sailor lingers by the board, his heavy pack set down by his feet, but his eyes bore into me. What's brought him to *The Turk's Head*, I wonders? I reckon Sarah's mind is running the same way, cos she takes her time clearing up, and when she's done, she saunters over to Black Jack and raises an eyebrow, as if asking a silent question.

'I'll come and give you a hand in a moment or two,' says Black Jack. He gives her a saucy slap on the arse as he turns her towards the kitchen door. His face lights up in a big grin.

It's plain she suspects we're up to somefink by her fierce look, her nostrils flared like an horse what means trouble, but she leaves wiv a sharp flick of her skirts, slamming the door behind her.

'Now Master Barnabas,' says Black Jack. He squats on his haunches so's he can speak low and look me in the face at the same time. 'Have you got anything for me today? You see, this gentleman—' he indicates the sailor wiv a nod, 'is willing to pay a good price for certain items you may have about you.'

I sticks me hand down me doublet and brings out a black cloth bag.

'Got some poppy,' I says, 'and some henbane. I've even got some nutmeg—but it's expensive.' I give Black Jack an hard stare when I says this, cos I ain't gonna be cheated by some poxy sailor.

Black Jack moves over to the sailor and they starts whispering. A moment later he's back at me side. 'He says, have you got any black pepper?'

I shakes me head. 'But I could get some for a price…' I looks up and catches the sailor's eye.

Plainly he understands, cos he tips me a nod and motions to Black Jack. When Black Jack comes back to me again he tells me the sailor'll pay me in silver and he names the price.

I nods and Jack holds out his hand for the bag. 'I want to see the coin,' I says. The sailor eventually agrees and we makes the exchange. Hey ho! I'm happy now. Business is booming since me and Jack set it up and I'm happy wiv the weight of me purse. It ain't enough to buy a place in Tom's wherry business just yet, but I have me hopes.

Later, I trots back through the streets towards Walbrook and I gets an edgy feeling—like someone's following me. It's an odd kind of prickling crawling up your spine and into your head what makes all your hair stand on end. I'm worried for me purse and I presses me hand to me chest to make sure it's still safe, aware of the pad of footsteps behind. Is it a thief?

By Horseshoe Bridge Street I decides it's time to take a chance. I sidles up a narrow alley by St John's Church and crouches down, waiting for the fellow to catch up. As soon as I hears footsteps, I pounces out like a cat, and stands in front of the runner, almost tripping him up.

'Do you want somefink?' I asks, wiv a snarl. I plant me feet wide so he can't get round me.

A spindly-legged feller in a brown doublet and hose stops and stares at me as if I'm an addle-wit. 'Get out my way, you scabby, little rat,' he says, giving me a push. 'I don't know who you are, but I've no wish to make your acquaintance. I'll call the Watch if you don't let me pass.'

'I think there's been a mistake,' says another voice, smooth and sly. 'I believe the lad wishes to speak to me.'

Out the corner of me eye I spots the dark-looking cove. The bloke what's been following me. He's leaning against a wall, a smirk on his pinched face and a nasty glint in his eye.

The other man snorts at us bof and moves away quick.

'Master Barnabas,' says the bloke. 'At last we meet. I've been searching for you for some time, you know.'

'And I've been trying to avoid you,' I says. Although me voice sounds bold enough, my heart's doing a little jig. 'What do you want? And why are you following me all the time?'

'Not all the time,' says the bloke.

Close up, his features is meaner than I first thought, and his brows is furrier. They straggle over his eyes like wisps of thatch, and make 'em seem darker and smaller—like little black beads. But those eyes is hard and fierce, red-rimmed as if he's used to lurking in dark, nasty places. He looks like the rat he is.

He takes me arm and steers me past the church. His touch gives me the shivers. He's strong, though, and he tows me alongside him as if he knows exactly what he wants. We go down a twisting lane, where he shoves me against a wall and pushes his face into mine.

'You seem to know a lot of interesting people, Master Barnabas,' he says. 'People of particular interest to me. First of all, you lodge at Jourdemaynes' farm at Eye where the renowned witch plies her trade. She, in turn, enjoys some familiarity with your mentor, Father Thomas Southwell of St Stephen's in Walbrook. I believe the scholarly Roger Bolingbroke also now numbers among her acquaintances. And what do all these people have in common? Don't look so ingenuous, my little imp. I know you for a sharp-witted knave, just as I know that your accomplices are skilled in the arts of necromancy.'

He leans in so close I can count the whiskers in the black mole on his face. There's no mistaking this man means business. His voice is full of menace.

'Don't know what 'in-gen-u-us' is,' I replies, feigning innocence, 'but I knows Father Thomas and Master Bolingbroke is alchemists—'

The bloke laughs and it sets me teef on edge.

'Don't pretend to be a fool, lad,' he says. 'Everyone in London knows you for a quick-witted young rogue. You've a reputation as a trickster—oh, I've some idea of what goes on between you and Master Hodgekiss too, but my business concerns someone of much higher rank than that. I believe you've met this fair lady yourself, and that she shares an interest in your mistress and her scholarly friends. My business is to discover what she intends by bringing these persons together—and I believe this is something you can help me to discover.'

'Me? Don't know how I can help you. Don't know nofink about no ladies—'

'Of course, I would make it worth your while to discover their intentions,' he says, ignoring me words. 'My employer is an eminent person who has the ear of the King himself. I'm sure you desire to serve our sovereign to the best of your ability, as any loyal citizen would.'

There's no mistaking his meaning. But the mention of making it worth me while to spy on Mistress Jourdemayne, Father Thomas and Master Bolingbroke ain't lost on me neither. And I knows the lady he's talking about must be Mistress Eleanor Cobham, the Duchess of Gloucester. But is it worf the skin on me back to help him, or is it more risky not to?

'Well, if I can do anyfink to help the King,' I says and gives him a grin and a shrug. 'How can I refuse?'

He seems satisfied wiv that and lets me on me way wiv a promise that he'll be looking for me answers soon enuf. I've bought meself a little time, though. Time to fink of some way out of this mess.

〜

It's raining hard by the time I makes me way down to Queenhithe and I pulls me head back further into me hood so's I can hardly see. I can smell the docks and the tang of the salt water already, though. I dodges in and out the carts that roll along the cobbles and nearly bang into a man coming the other way. It's slippery enough and I slow down a bit until I sees the docks and the Portugee caravel. Men are busy on the dock beside it, hoisting cargo aboard. I peers anxiously to see if Captain Flores is about.

I stops one of the sailors knotting a rope around a wooden box. 'Have you seen Captain Flores?'

The man stands up, babbles somefink and points to the ship. A man pushing a small cart stops and grins at me. 'You're wasting your time, lad,' he says wiv a laugh. 'None of these fellows speak English. 'But if you look yonder at the mainmast I think you'll spy your captain.'

I looks to where he's pointing and sees that Captain Flores has just appeared there. He spies me looking.

'Master Barnabas!' He greets me wiv a wide grin. 'You come to bid farewell?'

'You're leaving?' The realization hits me in the belly like I've swallowed a stone.

'On the next tide,' he says. 'I've delayed too long, as it is. The winter storms are nearly upon us. But why so sad, my friend?'

What can I say? That I don't want him to go? That's the truth, but why would that bother him? Captain Flores looks as jaunty as ever in his fine leather boots and diamond ear-ring. So I just shrugs and hangs me head.

'Come aboard, Master Barnabas,' Captain Flores says. 'Have a cup of ale with me before I go. Master al Qali is here, too, to say farewell.'

I makes me way on board and even wiv me troubles I still feels excited to be aboard ship, a trade ship. I take in all what's going on, watch the sailors lower the cargo into the hold and check the sails and ropes.

Captain Flores claps me on the back when I reaches him and leads me down into the small cabin below. Inside Master al Qali sits on a stool by a table wiv a map spread out.

He stands when he sees me. 'Master Barnabas, how good to see you. And under much better circumstances than when we last met. You are well?'

I nods and tries to grin. 'No more attackers?'

Master al Qali smiles at me joke. 'No more attackers. I fear the original attacker was after something we no longer had. And now he realizes it.'

Captain Flores touches his side. 'I would wish the man had bothered to find that out before he decided to stick a knife in me.'

'Is the wound better?' I asks.

Captain Flores bows. 'I am healed and fit enough to be at your service. What you did is a great thing. And if there is anything I can do to repay you, ask away.'

'Take me wiv you,' I says. It's out of me mouf before I knows it, but when it's out I'm glad. It's what I wants.

Captain Flores takes one of the stools and points to one for me. I sits and can feel tears come to me eyes cos I knows what his answer'll be.

'You know I can't do that.' His voice is kind and somehow that's worse. I feels meself choke up.

'My business is dangerous, Barnabas, and I wouldn't risk your life in following after me.'

'But I wants to go to sea,' I says. ' There's nofink for me here, not any more. I don't wanna be no farmer. And I don't wanna be no cunning-man either.'

'Cunning-man?' Captain Flores says. He frowns and Master al Qali leans towards me.

'She makes me look in her showstone,' I says in a mumble, a stab of fear deep in me gut. I knows I shouldn't have said noffink.

'Who, Mistress Jourdemayne?'

'Just sometimes,' I says. I tugs me hair, all nervous now. I wishes I could take back the words. 'Usually I just fetches and carries stuff or runs errands in the city.' I tries to shrug off me dangerous admission wiv a careless grin. 'You don't have to worry about me, I can look after meself.'

Captain Flores ain't convinced. I sees it in the way he and Master al Qali look at each ovver.

'Be careful, Barnabas,' he says, his face all serious. 'I think you need to tread very carefully and watch what you say and do. There are rumours going around London about Mistress Jourdemayne and they aren't good. But my business is pressing and I must leave. I shan't be long. I'll be back in England in three months or so. And then we'll speak of these matters again.'

Master al Qali puts a hand on mine. 'But in the meantime, my friend, if something does happen and you need some help, you may come to me. I will remain here for a time. If I am not in my rooms at *The Golden Lion*, you will find me at La Pleasaunce consulting with the Duke of Gloucester.'

I gives him a grateful nod. I don't like the fact that he is keeping company wiv the Duke, but he has been a true friend so far. It gives me some comfort.

'So, it's you, is it, Barnabas?'

Mistress Jourdemayne, her hair sticking out from the braid that hangs over her shoulder, seizes me by me arm and yanks me towards her.

'Come to filch more of my herbal stores, have you? Do you take me for a fool? I knew someone was stealing from the stillroom, but it was Cook who felt the lash of my tongue first.'

She eyes me closer. She catches sight of me bruise. A sweet one it is, thanks to Nick, who gave me a thrashing out in the yard for what reason I dunno.

'Sweet Jesu, what's happened to you?'

She lights a taper and holds it to me face. I tries not to flinch when she examines it, but it's tender as anyfink. I shudder. I'm cold now and don't know if it's cos she caught me stealing or that Nick's done me over good. All I knows is that I feels wretched.

'Who did this?'

'Dunno,' I mumbles. It's better to put up wiv it then rat on Nick.

'So you were looking for something to treat your bruise? Why didn't you ask me first? You know I wouldn't have begrudged it to you.'

'I didn't want to wake you,' I says. I lowers me eyes so she can't see 'em. See that I'm lying. I puts up wiv her poking and prodding and smearing ointment on me face. When she's done she gives me a light cuff on me head.

'There, that should do you. You were lucky this time. But there better not be a next time or I will not go so easy on you.' She gives me a look full of such meaning I knows I been tumbled. Me business is finished. She's watching me now and she'll know it's me if any more of her stuff goes missing.

CHAPTER TEN
Westminster Palace, Christmas 1440
ELEANOR

The air was filled with the scents of roasting meat and spices. Holly and ivy hung from beams and a large Yule log burned in the grate. Music gave a pleasant backdrop to the murmurs of conversation, and for a moment, Eleanor could feel some of the light-heartedness around her and she smiled. Mass was over and everyone was ready to enjoy themselves and forget the troubled events of the past year. At this moment there was no unrest, no lords at loggerheads, no crop failures and bad weather. There was only Christmas and the enjoyment to be had from the days to come.

Eleanor patted the veil draped over her hennin for reassurance. Her hennin cone was one of the tallest in the room and the veil over it made of the sheerest silk. She appreciated the stature it gave her and the support to her confidence. The veil and hennin were new this season and she was happy to have the opportunity to show it off with her new gown of russet brocade. Her hair was well hidden underneath her headdress and any stray tell-tale white hairs with it.

She searched the hall for her husband. She knew he would be with some group of lords. The room was filled with nobles. She spied Talbots, Percys, the Earl of Stafford and even the Neville women with young Warwick and the Duke of York escorting their wives. And of course the Dowager Duchess of Bedford with her second husband, Woodville. Beaufort and his group, including William de la Pole and Somerset, gathered around the King, talking with him, as if they were staking a claim. The King looked pale and almost fragile in his sober brown doublet that seemed too big for him. He plucked at his sleeve nervously while Beaufort talked to him in a heated manner.

A short distance away she spied her husband, talking with Talbot. She moved nearer and saw the Duke of York approach Humphrey, clearly in a bad humour, despite his handsome looks. The reason became clear when she drew up beside her husband. The three men gave her a brief nod and resumed their conversation, their voices low.

'Still, there is nothing for me, Uncle,' said York.

'It's an insult that you, someone in line for the throne, shouldn't have a more notable position. But it will do you no good asking me to speak on your behalf,' said Humphrey. 'The King hardly pays any attention to what I have to say any more.'

'But you have his ear, which is more than I have.'

'Only one of his ears.' Humphrey gave a bitter laugh. 'The other one is devoted to Cardinal Beaufort and William de la Pole. And it seems that ear is the one that counts, lately.'

'But what of your time in France? The peace negotiations have moved no further and the French remain weak. A good thing. The Duke of Burgundy still seems uninterested in helping them. Another good thing. And a good reason to continue the war and finish off the French. Secure the French throne for the King.'

'But these things are not good in Beaufort's eyes or William de la Pole's.'

The Duke of York sighed and nodded, clearly familiar with this issue.

'I agree with you, Richard. As a royal duke you should have a place in the Council,' said Humphrey. 'But others won't have it.'

'I know that's an impossible task, but if I could have some other position, worthy of my rank?'

'Would the King see fit to send York to France?' asked Eleanor. The suggestion only occurred to her. If York went to France it would surely mean her husband would remain home with her.

The three men looked at her.

'He might be open to that idea,' said Talbot. He was a seasoned soldier and an honourable man.

'I could suggest it,' said Humphrey. 'That is if you are agreeable, Richard.'

Richard gave a snort and nodded. 'Well it would be something, I suppose. If only he could be persuaded to abandon this damnable peace strategy in the meantime.'

'That is hardly likely,' said Talbot.

'Well, we must do what we can, given how little room we have to manoeuvre,' said Humphrey. He smiled wryly.

'It's a start,' said Richard. He turned and bowed to Eleanor. 'It was most kind of you to think of me, Aunt.' He gave her a warm grin.

Eleanor flushed, flattered by the attention of this handsome young man. She smoothed her gown and extended her hand, the rings on her fingers flashing with the movement. The Duke of York obliged and leaned over to kiss her hand.

'And now if you will all excuse me, I must find my wife,' he said.

He bowed and made his way across the room. Eleanor watched him go and gave a little sigh. Perhaps her looks had not faded as much as she'd thought. She turned to her husband and beamed at him. He caught her look and returned her smile with a warm one of his own.

'What are my great lords discussing so seriously?' asked the King, coming alongside of Humphrey. Tiny beads of sweat gathered at his brow under his simple crown. He had not worn even a jewel there, though today was a feast day, a day for show.

'Nothing of note, Your Highness,' said Humphrey. 'Richard was merely asking of my experiences in France.'

The King gave him an anxious smile. 'I am so glad you are returned safely. And I do want to hear about it myself.' He gave his uncle a nervous pat. 'I do understand that there were no serious outbreaks and skirmishes while you were there. You are to be commended.'

'Whenever Your Highness will permit, I would be happy to tell you everything. But I would mention as the Duke of York listened so closely to my words and seemed most astute in his assessment of the situation, perhaps he might do well to serve there for a time.'

The King gave a nervous glance towards Beaufort and William de la Pole who'd moved to the far side of the hall where the lords and ladies had begun to seat themselves at the many tables erected for the Christmas feast.

'It might be a good idea,' said the King. 'For now, it is time for other things.'

'Maybe if you pray on it, Your Highness,' said Humphrey. There was a hint of sarcasm in his voice that surprised Eleanor.

The King gave Humphrey a startled look. 'Yes, yes, maybe. Tonight, maybe. When all this is done.'

Eleanor sat at the high table, near the King, her head held regally. This time it was the Duke of York on her left side and his wife, Cecily Neville. She was surprised and displeased to see that Jacquetta, the Dowager Duchess of Bedford, was further down the table with her current husband, who wasn't even a baronet. It seemed the King had truly forgiven her for not seeking permission to marry that commoner. She saw Cecily spy Jacquetta and her subsequent frown. It looked as though Eleanor and Cecily could agree on something.

Despite the King's simple dress Eleanor was glad to see the banquet itself demonstrated the wealth and importance of a King who reigned over not only England, but most of France. Tables spilled from the hall to the chambers beyond and the guests numbered in the hundreds. Each table was laden with silver plate and goblets and the wine and food were of the best quality. The first course alone had seven different kinds of pottage along with capons and hams of wild boar. Following that there were ragouts made of pheasant, partridges, wild geese and swan all served with various sauces that made Eleanor's mouth water. She tried to eat sparingly, giving a thought to the fit of her gown, but it was too good to resist.

She flirted and made light conversation with both Humphrey and Richard. Above them, in the gallery, the musicians still played tirelessly. Eleanor's heart was light and she was enjoying herself more than she had in months. In such a good humour as this, she was certain that all the worries that had troubled her for so long would be easily resolved.

When the course was finished there was a pause for an *entremet*, one of the interludes of entertainment that came during a feast.

A man attired in embroidered crimson satin appeared astride a similarly caparisoned horse. In his hands he carried a silver plate with model garden made of wax which was filled with roses and a variety of other flowers. He dismounted and placed the garden before the King. The King, clearly delighted, thanked the man graciously.

Eleanor leaned forward to admire the beauty of the garden's workmanship. The detail and size were remarkable.

'Your Highness, you have outdone yourself this year. What a wonderful display.'

The King shook his head. 'Oh, it was none of my doing. You have William de la Pole to thank for this spectacle. It is all marvellous, isn't it?'

She nodded and sat back, making an effort to retain her smile. Never mind, she thought, she wouldn't let that piece of information ruin her enjoyment today.

The next course arrived moments later, with the steward leading the procession and the servants bearing the silver plates. They contained more fowl, only this time they were gilded, so that they sparkled in the light. Gasps came from around the hall. It seemed to Eleanor that each course and entertainment was more spectacular than the previous one. She wondered what the next *entremet* would be and found herself excited at the thought of it.

It arrived after the fifth course, which included tarts, fried oranges and other small sweet dishes. This *entremet* didn't disappoint, either. Twenty-four men carried a mountain with two fountains spouting rosewater into the hall. Suddenly, rabbits emerged from the mountain and scampered to the floor and live doves flew up into the hall's ceiling. Six girls and six boys came in and danced as the doves circled above them all.

Eleanor clapped and laughed at such a wonderful show and leaned towards Humphrey. 'It seems William de la Pole can do some things right,' she said. Humphrey nodded and patted her arm.

The last *entremet* came before the seventh and final course. A buzz of anticipation rose up among the guests. Twelve men wheeled in a wooden model castle containing a tower at each of the four corners and a large keep at the centre that flew heraldic banners bearing the King's arms. There were four windows in the keep and a richly attired lady sat at each one. At the top of each of the four towers a child sang. When the song was over the King clapped loudly, clearly delighted. Eleanor leaned over and smiled at him, her own pleasure just as great.

But it wasn't over yet. From the bottom door of one of the towers burst a masked female dwarf. She wore a large paper cone nearly twice her size on her head and her gown had a train just as long. She minced and pranced around the castle, barely holding onto the unmanageable cone. When she made a complete circle she reached inside one of the tower doors and pulled out a ball of silver. She stared into it and adjusted the cone on her head as if it were a mirror, and after a moment held it from her and gave it a shake. The ball dropped from her hands and she ran after it. Once the ball was back in the dwarf's hands, she placed it under her skirt, on her belly. But the ball fell out at once and the dwarf dropped to the floor and pretended to cry. After a moment, she held her hand up and went back inside the castle. She reappeared a short while later, her skirt belled out again over a mound that wriggled violently. The dwarf quickly reached under her skirts and withdrew a small puppy. The guests laughed and clapped, clearly delighted by the surprise. The dwarf bowed and withdrew into the castle. The spectacle had finished.

Eleanor sat in her seat in shock. There was no doubt in her mind that the dwarf was meant to represent her. Shame and embarrassment flooded her and tears gathered in her eyes. She wanted to weep and rage but she dared not. Not in front of all the guests, especially the nobles who would gloat over her distress. And most especially not in front of William de la Pole, who'd clearly arranged this huge insult. She would not give him the satisfaction of seeing how much it had upset her. She lifted her chin.

Further up the table she could hear the King congratulating de la Pole on the cleverness of the various *entremets*. She looked at the King. Clearly Henry had no idea about the true meaning of the dwarf's little mime. For once she could be thankful of his ignorance of fashion and the wider ways of the world. But someone would certainly enlighten him. That she wished for a child, she had no doubt would only make him sympathetic towards her. The fact that she would use a showstone in pursuit of this goal was an entirely different matter.

Humphrey leaned toward her and spoke in a low voice. 'William de la Pole will answer for this, Eleanor. Have no fear of that.'

She gave him a wan smile of thanks. A tear escaped and coursed down her cheek. 'Can we retire early tonight?' she asked.

'As soon as the music has finished,' he said. He squeezed her hand.

Humphrey's kindness was a small recompense for such a wretched insult and it did go some way to make her feel better.

*

Tears streamed down Eleanor's face as she watched from the bed as Humphrey paced the room, his anger growing.

'It is insufferable to think de la Pole could put on such a display with impunity,' he said. 'The King must make him apologize to you. In public.'

'In front of the King, yes, but not in public,' she said. 'I wouldn't want to call more attention to my humiliation.'

'But Eleanor, you don't understand. This is an affront to me, a royal duke. He must be seen to pay.'

'Please, Humphrey. The King hardly knew what he saw. And I'm sure many others had no idea.' It seemed ironic that she would be taking the part of that scum, William de la Pole. 'I think we must make him pay in other ways. We must tell the King in private about the meaning of the dwarf's charade, so that he will see nothing in the ball other than it represented first a mirror and then my wish for a child.'

Humphrey halted in his tracks. 'What else would it be?' He gave her a hard stare.

She flushed and caught herself. Humphrey had no idea about her attempts to see the future in the showstone and she must keep it that way. 'Nothing. But someone else might read other things into it. And we must guard against it.'

'We will,' he said, his voice softening. 'Leave it with me and I will find a way.' He moved over to the bed and laid his hand along her face. 'Come now. Dry your tears. You looked very comely tonight, my love, and I wouldn't have you spoil that now.' He ran his hand along her hair and cupped her breasts. 'Let's put our mind to other things now, shall we?'

CHAPTER ELEVEN
London, January 1441
BARNABAS

A hellish hubbub swells from the tavern and spills out into the alley what stinks of fish. I sees a drab lolling against a greasy wall wiv a tipsy seaman. Besides the noise in the tavern, I hears drums and a hurdy-gurdy playing. Sounds like Black Jack's dragged in a rowdy crew—probably some cog from the Low Countries has docked at Queenhithe today. I finks that maybe it ain't a good idea to come here so early, but I've business wiv Jack.

Smoke and fug surrounds me as soon as I steps inside.

'Thought you'd deserted us, Barney.'

Black Jack appears before me, big as a bearded giant from a folk tale. He takes me by me arm pulls me to a table in a dingy corner.

'I hope you've got somefink for me, you young imp. I've customers getting restless.' Winking, he taps his nose, and then shoves a three-legged stool under me bum. 'What have you got in that bag of yours, eh?'

The cat hops out on to the nearest barrel and sits wiv his ears laid back, hisses at me, green eyes blazing.

'Hold your tongue, Raggles. This boy is a good 'un.'

Jack leans over me then, his eyes sly in case Sarah's watching, but she's too busy jesting wiv some sailors by the hearth. Flemings by the sound of 'em—their harsh sounds are familiar. Like Petronella's when she talks her own lingo.

'I've only a few bits—' I says and digs in me bag. 'Here, there's the herbals you wanted.' I says this in a low voice, so he has to bend his ear close, 'I couldn't get no poppy, nor no henbane. And I can't get you no more. She's wise to me, now. Keeps it under lock and the key's wiv her all the time.'

Jack looks glances round the room and takes the small packet from me and sticks it up his sleeve.

'How much?'

I names me price.

Black Jack gives me a look. 'That's higher than last time.'

'That's precious since it's the last of it you'll get from me.' I shakes me head sadly. It's truly felt alright. I've no idea what I'll do to make money next and I needs it fast. I can feel me time's running short.

Black Jack claps me on me back. 'Ah, Barney. You'll come up wiv a way to keep fings going. I have every faith in you.' Fumbling in his purse, Black Jack pulls out a coin and I snatches it quick.

While he's gone to get me a drink, I watches the merry pack round the musicians. A couple of swarthy fellows, already in their cups, is performing a stomping kind of dance, linking arms and jigging around in a dizzy circle, raising their knees high and shaking their heads in time to the rhythm of the drums. Other rowdy folk is clapping their hands and shouting encouragement, and everybody joins in the chorus of the old song. It ain't tuneful, but everyone's in a fine humour, and I'm tapping me feet by the time Black Jack slaps a cup of weak ale on the barrel top table.

'Good for business,' says Black Jack, flicking his eyes towards the musicians. 'Jem and Wat's Sarah's cousins. Always bring in a crowd.'

The cat sniffs at me ale and shakes a paw as he backs off. Black Jack roars wiv laughter. A moment later, he turns to me, all serious now.

'Here, that shifty looking fellow's been asking after you, Barnabas,' he says. I can barely hear his voice above the roar of noise.

'I think I knows what he wants,' I says, pretending nonchalance. 'But he ain't no friend of mine.'

It's plain Black Jack wants to ask more, but a glassy-eyed rogue in a red hat claps him on the shoulder and asks for grub. Black Jack gives me a dark look and leads him away. I sits supping the rest of me ale for a little while, wondering how I'm to get out of the mess I'm in. There's no doubt the dark cove, the King's spy, is looking for me to see what information I have for him. Whatever I say there's danger. I'll have to make a dash for it somewhere. No use asking Father Thomas, either. Even if he did believe me now, what could he do? Probably chuck me in the river so's I won't talk. I downs the rest of me ale and slip out into the lane to go down to Queenhithe and Tom. He might know a place I can hide.

'Took your time, Master Barnabas.' His voice's a snarl. 'Cold out here in the wind.'

He grabs me arm and draws me down the lane, shivering in his threadbare cloak. His eyes are as mean as rat's. He pinches me arm.

'Now, what've you to tell me?'

I shrugs. 'Not much news. A lady visited Mistress Jourdemayne. Proper lady she was.' I'm trying to buy some time so I says the first thing that comes to me mind.

'And?'

'Me mistress told her she should keep taking the Lady's Mantle infusion—'

'What?'

'The lady's anxious to have a child—'

'Yes, we know that.' He waves his hand impatiently. 'What else? Did they look in the showstone? Meet with Master Bolingbroke or Dr Southwell?'

I'm scared now. I mumbles and shakes me head. 'I don't know nofink about that.'

He spits at me feet. 'Don't try codding me, Master Barnabas. I know all about you.' He puts his hand on me neck and shoves me up against the wall. 'I can take you with me and find other ways to make you talk.'

His eyes is glaring at me and I knows he means it. Just on me instinct I kicks him quick in his 'hey hos' and he doubles over. I dashes away then, afraid for me life and heads down to Queenhithe, dodging the carts and people that fills the lane.

I'm down at the dock in a trice and I runs up and down hoping to see Tom. I sees him just taking off and I gives a shout. He waves at me and shouts something back. I runs over to his usual place, hoping he'll come back. I looks back up the street and catches sight of the spy hobbling towards the docks. I waves to Tom urgently. I can see he's passengers taken on and knows that he wouldn't turn back usually, but this time I get lucky. He can see I'm upset. When he's nearly there I jumps into the wherry and almost knocks one of the gentleman over in me rush to scramble on the boat. Breathless, I offer me apologies to him and Tom and takes up the oar Tom offers me.

'In an awful hurry are you, Barney?'

'Sorry, Tom. Me business at *The Turk's Head* took longer than I thought and now I has to get back to me mistress afore she notices I'm gone.' I grins at him.

Tom raises his brows and nods. I'll have to tell him somefink later, when the passengers is gone. It don't take long, because I've the energy of a demon wiv me oar and we are free of them at White Friar's. Tom doesn't rush his questions though. He lets me tell him what I will, in me own good time.

'I'm in real trouble now,' I says, finally.

'I thought it were somefink serious.' He's a gentle feller, really. But he's got a wiry strength about him that you'd want on your side in a fight.

I nods. 'It's not of me own making. It's me mistress and Father Thomas what have got me in this pickle. They're involved wiv some important people and ovver important people wants to know more about it. So important I has to find somewhere to hide for a while.'

Tom gives me a look of pity. He shakes his head. 'That's terrible, lad. But I don't know what to say. I've nowhere to hide you that I can fink of really. I can't take you home wiv me. We share rooms wiv another family and the woman's such a busy body that they would know you were wiv me afore the day was out. And the whole of London the day after.'

Me heart sinks but I knows he's right. I fank him anyways.

'Well hold on, we'll fink of somefink, lad.'

He talks away, dredging up people I knows and one by one we sees that they won't do for one reason or anovver.

We ain't long off Greenwich when I comes up wiv an idea. Master al Qali.

Before I can fink of a reason not to, I gets Tom to let me off at Greenwich and head for the Duke's home.

'Pssssst. Alys!' I pops out of the shrubs I've been hiding in this past hour in hopes of figuring out some way to gets to Master al Qali. I blows on me hands and jumps up and down. It's been cold work staying hidden in this damp old winter weather.

Alys stops dead. She's so startled she drops the basket she's holding. 'Barnabas,' she says. 'What are you doing here?' She gives me a small smile, like she ain't certain if my being here is a good thing.

'Don't worry,' I says. 'It ain't nofink bad I wants.' Her titties is staring at me so ripe and plump, though, it's all I can do to keep me hands at me side.

She sees me looking and gives me a swat on the head. 'They're not for the likes of you.' She sticks her chin out at me.

'No, no. It's nofink like that. Honest. I just needs to ask you a question.'

'What question?' She gives me a suspicious look.

'Do you know Master al Qali? He's a Blackamoor.'

She nods and me hopes rise a little.

'Is he here? Can you fetch him for me? I needs to tell him somefink.'

She frowns and her eyes go soft and kind. 'I would if I could, but the gentleman ain't here, now.'

'He ain't here? Do you know where he is?' Me heart starts to sink.

'I've heard he's gone to Oxford, to the university men. He'll be back in a few days. Shall I tell him that you're looking for him when he returns?'

I stares at her for a moment, wondering what to do. Where will I hide until then? I'm just about to open me gob when someone grabs me from behind.

'Barnabas. Just the person I want.'

I turns me head and looks up into Father Thomas' face.

✁

The sound of the deep brass bell shatters the dark. It rips me from dreams of sunny places, dark-skinned men and birds wiv bright feathers. It sounds again, annoying as ever. I groan and burrow down, but I hit only a hard pallet, so I hugs the threadbare blanket tight round meself, squeezes me eyes shut and pretends I ain't heard nofink.

What am I doing in this place? Every frost-bitten day I asks meself this same question. Every day before dawn I'm woken by this great, clanging monster. And every day I curses Father Thomas.

Me, a monk? It's a laughable idea. But here I am, hidden away in the monastery at Westminster, under the watchful eye of Brother Richard, Master of the Novices. The oblates that I'm wiv, those monks in training, are mostly from noble families. But Father Thomas told 'em to take me and so they did. Father Thomas says I'm safe here. Safe from any lot that might put him in danger if they nab me and make me confess, is what he means. He don't fink what might happen to me if the monks find out I sees fings. So I has to be on me guard now, try and make sure that nofink happens. These monks will use any old excuse to say you're possessed by the devil. Brother

Richard already takes every chance to pinch me arm and twist me ear. So far, in the weeks that I've been stuck here, nofink's happened. 'Nothing,' I says to correct my thoughts. It's become a regular thing now, this correcting my speech all the time. And now I'm even doing it in me thoughts, that's how bad it is.

I rises from the bed, reluctantly, shivering with the cold. No fires allowed here and only a mangy blanket to cover us in the night, so we wear our long robe as well.

As usual, the water in the bowl is ice, so I have to break it to wash my hands. Shivering with the cold, I stumble with the rest of them to the chapel for Matins, the first service of the day, though daylight ain't for hours yet. Blind with sleep, I stands wiv me hood drawn low over me head, listening to the endless chanting, aware of me belly's low growl. Me feet are numb and me fingers stiff as twigs. I'm nearly afraid to move, or open me eyes in case Limpin' Sam comes out from behind the altar, or worse, Bethor pops up beside me, making a demand.

Later, in the Chapter House where they read from the Gospel, I sits still as a board, making my mind as empty as I can, but that just seems to make me thoughts busier than ever. I stares at Brother Richard's beaky nose instead and imagine it as a mountain wiv someone climbing it. It seems to work and I sigh with relief when another morning has passed wiv no sign of any appearances or visions.

When the chapter meeting is over Brother Richard nabs me by the arm and pulls me towards Brother John.

'Barnabas,' he says.

I can't for the life of me think why he might want from me. I only see him at a distance. I come up to the front and stand before the two of them.

'You are to work with Brother John in the Scriptorium,' he says in low, rusty tones. 'Father Thomas spoke highly of your penmanship.'

I'm too startled to say anything, not that they expect me to. He leads me away from the western cloister to the cold chamber nearby. There are several monks there sitting at high tables, near the windows, scratching away with their quills. Brother John seats me at an empty table wiv a quill, knife, and pot of ink. Brother John is short, wiv a grey ring of hair and jutting eyebrows. But his eyes are keen and they look me up and down.

'If you get on well with the copying, lad, we might have you learn how to do illumination. Perhaps even with gold leaf.' He pats me on the back and points to the sheaf of fresh parchment and the great tome beside it. 'You can start at the marked page there. Speak only if you have a question. I will be at my table.'

I takes me place on the stool and sets to work. It's tedious enough, but it's work that's familiar. Haven't I copied enough books on alchemy Father Thomas has borrowed? This book isn't as interesting, though, but I thinks maybe the pictures might be something to look forward to.

After hours of copying, when I'm starting a fresh page, I find meself drawing. It becomes a boat. A swirl of waves form and rise beneath the little boat and suddenly, Limpin' Sam leaps into me head, fast as a lightning bolt. Shocked, I sit rooted to the spot, pen frozen in me fingers. Limpin' Sam's building a fire. Wisps of wood, twigs and tree-bark grows into a pile. Using flint, he casts the sparks what catch the kindling, and soon smoke twists and spirals. Singing, he circles the fire, its red glow ruddying his features, its roar rising like a storm, until it drowns out all other sound. In the flames dark, winged shapes dance around—

The bell clangs loud, signalling prayers. I jump and Limpin' Sam vanishes. I look up and see Brother John is at me side. He looks at me suspiciously. I sees the drawing and cover it wiv me hand.

'You're very pale, Barnabas. You were muttering something, too. '

'I was?' I look at him blankly.

'Did you have a fit, lad?' He peers closely into me face. 'We must watch you. We wouldn't want the Devil finding his way into you, would we?'

Fear clenches my belly, driving away all me hunger. Only one thought is in my mind now. I'm not safe here anymore.

CHAPTER TWELVE
Greenwich, March 1441
ELEANOR

Eleanor smiled at her husband. He sat next to her in a chair at the head of the large chamber they used for small musical and literary gatherings such as this one. John Lydgate's words filled the air, fluid and melodious. The poem this time was a tribute to her husband's learning and her beauty. How could she find fault with any of it?

The room was crowded with her ladies in waiting, a few musicians and several scholars and poets, including Masters Hume, Bolingbroke and Southwell. Some of her husband's friends from court, lesser nobles and their wives also attended, each sitting quietly in their chair, listening patiently. When the poem ended, the applause was strong enough to please Lydgate and Eleanor. A brief discussion followed on the poem's merits and Lydgate responded warmly to the comments.

Eleanor was satisfied with the event. It was a pleasant way to pass a cold, damp evening at a time when winter seemed never to end. It had been a particularly wet winter too, delaying the ploughing and starting rumours of another year of crop failure. But Eleanor would not allow thoughts of disgruntled peasants to interfere with her pleasure, and she set them aside. She turned her mind to brighter things like Humphrey's loving attitude of late. After complaining bitterly to the King in private about the insult at Christmas, Humphrey had secured an apology from de la Pole. It was not the most earnest or sincere apology, but it was one, nevertheless, and it satisfied Humphrey.

For now, all she wanted was to keep Humphrey in a good humour so that he would continue to warm her bed. She still took the herbs provided by Mistress Jourdemayne, but she hadn't made any more attempts at the showstone or implemented any other suggestions Southwell had made to her. Better to proceed with things as they were. She was certain she would get results sometime soon.

Her husband made the signal to bring the evening to a close and she rose in her chair. Guests milled around, some greeting her courteously and others with a more ingratiating tone. Master Bolingbroke approached her and bowed.

'Your Grace, when you have a moment I would like to show you something that I think you'll find interesting.'

She smiled at him. 'Have you finished translating the Italian poems?'

'No, no,' he said. 'You gave that task to Master Hume.'

'Of course,' she said. 'I remember now.' She waved her hand. 'You may show me tomorrow, if you like. In the library. I think Master Lydgate and some of the other poets will be there as well.'

'I think you would prefer to see this in private, Your Grace,' he said. 'Perhaps you might like to see it now, if you've time.'

She looked at Bolingbroke closely, but she could read nothing from his face. Unease stirred in her. 'Meet me in the library in a half hour,' she said in a low voice. 'Bring there what it is you have to show me that is so important.'

He nodded to her, smiling widely and moved away. She watched him weave his way through the crowd and leave the room. Please God it is nothing, she thought.

It was later than half hour when she was finally able to slip away and go to the library. There was no fire in the grate and it was only the lone candle on the table, lit by the waiting Bolingbroke, that provided the feeble light to the room. She rested her own candle beside his and saw the parchment that lay unfurled before it.

Bolingbroke gestured towards it. 'See, as you requested. Finally.'

She looked at it closer and saw lines, angles and circles beside numbers and phrases. It took a few moments before she realized she knew what it was, but could only whisper the question. 'What do you mean?'

'The horoscope.'

'You've done my full horoscope?'

He shook his head. 'No, I explained how that was impossible. This is the King's.'

'The King's?' She couldn't keep the horror from her voice. 'But I never told you to cast the King's horoscope.'

'But you did, Your Grace. You said the King's birth would be known and there would be no trouble to cast his horoscope.'

'But I said no such thing!' Her voice was shrill with fear. 'What have you done?' She folded up the parchment quickly and shoved it into his hands.

'You must take it away. Get rid of it.' She glanced at the empty grate in frustration. 'Take it to your room and burn it immediately. No one must know you've done this.'

'But I've already consulted with Southwell on some of the points of calculation.'

'Southwell?' One more person to urge to silence. 'Is there anyone else? Hume? Did you consult with him?'

Bolingbroke made scornful sound. 'No, I wouldn't trust him to do it correctly.'

'You didn't tell anyone else?'

Bolingbroke shook his head. 'But Your Grace, listen to me a moment. You must hear what the horoscope had to say. The prediction is clear. The King will die in the twentieth year of his reign.'

Eleanor stared at him, too stunned to reply. 'No, no,' she said finally, feeling faint. 'Are you certain? Is there no mistake?'

'No mistake, Your Grace,' said Bolingbroke. 'I checked all my calculations carefully. That's one reason I found it necessary to have Southwell review them, too. I had to be certain before I told you.'

She took a seat and tried to take in his words as he opened the parchment once again and began explaining the chart to her. The words soon washed over her because she could only focus on one thing. If the King died in two years as predicted, Humphrey would be King and she would be Queen.

She stared up at Bolingbroke and then down at the parchment. It was a valuable piece of information. It was also dangerous. Too dangerous to be in anyone's hands, let alone hers. The penalty would be death. She had no doubts about that. She stood abruptly and gathered up the parchment again, Bolingbroke still finishing a sentence.

'You must burn this immediately.'

'But Your Grace, the work, the proof—'

'Burn it or it will condemn us both.'

Bolingbroke paled a moment. 'But only you and a few others of us know it. We can prepare, ensure all is ready for when the time comes.' He gestured to her belly and she flushed.

'Do as I say and leave the rest of any "preparation" to me. And keep your mouth shut, if you value your life.'

'But I must tell you that Dr Southwell would like to see you tomorrow. He has something he must tell you.'

'And what is that?' she asked.

'I don't know. But he said it was important.'

She looked at him uneasily and gave a reluctant nod. 'Tell him to come to my apartments tomorrow afternoon.'

Bolingbroke nodded and took his leave, the parchment clutched to his chest. She watched him close the door and wished she could follow him to make sure he destroyed the chart. She would have to trust him, because there was more danger bringing it back to her apartments where women with piercing eyes and wagging tongues acted as her ladies in waiting.

♈︎

Eleanor crouched in the shadow cast by moonlight shining on St Sepulchre's church tower. Above her, an owl hooted and she jumped. Southwell squatted next to her and intoned some prayer in Latin while Mistress Jourdemayne and Bolingbroke looked on like crows. A small fire flickered in the centre of their little circle, uncertain in the chill wind. Eleanor pulled her face back into her hood against the cold and hoped the night's work would end soon and she could return to her bed.

It wasn't Southwell's persuasiveness that got her here. Rather it was her fear that he might tell someone about the ritual that he and Margery Jourdemayne insisted was necessary for her to conceive a child and secure her future.

When Southwell finished his prayer Mistress Jourdemayne knelt closer and traced a circle around them. She muttered some words that Eleanor couldn't make out. Eleanor licked her lips and tried to reassure herself that there was nothing wrong in what they did. Southwell was a member of the clergy and he would be well aware of what was permitted and what wasn't.

Bolingbroke shifted nervously and edged away a fraction. She took no comfort in his presence and she could sense his unease from where she crouched. Mistress Jourdemayne, her mumbling finished, started digging a small hole inside the circle with her hands. When that was completed, she reached for the small bag tied at her side, withdrew a wax figure and laid it in the hole.

Eleanor gave a small gasp. The wax figure was the one she had made. She was certain of it. Sweat gathered on her forehead, despite the cold. She'd forgotten about the figure. She touched her stomach.

'Is this to help me have a child?' she asked. She could hear the fear in her voice.

Mistress Jourdemayne gave Southwell a nervous glance and looked down, avoiding Eleanor's eyes. 'Yes, of course, Your Grace. It is the custom. A poppet in shape of the child, buried in hallowed ground.'

Eleanor stared at her a moment, willing her to look in her direction. But it was no use and Eleanor didn't make the effort for long. Her fears started to overwhelm her and she found she didn't really want to know. It was better not to.

CHAPTER THIRTEEN
London, March 1441
BARNABAS

I walks quickly, head down, past Grey Friars and along. Me sandals slap the cobbles loudly and echo against the walls of the Friary. I pulls me hood lower and hope that I seem like an innocent novice out on an errand for the good brothers.

It's when I gets closer to Cripplegate and *The Golden Lion* that I starts to feel me nerves rise up a little. I rehearses me words in me mind. Words that will convince the innkeeper I will be welcome. Me belly growls loudly and I hopes it will be calmer by the time I get there, but I haven't eaten since the day before. With such an empty belly I feel the cold even more and I sticks me hands deeper into me sleeves so that they are tucked under me armpits. I spies the sign for *The Golden Lion* and I nearly cries with relief. But the moment of truth is here, too and if this doesn't work out, I don't know what I'll do.

I opens the door and peers in. Through the dim light I sees the innkeeper hunched over a heel of bread and a tankard of ale. There's a strong stink of the night before in the air, but the place seems respectable. The man's apron is clean and so are his hands. I offers a greeting in a low voice and he turns to me and wipes his mouth on his sleeve.

'What have we here?' he says.

'Begging your pardon, sir, but I am sent here on behalf of Brother John to inquire after a Master al Qali.'

He studies me for a moment and I tries to keep my face blank. 'Master al Qali?' he says.

I nods. 'The brothers would like to speak with him about some manuscripts.'

'Oh he does a lot of that, so he does,' says the innkeeper. 'Always coming and going, that one. Always carrying bundles wiv him. Don't say much, but he pays his way. Don't know why the brothers want to have dealings wiv a foreigner. Can't see that he would have anything they'd want.'

'He is good at translating,' I says. I am working hard to keep my speech proper, lest he suspect that I am not who I am supposed to be, a novice from the higher ranks.

The innkeeper sighs and moves off his stool. 'He's still up above. I'll just knock and tell him you're here.'

I watches the man heave himself up the stairs like he's ancient, though he has a full head of hair and his legs seem sound. It seems ages before I hear any sound but the knock on the door. A moment later they talk in low voices so's I can't make out the words. Then I hear footsteps. The innkeeper comes down the stairs, just as slow and maybe even slower, but behind him is Master al Qali, a look of puzzlement on his face.

Me whole insides light up when I sees Master al Qali and I realize then how much I feared he would be gone. I pull back me hood a little for a moment, just enough so that he can see me face. I tries to put on the cheeky smile he knew me for, just to help him remember who I am.

He comes to me side and greets me warmly. 'You are cold. It is a long walk from the monastery. Come up to my room to warm yourself and have some refreshment.'

Master al Qali asks the innkeeper to light a fire in the brazier and bring food. His words are so polite and clever, the man can hardly refuse and offers to warm the ale. I nods me head gratefully when Master al Qali passes the question on to me.

Master al Qali waits until the fire is lit and the food brought before he asks me anyfink.

'Now, Master Barnabas, you may tell me the real purpose of your visit.'

I make sure I've had a good chunk of bread swallowed and taken a hefty swig of the ale before I starts me tale of woe. He listens carefully, waiting 'til I'm finished before he says anything.

'And how did you escape the monastery?'

I smiles at this. 'That was easy in the end, though it took me months before I was able to get a chance to escape. I sneaked out in a farmer's cart. I hid under some sacking and jumped out as soon as I could without causing attention. Then I stayed there until it was night and made my way to the city walls and waited for morning.'

'You are a resourceful boy indeed. But I never had any doubt of that.' He leaned forward and studies me face. 'And now we must decide what to do with you.'

'You will help me, won't you? You did say if I needed help to come to you,' I says. Me voice squeaks at the end. It's been doing that a lot lately, when I'm nervous.

'Don't worry, Barnabas. I keep my word.' He smiles kindly at me and small crinkles appear at the corner of his dark eyes. He places a hand on me own. It looks so dark against me white skin, but it feels nice. Like he's telling me everything will be fine.

'Will you hide me here?' I asks, squeaking again. 'I knows you can't do it for good, an all, but just for a while. 'Til I can figure somefink out.' I falls back into me bad speaking habits I'm so nervous again. Cos what could he do wiv me?

'Oh, I think I there is something that can be arranged.' He puts his hand under me chin and studies me face hard. 'Your eyes are dark, which is a help. And you have fine bones, I see. The nose isn't bad either. I think, soon, it will be long and narrow.'

'Is that good?' I asks.

'It is good indeed, Barnabas.' He stops a moment. 'No, not Barnabas. Giacomo, I think. Giacomo Bonavillagio.'

'Giacomo Bonavillagio? Who's he?'

'Why you, my friend. Your father, Signore Bonavallagio, is a rich merchant from Venice who has lived here in London for some time, pursuing his business. Or was a rich merchant, for alas, he has died, leaving you to await the return of your brother Pietro, who is on a trading voyage with Captain Flores.'

I stares at him a moment. 'But …. I don't know Italian. I don't know nofink about Venice.'

'Ah, but neither does Master Kyd, the innkeeper. Besides, we will say you have grown up here and so have a good command of English. And the word is "nothing", or rather the proper use is "anything". You must mind your language now, my dear friend.'

I nods at his last words. I feels a bit better about the idea. 'Am I to stay here with you, then?'

Master al Qali nods. 'Yes, for you see, your father entrusted you to me, until you can be re-united with your brother.'

'Pietro,' I says.

'I see you are as quick as I hoped.' He pats me knee. 'But now we must do something about your clothes.' He shoves the hood off me face completely. 'I see they shaved your hair. All the better. We shall get you a fine hat and with a new doublet, cloak, hose and shoes, I think Barnabas will be gone completely.'

'I gets a new doublet and a cloak?' Me eyes are shining at the idea of warm clothes.

'I see you still need to work on your speech, more. I'm sure your father wouldn't have you speak incorrectly, Giacomo.'

Me face turns red and I clap me hand on me mouth. 'Yes, sir. Sorry. It won't happen again.'

'I have every faith in you, lad,' says Master al Qali.

❧

'Twas a very fine young gentleman that owned this doublet,' says the shopkeeper. He gives Master al Qali a dubious look and points to the doublet he has laid across a chest next to a soft white shirt. 'And this shirt is made of cloth of Rennes.'

I finger the doublet's fine silk cloth and at the same time admire the hanging sleeves on the shirt. Such luxury I could never imagine. 'It is a good fit,' is all I can manage to say. I look at Master al Qali. 'What do you think?'

'I think you have gone very tall, Master Giacomo, since you entered the school. Perhaps something a little longer in the waist would be better. We wouldn't want all the girls to know how well-endowed you are yet.' He gives a hearty laugh.

My ears are burning and my face is hot from his joke, but I still can't take my eyes off of the doublet. I sigh, knowing that, in the end, I will be wearing what Master al Qali chooses. The last few shops we'd visited had proven that. Despite the looks of curiosity, distrust and reticent demeanours from the shop keepers at the presence of Master Al Qali, his gold speaks loudly and they show him the wares.

'The shirt, I think, would be a fine addition, though,' says the shop keeper.

I give him a beaming smile, suddenly happy at the thought of such a fine shirt on my back.

Determined to make as much of the sale as possible, the shopkeeper pulls another doublet out from the chest. 'Perhaps this one would suit?' he asks.

It's more sober than the other doublet, a deep burgundy with no trim, but made of silk just the same. Master al Qali gives his approval and puts it up against me.

The shop keeper points to a spot on the front. 'Just a small mend here, you see. But once it is on, and the belt brings the cloth into folds at the waist, you would never see it.'

I finger the cloth where the small tear was made and notice it's the shape a knife would make and it falls just where a knife would enter if it was to stick up under your ribs to aim for your heart. I shudder a moment, imagining the scene.

'That will suit us perfectly,' says Master al Qali. 'We'll take it. I know your father would approve of the quality of this silk, Master Giacomo.'

A short while later, I'm dressed in the fine cloth shirt with hanging sleeves, fine hose, shoes of Moroccan leather and a short cape with a silk lining. And of course the doublet with its suspicious past. The sleeves of this doublet have openings for the shirt sleeves to puff out. I decide I like the way it looks. The shopkeeper hands me a hat. It's a hood of sorts with the 'liripipe' end twisted around that folds over on itself and hangs down from the brim it forms. The shopkeeper hands me a burnished brass plate to see what I look like. All I see is a young coxcomb, someone who can't be me. What would Alys make of me now?

'Well, Master Giacomo,' says Master al-Qali. 'I think you are ready to face the world.'

~

I watch Master al Qali at his table by the window. The table is filled with books and various pieces of parchment. Numbers, circles, triangles and squares crowd each other out on some of the parchments, while others are filled with words. He looks up at me and motions me to the table. My eyes light up and I cross the room quickly. I've been waiting patiently for this time all day. It comes every day, now, when evening is nearly upon us, after Master al Qali has done his work or met with others while I study in the room. He has taken me out on a few occasions, as an interested young scholar attending him.

'Mathematics today, Giacomo? Or would you rather we spent time on your Italian?'

I want to say mathematics, but I know he wants me to learn as much Italian as I can, so that there is less danger my new identity would be proven false. In the six weeks since I've come here, he has praised me often for my quickness and my grasp of the language, but he is anxious that I learn all I can. It seems more than necessary for the role I'm playing, but I enjoy it, so I say nothing. What will happen to me once Captain Flores returns for Master al

Qali, I can't say. In the meantime I will enjoy what time I have with this learned man.

'Italian,' I say to him. He nods, and grins widely, his teeth showing white against his dark skin.

We spend the next hour speaking in Italian. He talks about Venice, its merchant trade with the East; the glass, the fine spices and silks that come through its ports. He also explains the art and music that are blossoming in that city and the nobles who patronize them. I drink it all in, asking questions where I need to. He turns to my own story, as he always does, the life of Giacomo Bonavillagio, brother of Pietro. He spins such a tale and is so convincing that I am certain at the end it must be my own life.

'And what will happen when Pietro returns?' I ask.

'We will see. I don't know what Pietro might plan for you. Return to Venice, perhaps? Or he might decide to take you with him on his next voyage. You are old enough, I think.'

At this moment I feel I should be old enough. I puff out my chest. 'I'm sure Pietro would agree to take me.'

Master al Qali's eyes light up with amusement. 'I think for now, though, it's time for bed. It's very late.'

I see the fire in the brazier has gone out and Master al Qali has lit a candle that is now nearly a stump. I stretch a moment and realize that I'm very tired. It has been a long day.

∿

Wind and rain lashed against the ship, ripping at the sails. Huge waves rolled the ship from side to side. Men shouted and screamed, trying to be heard over the storm. Bodies hung from tangled rigging. The ship moaned in protest at such treatment. A mast cracked and fell, crashing against the side of the ship.

'Captain Flores!' I screamed, fighting to see my way clear to the wheel. A moment later I'm tossed overboard, into the sea, plunging downward.

Someone clutches my arm and shouts at me. I open my eyes and see I'm in the room at *The Golden Lion*, and Master al Qali is leaning over me, shaking me awake.

'Giacomo,' he says. 'Calm yourself. It was a dream. You are awake now, safe in the room.'

I blink my eyes a few times, still somewhere back in the water, drowning. 'It was terrible, Master al-Qali. A nightmare, so real—I stop a moment and realize what I'm saying. 'It's Captain Flores, something terrible has happened. I'm sure of it.'

Master al Qali's face becomes full of concern. 'Tell me then. What exactly did you dream?'

I recount everything I can remember, speaking slowly so that I leave nothing out. When I'm done, he nods, satisfied. 'Very good. This is important and you've done well in your explanation.'

'What do you think it means?'

He pauses a moment, looking at me intently. 'It seems that you have had some kind of warning about the fate of Captain Flores' ship. Whether it is in the future or it happened some time ago, is not clear. I will make some inquiries in the morning to see if anything has been reported.' He takes my hand a moment. 'But now, if I put you before a bowl of water, do you think you might scry for me and see if you can see anything more?'

I take a deep breath and then sigh. I had promised myself I would never scry again. It always seemed to lead me into danger and to people who really cared nothing for my wellbeing. But Master al Qali is different. I will do it for him. I give him a nod.

A moment later, I'm sitting at the table surrounded by candles and a bowl of water in front of me. I stare into it as I used to do with Father Thomas and look for Limpin' Sam. For a moment all I can see is my close-shaved head and my large eyes peering back at me. Then it clears and a stormy sea forms and in the next few moments I see all that was in my dream. I look desperately for Captain Flores but again he's not in sight. The sight fades a while later and I look up and shake my head.

'Did you see anything at all?' asks Master al Qali.

'Just what I saw in the dream. Nothing more than that.'

He pats me on the shoulder. 'Never mind. You've done well, my friend. We'll see what we can find out in the morning.'

CHAPTER FOURTEEN
London, 28 June 1441
ELEANOR

The sun beat down with the strength of full summer. Eleanor could feel the sweat trickle down her back under her rich purple gown. Under a gilt filigree cap shaped like a crown, her hair blazed like spun gold, giving extra colour to her cheeks. She wished for a moment that she hadn't decided to wear her ermine-trimmed cloak, but she loved how it framed her neck and face. And it was important she look well alongside her husband. She'd ensured the white palfrey she rode had been brushed to a shine to give her appearance that extra lustre. Here, among all the other nobles in the procession, the Beauforts, the Nevilles, the Talbots and even Dowager Duchess Jacquetta, she could take her place as befit her rank as Duchess of Gloucester.

They approached Chepeside and she could see the swelling, sweating crowds jostling each other under the hot sun. The excitement was palpable. A few cheers rose up for the Duke of York. York was popular in London, she knew, but her husband was even more so. He was always cheered heartily whenever he passed through the city. She smiled widely at the thought and glanced over at her husband.

A cry came from someone in the crowd near her. 'There she is! The witch!'

'Harlot! There she goes, stuck-up Nelly Cobham, flaunting herself like a queen!' The growing sound of jeering drowned out any further words. A cabbage was flung and hit her horse. The horse started for a moment until Eleanor got it under control.

Shocked, Eleanor could only stare out at the crowd in horror. How was it possible? Why? What had she done to them that they should treat her in this manner? Her husband loved her, couldn't they see that? She glanced over at Humphrey, but he stared straight ahead. She fought back the tears that gathered in her eyes. She wouldn't let them see how much their actions upset her. She stiffened her back and lifted her chin. It was only a small group of hot, bored people. They would soon forget why or who they felt such animosity towards. That was the way of Londoners.

These thoughts comforted her as she made her way along Chepeside to the end of their journey at *The King's Head*. It was meant to be a jolly outing. A good meal with some music and laughter among the people of London. She was determined that it should still be the case. When they arrived at *The King's Head*, Humphrey assisted her from her horse, but refused to look at her directly. She could see the anger in his eyes and hoped it was directed at the crowd and not her.

The landlord himself escorted Eleanor, her husband and the rest of the nobles into the inn, while burly men with staves dared any of the jeering crowd to approach. Once inside, Eleanor forced herself to take pleasure in the smell of roasting meat basted in hippocras and sat beside her husband at the head of a long trestle table. The other guests took their places and chattered away loudly about trivial matters. Eleanor could feel them steal furtive looks at her, though, and the pleasure that most of them took from her discomfort was palpable.

She had to take several sips of her wine before she was able to relax even the smallest bit. But the plates of food that were set before her, so much anticipated this morning, she could hardly touch. The sight of the meat turned her stomach, and for a moment, she thought she might be pregnant. That glimmer of happiness gave her the courage to look once again to Humphrey and put her hand over his.

He smiled at her and allowed her hand to remain there, but the smile hadn't reached his eyes. She turned away before the tears would come again. She lifted her chin and stared down the table at Duchess Cecily. Cecily raised her brow slightly and a faint smile appeared on her face. Was she a kindred spirit? Her husband, the Duke of York, scorned by the Beauforts and ignored by the King, gave them something in common. Next to Cecily, a man leaned over and whispered something in her ear. She looked across to the doorway where three people gathered, deep in conversation. A moment later, Cecily looked again at Eleanor, curiosity on her face.

'Your Grace, interesting news has come to light,' she said, addressing Humphrey.

'News?' said Humphrey.

'It concerns some men who I think are part of your learned circle,' said Cecily.

'Who?'

'Dr Southwell and Masters Hume and Bolingbroke. It seems they've been arrested.' Cecily looked at Eleanor again. 'I think they are also your friends, too.'

Eleanor paled. Arrested? Why? How? The questions raced through her mind and she tried to fight off the panic that threatened to seize her.

Humphrey frowned. 'On what charge were they arrested?'

'They are accused of trying to harm the King.'

Humphrey snorted. 'Why on earth would they want to harm the King?'

'I don't know, Your Grace.'

Cecily looked at Eleanor again, but Eleanor couldn't read her expression. Was this woman set out to harm her? Eleanor sat numbly, unable to think or move. Conversation buzzed around her excitedly, but she heard none of it.

'It is probably a false rumour,' said Humphrey in a firm voice. 'I can't imagine those men would be involved in anything remotely treasonous.'

'I'm sure you're right, Your Grace,' said Cecily. Her smile was reassuring.

But Eleanor knew it was the truth. She knew exactly the reason that would have led to their arrest. Someone had informed on them. And she had no doubt it was only a matter of time before the one of them informed on her.

The thought made her physically sick. She put her hand to her mouth, fighting the bile that rose there and tried to breathe deeply. She knew it had nothing to do with a possible pregnancy. 'I'm sorry, Humphrey, I'm not feeling very well. If you don't mind, I think I'll return home.'

'You are looking pale,' said Humphrey. 'Perhaps you should. I'll have your horse brought round.'

'No, no. I think I'll make my way by wherry. I think the air might do me some good.'

'Don't be foolish, the smells from the river at this time of year will hardly settle your stomach.'

'But it will be quicker. The tide is in my favour. I'll just take one of the servants with me. I don't want a fuss.'

He gave her an odd look and then nodded. 'Very well. I'll see to it.'

The words were spoken low and with as little attention as possible, for which Eleanor was grateful. She took up one of her ladies' light cloaks and pulled it over her, concealing her beautifully arranged hair and rich gown. No one would take her for the Duchess of Gloucester now, she hoped.

~

'What have you heard?' Eleanor asked Alys. She'd risen from her chair as soon as Alys opened the doors to her bedchamber and started pacing the room. 'Is it true? Are they arrested?'

Alys curtseyed. 'Yes, Your Grace. I'm afraid it's true. They arrested Dr Southwell this morning and Masters Bolingbroke and Hume this afternoon, just after you left for the city.'

'They waited until Humphrey and I had left,' said Eleanor. She wrung her hands. 'Anything more about why they were arrested?'

Alys gave her a nervous look. 'Only that they are charged with conspiring to harm the King.'

Eleanor nodded and bit her lip. She couldn't be certain it was anything at all connected with her. It might be something entirely different. Something of their own making. And it might come to nothing.

Alys took up her hand. 'Oh, Your Grace, what will you do?'

Eleanor looked down at Alys. 'Do? I will do nothing. I have done nothing.'

Alys nodded, but her eyes were full of doubt and fear. 'You have nothing to fear from me, Your Grace. I will hold my tongue. You can count on me.'

'Why should I worry when I am innocent of any action that might be seen as harmful to the King? Besides, I have my husband to protect me.' It was that thought that calmed her now. He would ensure that anything these three men might say against her would be dismissed. This thought had calmed her as she made her way back from *The King's Head*. It had stopped her from running full pelt to the wherry and to take the oar herself while she was ferried upriver to Greenwich.

'I hope what you say is true,' said Alys.

CHAPTER FIFTEEN
London, 29 June 1441
BARNABAS

I look up in surprise from my writing when Master al Qali opens the door and enters.

'You're back earlier than I thought,' I say. 'I haven't finished the translation yet, I'm afraid. If you give me another hour—'

'There is no need to concern yourself with that,' says Master al Qali. 'I have something else I wish you to help me with.'

'Of course,' I say. 'What is it?'

'I have just heard some disturbing news. Masters Bolingbroke and Hume were arrested, along with your friend, Father Thomas.'

I'm so shocked I can only stare at him for a moment. 'Father Thomas has been arrested? What for?'

'For conspiring to harm the King.'

'But how?' The words are out of my mouth before I can think. Of course I know. I have known deep down that it was only a matter of time before something like this would happen.

'The "how" is not the issue for us at the moment. Now, we must think carefully and ensure that we are protected from what might come about.'

'What do you think will happen?' I ask in a whisper. I have a good idea, but I can't say the words myself.

'It will not be a happy end, my friend. And we must be certain that we don't find ourselves on the same path. So, for now I need you to tell me carefully everything that happened between you and Father Thomas, especially if it involved Masters Bolingbroke and Hume.'

It takes me an hour at least to explain it all to him. He would interrupt occasionally, especially when it came to the part Mistress Jourdemayne played in the story. It's then, as I tell him that part, that I realize how he might be in danger, too.

'The showstone,' I say. 'You and Captain Flores sold her the showstone.'

Master al Qali nodded. 'This is a link to both of us, Giacomo, and we must find a way to break it. You must go to her. I cannot because my presence is always too well remarked upon.'

'I'll tell her to get rid of it.'

'Ah, but can we trust her to do that?' Master al Qali shook his head. 'No, I think it is best if you were to go to her and persuade her to give you the showstone and say you will get rid of it.'

I nod. I know it's a risk for her to see me in my new disguise, but it's important to go and get the showstone. There's no choice in the matter. Master al Qali is too noticeable to go to Mistress Jourdemayne's house for a task like this. But I have an idea that might reduce the risk Mistress Jourdemayne would be able to find me again.

I waste little time and am making my way towards the docks to take the wherry there. It's safer on foot, but faster to go by wherry. Before I go far, though, in a small alley I change into the sober novitiate's habit and bundle my clothes into the sack I've brought along.

When I arrive at the docks I see it's Tom's wherry that's nearest and available and my heart sinks. It would be noticed if I took a different one, so with my heart in my mouth, I step aboard, hand him my money and tell him my destination in the best quality voice I can. My voice has dropped now, and it's only certain times when I'm nervous that it squeaks and breaks. Times like this. So though Tom tries to chat with me, I say little and keep my head back in my hood.

The river is stinking and the heat is fierce, and after a while I can't help but feel I'm boiling alive. There's not a breath of wind today. I scratch under my arm where the wool is particularly irritating and pray the river currents will take me to Eye quickly.

∽

'Mistress?'

'Barnabas?' Margery Jourdemayne almost drops the flask she's holding when she catches sight of me on the threshold to her stillroom. I've thrown back my hood so she can get a full view of my face. I nod to her.

'Where have you been?'

'No time for that now, Mistress. I comes to warn you.' I try to pitch my voice high, as before, but still it cracks. 'You have to get rid of everyfink. Father Thomas and Master Bolingbroke have been taken.'

'What?'

'I just heard and I came to warn you. They took Father Thomas and Master Bolingbroke yesterday. Along wiv Master Hume.'

'Mother of God,' says Mistress Jourdemayne. She moves to a bench and sits on it hard. 'On what charge?'

'Somefink about wanting to harm the King,' I say.

Mistress Jourdemayne pales even more and moans. 'Harm the King? Oh, what will I do? They are sure to say something about me.'

'We needs to get rid of anyfink what might be dangerous,' I tell her. 'All your herbs, ointments, philtres, all of it.'

She rises and starts to pace the room. 'Yes, yes, you're right. I must get rid of it all. Leave only the simple herbs. Ones that every housewife would keep.'

'And the showstones, mistress. You can't be found wiv that.'

She looks at me, fear filling her face. 'No, no. Oh God. They mustn't find that. She makes her way to the press, fumbling with the keys hanging from her girdle. Lifting out the boxes, she stumbles and drops the new one and the lid flips open. The crystal globe, shed of its black velvet cover, rolls out among the rushes.

Mistress Jourdemayne chases after it like a child with its ball, and catches it by the bench leg. 'Oh this bodes ill, Barnabas.' Her hands are shaking as she raises the ball in her hands and gives it to me as if it was on fire. She hands me the other box with the smaller one, too. 'You get rid of them, Barnabas. Dump them in the Thames. No one will find them there.'

I take the showstones and put them into my sack and nestle them safely among my clothes.

She gives me a calculating look, reaches into a jar on one of the shelves and withdraws a few coins. 'Take this,' she says and presses the coins into my hand. 'After you've gotten rid of the showstones, go straight back to your friary, or wherever you've been hiding, until this dies down. Tell no one about this or anything else connected with it.' She gives me a knowing look. 'You understand my meaning? You will be rewarded well, lad. I promise you.'

I nod to her and try to look grateful. 'I will, mistress.'

She pauses a moment and pats my face. 'You're a good little imp, Barnabas. Though, you're not much of an imp anymore, are you?'

I give her a cheeky grin, like the old times, and take myself off.

⌘

Master al Qali meets me at the door when I return.

'You have it?' he asks and I can hear the anxiety in his voice.

'I have, Master.' I hold up the sack. It only holds the one, now. The old one I dumped in the river like Mistress Jourdemayne said. 'I didn't know if you wanted me to dump it in the river, so I brought it here. But I can go back and do that now, if you wish.'

'No, no,' he says and takes the sack from me.

Carefully, he withdraws the habit from the sack and unfolds it on the table. The showstone glints in the light. It is so beautiful I can't help but be drawn to it. The two of us gaze at it for what seems like an age. Master al Qali sighs.

'How could anyone think of destroying such a thing?' He rests his hand on the showstone and runs his hand along it. 'No, we will do nothing so foolish as to throw such a valuable object in the river.'

'But what will you do with it?'

'For now, we will keep it wrapped up and hidden. I will find a safe place for it.' He gives me a smile. 'A place I will tell you nothing about. For your own protection.'

I nod. 'But what use is it to you for anything more than a beautiful object? You can't scry, otherwise you wouldn't have asked me to look to see if I could find out anything more of Captain Flores' ship.'

His face darkens at the mention of the ship. 'You are right, my friend. I cannot scry. I only wish I could, because at this moment it would be better if we knew what the future could tell us in that regard. All these weeks and still no word.'

He looks over and studies me a moment. 'Perhaps you might have more success with the showstone,' he says with a murmur.

I frown. I look over at the showstone and try to find a way to say no to him. I have a terrible feeling about the showstone. I've never liked peering into it, but up to now I always thought it was because of Mistress Jourdemayne and her antics pretending with the Duchess. But since carrying it back with me from her place I know it's something more. The stone itself seems harmless when you look at it, but I feel a certain coldness deep inside me when I go near it. Still, it's for Master al Qali, and after all he's done for me, I can't refuse.

Reluctantly I go to the table and sit down beside the showstone. I take a deep breath and clear my mind. Carefully, I focus on the stone, letting my sight sink deeper into it. I stay that way for a long time, searching intently, but there is nothing. Finally, I look up and shake my head. 'Nothing,' I say.

'You see nothing?' There's disbelief in his voice.

'Truly, Master al Qali. I could see no image.'

He pauses a moment and then nods. 'Perhaps it's the strain of today. We'll try another time.' He pats me on the back. 'It would be well, though to find out if we must leave sooner rather than later.'

'But won't you wait for Captain Flores?'

'Not if things become too… complicated here.'

My heart sinks when I hear those words. 'You would leave me?' I whisper.

His eyes narrow a moment and then he laughs. 'Never fear, Giacomo. I won't abandon you. I have great plans for you.'

It takes a moment for the words to sink in, I was so certain he would tell me it would soon be time for me to go and find my own way. When I realize what he's said my whole heart lightens and I can't help but break into a big grin. 'Really, Master al Qali? You won't abandon me?'

'Why would I abandon my greatest scholar? No, my boy, there is much in your future. You're far too much of an asset to leave to the back alleys of London.'

CHAPTER SIXTEEN
Greenwich, 10 July 1441
ELEANOR

'They have imprisoned Southwell in the Tower of London,' said Humphrey. He'd entered the solar a moment before, his face a thundercloud.

Eleanor sat among her ladies, her embroidery needle poised in mid air.

'Imprisoned in the Tower?' Her voice trembled.

'In the Tower. This doesn't bode well for him. He's been charged specifically with saying mass unlawfully. And also that he used heretical implements when he did.'

'He would never do that,' she said with a conviction she didn't feel. 'He was a most learned man.' Eleanor glanced at her ladies and tried to judge their reaction. Most continued sewing with their heads down. Only Lady Margaret gave her a sceptical look.

Humphrey paced the room. 'He is a learned man. His interests took him to dabble in a variety of things. Literature, astronomy, alchemy and astrology.' He looked at Eleanor meaningfully.

'But you were interested in all those subjects, including astrology.'

'I did. The astrology I found only a curiosity, though.'

Eleanor pressed her lips together. She wouldn't say anything more on the subject, not with her ladies present. But his meaning was clear enough. He wanted to know if Southwell was involved in any way when Bolingbroke drew up her astrological chart. She would tell him no and hope it was the truth. Her nerves had suffered these last ten days while she waited for further news of the arrests. This was the first new bit of information and it did nothing to calm her. She tugged at her bodice. The room had grown hot and muggy in the last hour and there wasn't a breath of wind coming from the open window.

'Will he stand trial?' she asked.

'It's a matter of heresy, so he will be under ecclesiastical law and it will be for the Church to decide.'

His voice was still angry and Eleanor had no idea whether it was directed at her, the King or Southwell. He stopped pacing a moment, clenched his fists.

'Baaah,' he said. 'It's all a mess. The King won't see me, let alone listen to anything I have to say, whether it be on the matter of Southwell, Bolingbroke and Hume or something else entirely. The Beauforts have him tight in their clutches.'

'Surely the King will give in and see you soon,' said Eleanor.

'It has been over ten days, Eleanor! I've never gone this long without seeing Henry. Something is wrong. He's angry at me for some reason, I can feel it. And I can't get near him to find out why.'

Eleanor suddenly felt a knot of fear grow inside her. A bead of sweat trickled down the side of her face. Humphrey was right, it wasn't a good sign at all if the

King wouldn't even see her husband. 'What of Hume? Have they questioned him?'

Humphrey shook his head. 'No, he's still being kept to his apartments at Westminster. But no more than that.'

'And Bolingbroke, is there any news on him?'

'Nothing new. Like Hume, he's still at Westminster, where they're watching him closely. There are rumours though. Rumours of heresy.'

'Heresy again?' The knot of fear grew bigger.

Humphrey waved his hand. 'It's just a rumour.'

Outside, the sky darkened, as if responding to the mood in the room. To Eleanor it felt almost like an omen of things to come. A flash of lightning lit the sky and illuminated the room as bright as if the sun were present. A huge crash sounded. Eleanor could feel it vibrate in her chest. The skies opened up and large hailstones fell, pelting the windows and the ground below. Everyone ran to the window to see the strange sight.

'Wasn't the King processing to the guildhall today?' asked Eleanor.

Humphrey nodded. 'Please God he's not caught in this. It would scare the horses.'

'And ruin all the finery,' said Eleanor. Privately, she hoped he and all the nobles who supported Beaufort were out in this. And with a little luck Beaufort's horse would bolt and throw him and he would die.

Humphrey pulled the window shut against hail that started to blow in. Eleanor stared at the small balls of hail that clung to the frame inside as they slowly melted in the heat of the room. She imagined they were hard and painful if they should hit someone with force.

⁓

'Alys, whatever is the matter?' said Eleanor.

She shook out her hair and allowed Alys to begin running the comb through it. The room was dark and soothing to her. Humphrey was still somewhere drinking with some of his supporters. It would be some time before he came to their chamber. If he did. She took a sip of her spiced wine and saw that her hand was trembling. She took another sip. It was her third cup and still her nerves hadn't calmed.

'I'm sorry, Your Grace. I didn't like to say anything, but there has been more news. I heard it today when I was in the kitchen.'

'News? What news?'

'It was the kitchen lad. He went to see his mother who lives in the city. It was his day off.'

Alys rambled on for a bit and Eleanor did nothing to stop her, dreading the words that she would eventually speak. She drank the last of her wine and swallowed hard.

'And what was his news?' she asked quietly.

'Well, all the city talked about the storm earlier. When there was that thunder and lightning and then the hail. Large as pebbles they were. And the King caught right in the middle of it. Horses rearing, men shouting and people running for fear of being trod on. It was a miracle the King wasn't harmed.'

Eleanor nodded slowly, unable to say anything.

'It was so strange, not like anything that's ever happened before. It wasn't natural. People started saying it was witchcraft. That it was caused by Mistress Jourdemayne.'

'Mistress Jourdemayne? Why should she have anything to do with it?'

Alys paused her combing. 'Well, everyone knows the Witch of Eye, and they say she's a powerful witch and she would like to see the King harmed so that they can set another on the throne.'

'Another? You mean the Duke of Gloucester.'

'Yes.' Alys' voice trembled. 'I'm so sorry, Your Grace. But they do say that since you and Mistress Jourdemayne are great friends she would have much more influence and power if your husband was to be on the throne.'

Eleanor turned to stare at Alys, feeling numb. The horror her words evoked rose slowly inside her. She sniffed. Surely it was only a rumour. And rumour could be spiteful, but nothing more than that.

'I'm sure it's just a group of busybody wives who have nothing better to do with their time than gossip.'

Tears formed in Alys' eyes. 'There's more, Your Grace.'

'More?'

'It's Master Bolingbroke. He's to appear before the King's Council to answer questions of sorcery and treason.'

'Sorcery and treason?' The words came out of her with a squeak. 'But how did that happen?'

'I don't know, Your Grace. It's what the boy said.'

Eleanor tried to take a deep breath, but it was impossible. Terror gripped her. Treason! That was too close to the bone. Treason meant there was no ecclesiastical court to decide. Treason, if convicted, meant only one thing. Death. But before that there was a long period of questioning. Questioning that was often so painful anything would be said to end the pain. Accomplices named. Events described in detail. Eleanor shuddered and let out a long moan.

'Put me to bed, now, Alys. I'm not feeling well at all.' She would allow herself this indulgence for the moment, but in the morning she would have to think hard about what to do. She couldn't afford to let events fall where they may. She hadn't come to be Duchess of Gloucester by just lying back and waiting for it to happen.

CHAPTER SEVENTEEN
London, 23 July 1441
BARNABAS

I glance nervously around me as I make my way down through Wood Street. It's the first time I've been out since I went to Mistress Jourdemayne's. I've lost my nerve. I'm afraid someone will recognize me and know my connection to Father Thomas, who is still imprisoned in the Tower. But at this moment a desperate need for news has driven me out into the street. I've slipped out while Master al Qali has gone to Oxford for a few days.

I'm barely at Chepeside and already the crowd is growing large. It carries me along like a fierce tide. It has purpose, this crowd, and they take little note of my handsome doublet and short cape, or my fine Moroccan leather shoes and wooden pattens.

I try to make sense of the words that are flung about to find out where this crowd is headed, and what's going on. My heart goes to my mouth when I hear the name, 'Bolingbroke'. It's not long, though, before I sight the cathedral and see that everyone is heading there, trying to squeeze themselves through the gate.

Something makes me push my way ahead and force myself through the gate. It's then, beyond the bell tower, at the cross, I see a platform. Church magnates, dressed in all their finery, are seated on the platform. One of them I suppose to be the Archbishop of Canterbury. Beside him is the Lord Mayor of London. Someone next to me points out Cardinal Beaufort, the Duke of Gloucester's enemy. It's 'sermon time,' he tells me. A time when the Archbishop of Canterbury and other Church officials tell the people of London what sin they have committed and why, and make a lesson of it. This time, it seems, they have one particular person in mind to make a lesson of. Master Roger Bolingbroke.

A roar from the crowd makes me look up. Surplice flapping, Master Bolingbroke climbs up the high platform. A chair painted with strange signs is placed in front of him and he's forced to sit in it. A man shoves a paper crown on his head and they give him a sword to hold in one hand and a sceptre for the other. I pale at the sight of it, recognizing the scene before me. It seems such a long time ago, but I know it's less than a year since I saw that image in a vision Limpin' Sam showed me.

Jeering laughter erupts around me while Master Bolingbroke looks out on the crowd, clearly frightened. Here's a man that will do poorly under torture, I think. But what does that mean for me? It's Father Thomas I'm worried about. I've had no real dealings with Master Bolingbroke.

A moment later a man holds up an astrolabe and parades it across the platform. Another man holds up glass vials and flagons containing liquids of bright red and blue. I can't imagine what they might be and can think only that they're easily seen and will make an impact with the crowd. The third man waves something around. It's a little difficult to make out what he's holding but his words are clear enough. It's a waxen image. And it's the image of the King.

I push closer, determined to see the exact shape of the wax figure. I'm holding my breath, hoping that it isn't one of the ones that Mistress Jourdemayne used in her work. I can't get close enough to tell, but I can hear the words being said when the Archbishop rises.

'This man stands accused of the serious crime of sorcery and treason. He has been examined fully by us, the Church authorities, and he has confessed to his crime of sorcery. He is here, surrounded by his instruments of magic, to make his public confession.'

I can take no comfort from the words, and looking at Master Bolingbroke, he seems no lighter in mind for his confession. Two servants force him to his feet and he addresses the crowd. At first his words are barely audible until the Archbishop prompts him to start again and speak up.

'I, Roger Bolingbroke, do hereby confess to almighty God of my sins of sorcery.'

A huge gasp rises up from the crowd.

'Although used to summoning angels and conversing with spirits in order to gain knowledge, I now admit my actions incompatible with Christianity. I hereby promise to forsake the devil and all his works.'

The people sigh, disappointed. What did they expect? That he'd conjure demons?

'But—' He holds up his sword, and every eye goggles. 'I want to emphasize that it was the Duchess of Gloucester who first urged me to this conjuring because she wished to know to her future.'

Loud mumblings ripple through the crowd. I glance around nervously, waiting for what he would say next.

'She commanded me to cast her horoscope and also that of the King, to see whether he would remain childless and whether her husband might therefore accede to the throne. Her ambition and pride knew no bounds. And she caused others to create waxen images such as these you see here now, in order to bring about the King's demise—'

A roar goes up in the crowd. Shouts are hurled at the platform. 'Shame!' Burn the witch!'

Cardinal Beaufort rises to his feet, shouting over the noise. 'I demand the Duchess of Gloucester be called to answer these terrible accusations.'

The crowd cheers its approval and more shouts of 'Burn the witch' are hurled to the front. I turn away and start to push through the crowd. I have to get back and somehow get a message to Master al Qali. With Bolingbroke accusing the Duchess of Gloucester in public it will probably be only a matter of time before she is questioned. Cardinal Beaufort would see to that. He's far too powerful for the Duchess to escape that much. And with the Duchess under questioning there's more chance that Mistress Jourdemayne's name would come up. And with her name, my own isn't far behind. And what of Alys? I think of her soft, lovely face and her round firm breasts and hope she has the sense to go somewhere safe. For a moment I think to go to her, warn her to leave London, but I know it's a foolish thought.

A man grabs my arm and swings me around to look at him. He seems familiar, but I can't place him immediately. Then I remember. *The Turk's Head.* One of my customers.

'Don't I know you from somewhere?' He looks me up and down, his face puzzled. There are stains on his doublet, but he's wearing hose and there's a dagger at his belt.

I give him a puzzled look. '*Non capisco*,' I say in Italian. I give him a small bow and move forward, praying that he makes no more of it.

I'm in luck. The man is all humble apologies. 'I'm sorry. I realize I was mistaken. Please forgive me.'

I toss back a smile and then push forward, away from him. It's not until I'm outside and making my way up Wood Street that I feel any sense of relief. It's all I can do not to run all the way back to *The Golden Lion*.

∽

'Should we prepare to leave soon?' I ask.

Master al Qali has only been in the door a short while. I know he's tired and I tried to wait until he'd had some food before I told him the news, but the words tumbled out my mouth as soon as he sat down. He remained there quietly while I spilled out the tale of the confession at St Paul's cross.

Now he shakes his head wearily. 'It is true, this is not good news. The Duchess could very well be taken for questioning with Cardinal Beaufort demanding it. He has the King's ear now, I understand from my Oxford friends. But there is no real danger for us yet. I think we will wait a while yet.'

'But she will mention Mistress Jourdemayne. Even now the word around London is that Mistress Jourdemayne used witchcraft to cause the strange hailstorm the King was in. And I met the Duchess of Gloucester. I looked in the showstone for her. Twice. She won't forget me.' I can hardly keep the wail out of my

185

voice. I know I sound like a baby and I hate myself for it. I bow my head, ashamed.

'Now, now. You mustn't worry yourself. The Duchess has never met you, Giacomo Bonavillagio, and nor has Mistress Joudemayne. That other fellow, Barnabas, well he has disappeared.'

'But Mistress Jourdemayne saw me when I went to get the showstone.'

'Yes, and you cleverly dressed in a monk's habit and spoke as you used to. I promise you, she would no more recognize you than your own mother would.'

I give him a dark look. My own mother would never recognize me because the last time she saw me I was a babe. But his words make sense and I can draw some comfort from them.

'I have my own news for you,' Master al Qali says. 'When I was up at Oxford I talked with some wool merchants. They have news of some of their own ships that were heading through the same area as Captain Flores. Apparently there was a storm and some ships were lost. One of their own, most certainly. They are still waiting for an exact account.'

There's a knock at the door and the innkeeper comes in bearing a heavy tray of food. He nods to us both and retreats quickly. He's used to our private ways by now and the money he gets for his discretion is encouragement enough to respect it to its full.

Master al Qali motions me to join him at the table and share in the meal. I've little appetite but I know better than to argue. Food is there to be eaten, not wasted, in Master al Qali's view. It's a view that I normally share and only a short time ago never wavered from. At the moment, though, I can only think of the fate of Captain Flores.

'Were there any survivors of the wool merchant ship?'

'There were. And it is these survivors they are awaiting. And when they arrive in London they will allow me to be present when they are interviewed.'

I take some hope from these words. I need this hope. Everything has been so awful in the past weeks. I don't want to think that there is any possibility Captain Flores is dead.

'Do you have any idea when they will arrive?'

Master al Qali shakes his head. 'A few weeks? A month, perhaps? It's hard to say. There are many things that could slow their journey and just as many that could speed it up.'

'May I come with you when you go to the interview?'

'We shall see. In the meantime I think it's time you began to learn something of astronomy. Did you have any instruction in it under your former mentor?'

I think of Father Thomas, still imprisoned in the Tower. What use is all his knowledge of alchemy, astrology and astronomy now? 'He explained only the basic ideas to me. Enough so that I would understand something of the astrological charts he cast sometimes.'

'So you know something of astrology too? Excellent.'

'I know enough to understand that right now I wish I knew nothing.'

Master al Qali gripped my wrist tightly. 'Never turn down a chance to acquire knowledge, Giacomo. Knowledge can be a powerful tool. And we make it serve us. Rather than have us serve others from lack of it. That's the part your former mentor forgot.'

CHAPTER EIGHTEEN
Westminster, 24 July 1441
ELEANOR

Outside, the light was fading. Soon the moon would rise and provide its own light to the darkening sky. Eleanor looked away from the window and turned to Alys.

'Pack my clothes and jewels at once. There's no time to lose.'

'All of your clothes, Your Grace?'

'No, just my summer gowns. But hurry. And tell no one.'

Alys placed the jug she had on the table by the window and began to pull out one of the chests in the room. 'Shall I at least order a wagon to be brought?'

Eleanor glanced nervously out of the window again. 'No. On second thought, just put a few underclothes in a sack and order two horses and one for the groom. I'll see to my jewels.'

Alys nodded and hastily did as she was ordered. When the sack was full, she left the bedroom and went to give the order for the horses. Eleanor used the time to get out her jewel casket from the press by the bed and put it in a velvet sack. When Alys returned Eleanor had her dark cloak on and she handed Alys another.

'Put this on. I want you to come with me.'

'Me, Your Grace? But where are we going?'

'You'll see soon enough.'

Alys nodded obediently, but Eleanor could see the question in her eyes. She knew she could count on Alys, though, like she could no other woman. She'd decided it would be best to leave her ladies and the other servants behind. With Humphrey still trying to gain access to the King at the palace and answering none of her requests for advice or help, she must act herself.

She made her way downstairs, nodding to any of the servants she encountered. Alys followed her silently, both sacks hidden under her cloak. Outside, the horses stood waiting, the groom holding the reins. Eleanor took the sacks from Alys and had the groom tie the sacks onto the saddle.

'The other horse is for you,' Eleanor said to Alys.

Alys' eyes widened. 'Me? But—'

Eleanor gave her a firm little push forward. 'You'll be fine. I'm sure you've ridden before.'

'Only a pony, when I was young,' she said in a low voice.

'There, see?' Eleanor turned to the groom and motioned for assistance. He helped her mount her white palfrey and then Alys on the horse behind.

'We must make good time. I want to reach Westminster before the moon has risen.'

'We're going to the palace?' asked Alys.

'No. We're going to the Abbey of St Peter. For Sanctuary.'

Alys opened her mouth in shock, but had no time to say anything because Eleanor kicked her palfrey forward at a smart pace. Alys' horse took off behind and the groom brought up the rear. They rode in silence for a while. Eventually Eleanor allowed the pace to slacken and she pulled up beside Alys.

'It won't be long, now, before you're there. You're to say nothing, you understand me? Should anyone ask you a question directly just say they must talk to me.'

'Is the situation so bad you must seek sanctuary?'

'Worse than bad. Bolingbroke made a public confession yesterday and named me as the person behind all his misdeeds. Me! As if he had no say in the matter. As if he didn't take it upon himself to do more than he was asked.' Eleanor could hear the tremor in her voice and she fought to control it.

'Oh, Your Grace,' Alys said. 'Will sanctuary really protect you from Master Bolingbroke's accusations?'

'Yes.' She said it with more conviction than she felt. It was the only alternative she could think of she could only pray that it would be granted and upheld.

At the abbey, after the groom helped her dismount and took the horses away to find the stables, Eleanor pounded on the abbey door. One of the monks opened the door and stared at her in wonder. She straightened and threw back her hood to reveal her face.

'I am the Duchess of Gloucester and I come here, a good Christian woman, to seek sanctuary from those that persecute me.'

The monk said nothing for a moment and then stood aside. 'You are welcome, Your Grace.'

He led her through to a small chamber and indicated a low bench against the wall. 'If you will wait here I will get the Abbot,' he said.

Eleanor took the bench indicated and lowered herself nervously. Alys remained standing, the sacks at her feet. She'd told the groom to make his way back to Greenwich and had no doubt she wouldn't see him again.

The Abbot appeared, his white robes catching the light from the mullioned window. A large gold cross hung from his neck down to the rope that was tied around his middle. His face betrayed nothing. He bowed to Eleanor.

'Your Grace. Brother Paul tells me that you have come seeking sanctuary.'

'I have, and pray that you will grant it to me.'

'Of course. I will uphold it for as long as I can.'

'Thank you. I only have a maidservant with me. If you could provide for us both I will gladly give you a large contribution.'

'And it will be gratefully received.' He made an effort at a smile, but there was no warmth in it. 'I have made arrangements for some bedding and other necessities to be brought for you. So you won't be too uncomfortable during your stay.'

'Thank you. You are kind.'

The abbot bowed and left the room. Eleanor sighed. It wasn't the warmest reception, but it was the best she could hope for.

'Well, Alys, we must make ourselves comfortable. This is our home now, for the time being.'

Alys gave her a doubtful look. 'Yes, Your Grace.'

The outlook the next morning proved little better. Eleanor was stiff from the uncomfortable pallet that did nothing to keep out the cold from the stone floor. Alys had managed to bring her a jug of water and a small bowl in which she could wash away some of the grogginess from the poor night, but it did little for the pounding headache she had.

She toyed with the chunk of bread on the plate before her. The small table it sat on was scarred with years of use and one of its legs wobbled. To be reduced to such a state made her want to cry. There was only weak ale in her cup, so she couldn't numb herself from the empty day that lay before her. But at least she was safe now and she must be grateful for that.

'Your Grace, have you seen the windows?'

'The windows?' Eleanor glanced around the room. There were no windows here.

'The window above the altar, especially. The colours, did you see the colours there?'

Eleanor gave Alys a feeble smile. It was kind of the girl to try and distract her with the images in the stained glass windows, but to be truthful, she couldn't recall them. 'I'm glad you can admire them. What is it about them you like so much?'

'Just everything.' Alys' face came alive and her eyes lit with pleasure. 'The folds of the cloth on the figures, the deep colour of the blues and the reds and even the golds. The manner in which they depict the faces. Such beauty. And the hands.' Alys held up her own hand and traced its outline with the finger of her other hand. 'They are able to show the curve of the fingers so well and the shape of the thumb.'

Eleanor struggled to recall the images in the stained glass and found she could only picture a vague image. Was this the first time Alys had ever been in the church? Perhaps it was. A maid of her sort wouldn't ordinarily attend mass when she did. She studied Alys, saw the soft curves of her face, the small mouth and fine nose. There was nothing coarse here.

There was a knock at the door. Alys opened it and one of the monks entered.

'The Abbot would like to see you in his study, Your Grace. If you would like to come with me, I'll show you the way.'

Eleanor rose from her seat. The hour was early. What could the Abbot possibly want with her? Were there hours so marked by prayer he wouldn't remember that most people would have hardly had their morning meal yet?

The Abbot looked up from his desk when she entered his room. There were papers scattered across the desk and an open ledger at one side. He held a letter in his hand. The Abbot rose when she entered.

'Come in, Your Grace. Be seated.' He gestured to the chair in front of her.

She took the seat and stared nervously at the letter in his hand. She couldn't see what was in it, but the frown on the Abbot's face didn't encourage her.

'You have news?' she asked.

'I have, and I fear it's not entirely encouraging for you. It seems the King is aware you have taken sanctuary here and you're now summoned to appear tomorrow before an ecclesiastical court presided over by the Archbishop of Canterbury.'

'But they can't do that. I've taken sanctuary here.'

'They can and they are. You can't invoke sanctuary for ecclesiastical offences. It seems you are to face charges of heresy, witchcraft and treason.'

'But that's not possible. I am innocent!'

'Nevertheless you must appear before the court tomorrow and they will be the judge of your innocence. I'm sorry.'

His face was unreadable once more and Eleanor could only imagine what he was thinking. Something unkind, she was sure.

'Will I be allowed to return here at night while the court examines me?' She knew that it was important to remain at the abbey. Even though the sanctuary didn't apply to ecclesiastical offences, it certainly did apply to treason.

'That will be for the court to decide, I'm afraid.'

'And you won't refuse me if they permit it?'

He frowned. 'No, of course not. You are welcome here as long as they allow it. In the meantime someone will arrive first thing tomorrow to escort you to St Stephen's chapel, where the court will be convening.'

Eleanor nodded and took her leave of the Abbot. She had a whole day to think of what she would say in her defence. There was no one else to advise her, no books she could consult; she had only herself to rely on. But she would think of something. She had to. Her life depended on it.

Eleanor watched Alys give her gown one last brush. It was a deep russet, with few trimmings on it and was the soberest colour she owned. It was important to strike the right balance when she appeared before the Churchmen, so she avoided striking colours, over rich fabrics and low cut bodices. Still, she didn't want them to forget that she was a duchess and her husband a royal duke.

Once brushed, Alys put the gown ready for her to step into and lace, a process that seemed to take longer than usual under Alys' nervous fingers. 'It will be fine, Alys,' said Eleanor with a calm she didn't feel. 'I'm sure the proceedings are only a formality, given that the fool Bolingbroke has seen fit to shift the blame for his own wrongdoing on to my shoulders.'

Alys gave her a sceptical look but said nothing. She sighed. It was just as well, she supposed, that Alys didn't believe her. She alone knew how closely Eleanor skirted the edge of disaster.

'I can count on you, Alys, can't I?' This time she let the tremor come into her voice. Anything to keep the girl on her side.

'Of course, Your Grace,' Alys said. 'I'm entirely loyal to you.'

Eleanor examined Alys' face. She could detect no guile in her, no sense that she was frightened enough to go running directly to the nearest priest or King's man and spill everything to save her own skin. But what did Alys know? She was with her at the Jourdemayne woman's home, took her herbals and looked in the showstone, but nothing more than that. That wasn't treason or heresy and it could hardly be called witchcraft, not really.

Feeling more comforted Eleanor sat patiently while Alys fixed her hair in simple braid that she coiled under a low hennin hat. A small linen veil topped it off. Eleanor gave it a small pat and was satisfied.

'There, I think I'm ready now.'

Her escort and guard arrived soon after and they took her to St Stephen's Chapel. Alys wasn't allowed to accompany her, and in some ways Eleanor was glad not to risk Alys' presence in the chapel because it might fuel her fears. Eleanor could rely on no one but herself for support, though, and it was a dismal thought. She'd heard nothing from her husband, and unless Humphrey was allowed access to the King soon, she had no doubt that Beaufort would do his best to keep Humphrey from her.

Her fears were confirmed when she was brought into the presence of the high ranking clerics there in the chapel. All of them were seated in the choir, with the exception of the Archbishop and Cardinal Beaufort, who were given the chairs in the front. She was made to stand at the edge facing the two men.

She moved forward and kissed the Archbishop's ring and the Cardinal's ring. With a small bow she retreated to her place and clasped her hands together in front, determined not to let these men see that they were trembling.

'You are here before us to answer for some very serious accusations,' said the Archbishop. The Archbishop was a lean man under his flowing robes and heavy gold cross that hung from his neck. His blues eyes were hard and showed no compassion as he examined her. A becoming gown and a winsome smile would do nothing with him.

'I would hear those charges and answer them, Your Grace,' said Eleanor.

The Archbishop nodded to a man seated at a small table in the corner, a quill in his hand and sheaves of parchment before him. He picked up one long piece of parchment and stood. He paused a moment to clear his throat before beginning.

'The Ecclesiastical Court, presided over by the Archbishop of Canterbury, His Grace the Right Honourable Richard Chicele, brings charges of witchcraft, heresy and treason against Eleanor Cobham, the Duchess of Gloucester.'

The words rang out and echoed through the church and seemed even more powerful with such a delivery. Up to this point Eleanor could somehow believe that it was all just a mistake or a dream, but hearing these words of her supposed misdeeds penetrated her mind and showed her like nothing else how much her life hung in the balance. One by one the clerk read the charges. Conspiracy to commit witchcraft, consorting with witches, conspiring to commit heretical acts with waxen images, geomancy, necromancy—on and on the list went, until the last and most serious of all charges—conspiring to bring harm to the King and make herself Queen.

When she heard the final charge it sent a shock wave through her. She looked around wildly at the assembled group in a feeble hope she might find Humphrey among them. There was no sign of him, or anyone else that might speak in her defence, or lend some sort of support. A wave of dizziness washed over her.

'Are you ready to answer the charges?' asked the Cardinal.

Eleanor looked across at the Cardinal sitting in his chair. Rings adorned every one of his sausage-like fingers that were folded over his huge belly. The man was a pig. Even the eyes in his fat face were slanted like those of a pig. But it wasn't his huge size, or his opulent robes and numerous rings that annoyed Eleanor, it was the smug look on his face and the dismissive tone of his voice. Like she was some piece of dirt shortly to be swept away forever. That she might be beneath him, that trumped up fellow. Her Humphrey was the heir to the throne.

She stiffened her spine. She would win this, show them that she was a Duchess, worthy to be Humphrey's wife. 'I answer these charges willingly and eagerly,' she said. 'I am innocent of all of them.' She let her voice ring out loudly, so its strength matched that of the clerk's.

The Cardinal gave her a disdainful look and pursed his mouth. The Archbishop nodded. 'Very well,' he said. 'You have heard the charges and answered them as you saw fit. You may return to your sanctuary, now, but tomorrow you'll return, where you will hear the evidence gathered against you.'

Eleanor stood stunned as the two guards led her away, back to the abbey chapel. Her mind spun through the Archbishop's final words over and over. Evidence. What evidence? Whose evidence? Southwell's? Bolingbroke's? What would they say? What lies would they make up or truth would they twist and elaborate upon?

～

She slept badly that night. The hard stone underneath her pallet didn't help her comfort, but it was her racing mind that kept any kind of rest at bay. She couldn't stop imagining Cardinal Beaufort's fat fingers around her throat, squeezing and squeezing while he screamed at her to confess.

When the day dawned she was stiff and cloudy-headed. Alys put a wet cloth to her neck and brow, but it made little difference to how wretched she felt. She left most of the food on her plate, which made Alys fret at her, until Eleanor told her to hold her tongue.

Her escort came at the same time as before, their faces grim and saying few words. When she arrived at the chapel, the assembled group remained unchanged. They sat in their clerical robes, all of them eyeing her with prim expressions on their faces. Except for Cardinal Beaufort, who wore a triumphant look that Eleanor found unsettling. She moved forward and kissed Archbishop Chichele's ring, giving him a tremulous smile. He frowned in response.

'Yesterday we read out the charges against you and you denied them,' he said to Eleanor when she resumed her place from the day before. 'Do you still deny them?'

'I do, Your Grace.'

'Very well.' He motioned to one of the guards. 'Bring in the prisoner.'

A moment later, Bolingbroke entered with two armed guards on either side and was brought to stand a few feet to her left. His robes and hair were well kept, but his face was drawn and grey. He studied his hands, avoiding her eyes.

'Master Bolingbroke, you were brought before the Church to be examined for heresy, and during that examination you confessed publicly to using instruments of magic, practices inconsistent with the Christian faith. Is that true?'

Bolingbroke raised his head briefly to look at the Archibishop. 'It is, Your Grace.'

'And you state that these practices were at the request of Eleanor Cobham, the Duchess of Gloucester. Is that also true?'

'It is,' said Bolingbroke. He stole a brief glance at Eleanor and she glared at him.

'What specifically did she ask you to do?'

'A horoscope, Your Grace. She asked me to cast a horoscope so that she could know what the future would bring.'

Cardinal Beaufort leaned forward. 'The future? She would dare to know what would happen to our beloved King, you mean.'

Bolingbroke paled even more. 'P-perhaps. I don't know for sure. I tried to do as she asked, but I didn't have enough information for her birth, but I prepared what I could. She wasn't happy with the result. She asked me instead to cast the King's horoscope, because his time and date of birth were known.'

Eleanor gasped. 'He lies, Your Grace. I did no such thing.'

'Hold your tongue, woman,' said Beaufort.

'Your time will come,' said Archbishop Chichele. 'For now, we will hear Master Bolingbroke speak.' He nodded to Bolingbroke. 'Continue.'

'She wanted desperately to determine the future and was happy to use whatever means she could. It's well known she's been consorting for years with the witch Margery Jourdemayne to that end. But her efforts lately hadn't produced the desired results—to conceive a child.'

'You mean she wanted a child, a true heir that might one day sit on the throne,' said Cardinal Beaufort.

'No!' The words were out of Eleanor's mouth before she could stop them. 'Please, it's not true.'

'Madam, I won't remind you again to remain quiet,' said Archbishop Chichele.

Eleanor clamped her mouth shut, nearly biting her tongue in frustration. How the words were twisted, the truth becoming something much more ugly than her intent.

'I cannot say whether that was her intent in wanting a child,' said Bolingbroke. 'But the manner in which she obtained the Duke was certainly clearly guided by Mistress Jourdemayne.'

'And have you met with this Mistress Jourdemayne?' asked the Archbishop.

'Only on behalf of the Duchess. She would have me help her with some of these efforts in addition to consulting the horoscope I drew up.'

'And what did that horoscope say?'

Bolingbroke frowned and looked over at Cardinal Beaufort. 'It is only what the calculations revealed. I assure you I had no control over the outcome. Mistress Jourdemayne saw it too.'

'What did she see?' asked Cardinal Beaufort. 'State it now, if you please.'

'That the King would die in the twentieth year of his reign.'

He'd muttered the words, but they could still be heard, and the result was powerful. There was a great intake of breath followed by low murmurs and words of condemnation. The Archbishop threw up his hand for silence.

'And do you still believe this horoscope is accurate?'

'There is always a certain amount of error that can occur.' Bolingbroke stumbled over his words. 'My experience is somewhat limited, and of course I was told to cast it as quickly as possible, so that in my haste, I might have easily overlooked some minor calculation.'

Eleanor sniffed. The man was backtracking so much he would likely fall over. It was obvious he had swiftly become Cardinal Beaufort's toady and would say whatever pleased the Cardinal.

The Archbishop thanked Bolingbroke and turned his attention to Eleanor. 'You have now heard Bolingbroke's testimony and he has countered your assertion of innocence with some very serious evidence. What do you have to say to this?'

'I would say that Master Bolingbroke has twisted the truth to suit others' purposes.'

'What truth is that?'

'I have never asked him to cast the King's horoscope.'

'Yet you did ask him to cast a horoscope.'

'Not the King's. He did that of his own accord.'

'But you don't deny consorting with the witch Margery Jourdemayne?'

'It's true I have visited Mistress Jourdemayne over the years for herbs and simples that might help me conceive. She is well known for that.'

'There was no other reason to visit Mistress Jourdemayne?' asked Beaufort.

She gave Beaufort a steady look. 'I visited Mistress Jourdemayne for her assistance in helping me conceive.'

'And that assistance included magical practices?' asked Beaufort.

Eleanor blanched. 'She used a variety of approaches.'

'Describe them.'

'She gave me herbs, philtres, ointments and on occasion she would look in her showstone.' She said the last words in a low voice, but the mutterings that followed left her in no doubt of their impact.

'So you admit to consorting with witches and witchcraft,' said Cardinal Beaufort. 'That would be considered sorcery and heresy.'

'I admit to the seeking the assistance of the Witch of Eye over many years, and that it was common knowledge and accepted by all members of the royal court.'

'In the light of this admission, I think you must reconsider your plea of innocence to at least some of the charges,' said Archbishop Chichele.

Eleanor took a deep breath. Would it be better to plea to the lesser charges and hope that it would make it easier to avoid the charge of treason and the greater charges of heresy and sorcery? It was a gamble.

'I will reconsider, Your Grace.' She cleared her throat and thought quickly. 'I will then plead guilty to some of the charges. She named the lesser charges that related to her association with Margery Jourdemayne.

The Archbishop heard her with a solemn face. Beside him, Cardinal Beaufort looked at her suspiciously.

'In light of this new plea, and the information you've given us today, we will allow you to return to sanctuary and await our decision.' He turned to Bolingbroke. 'You may go to your quarters at Westminster, for now. We may need you yet again for questioning.'

Eleanor released the breath she'd not realized she'd been holding. She had gained some time at least. And time was something to value. She must figure out how to use it wisely.

～

She wiped an ink stain from her finger. The quill had split from pressing down against the page and she needed Alys to sharpen it again for her. She found writing difficult and she hated it. The letters came slowly under her unpractised hand and looked more like chicken scratchings than anything that might be a letter. But it must be done and quickly. Words crowded her mind and she tried to choose them as carefully as she could. People other than her husband would read this letter, she had no doubt. She only hoped that Humphrey might actually see it. It was her best chance. To plead for his help and ask that he persuade the King to be merciful towards her.

When the letter was finally done, she blotted it and folded it into a small packet. Wax sealed it, but there was no insignia to press into it, so she left it as a plain blob on the parchment. She gave the letter to Alys and asked her to ensure its delivery. That completed, she sat back and sighed.

Five days had passed since she'd been examined in front of the ecclesiastical court, and still no news. The monks and Abbot had seen to her basic needs but they had very little to do with her. She knew it was as much by choice as the fact they had their daily obligations and duties. Alys had tried to find out what she could the few times she had managed to slip out, but she'd returned with rumours that were so frightening Eleanor refused to let her try any more.

A tap on the door roused her from her musings. A moment later the Abbot entered. He withdrew a small folded packet from his sleeve and for a brief time Eleanor thought it was her letter.

'This has come for you,' he said. 'It's from the Archbishop.'

She thanked him and took the letter, noting the slight tremble in her hand. Was this her fate scratched out in ink in this letter? Carefully, she broke the seal and unfolded it. The Abbot stood beside her while she skimmed the contents. She gave a bitter laugh.

'It seems that the King has commissioned a horoscope from John Langton and the Duke of Somerset and it's now completed. It counters Bolingbroke's and clearly shows that the King will not die in the twentieth year of his reign.'

'That is good news,' said the Abbot.

There was a trace of humour to his tone and she glanced up at him and saw a gleam there. 'Yes, it is good news, isn't it?' With such a dire prediction defused by a second horoscope, perhaps it increased her chances of escaping any further investigation and danger. She read on and her smile slipped away.

'I am to be taken in two day's time to Leeds Castle in Kent to await another hearing. It seems they need time to investigate all the evidence that has come to light.'

She tossed the letter on the table in front of her. 'More investigations. More time to dig up lies and people who will support those lies. Beaufort will see to that. He wants me burned as a witch, humiliated for all to see, and then permanently out of the way.'

'Through your disgrace the Duke of Gloucester's standing comes into question.'

Eleanor stared at the Abbot, the fog of fear clearing for a moment. 'Yes, you're right. They want to bring down Humphrey.' She pursed her mouth. 'But the King loves Humphrey. He's his uncle.'

'The King is being fed many different tales. He wants to make decisions, to act the King now, yet he isn't able to understand the difference between flattery, lies and truth.'

Fear gripped her again and she saw the full scale of the danger she faced. 'Humphrey may not be able to help me.'

'No. But you may be assured that they can't make you answer the charge of treason in an ecclesiastical court. It is not a religious crime. And you are a peeress of the realm. No one has ever tried a royal duchess, and they would be loath to do so now.'

His words were cold comfort, but they were still reassuring and she gave him a weak smile. 'I thank you kindly for your insight. You may be right. Or they may see fit to make an example of this duchess. The Cardinal's ambition knows no end.'

The Abbot bowed. 'For that, my lady, you can only pray. God hears all our prayers.'

'A thousand candles lit might make the difference for me, Lord Abbot, but at the moment, I've very little with me but my own knees and clasped hands.'

The Abbot smiled. 'A lone voice may work many wonders.' He blessed her and made to go. She gave a sigh, watching his retreating figure. It was true. Prayers were all she had now. Humphrey wouldn't be able to help any longer.

CHAPTER NINETEEN
Westminster, 30 July 1441
BARNABAS

The cold of the stone wall is chilling my skin and seeping into my bones, despite the heat that has been raging across the city for the past week. The rank smells of the river and the sewage of the nearby palace seem trapped in the confines of the church cloisters and I have to cover my nose from time to time. I've been here all the morning, hoping for Alys to appear, and now I'm ready to give up. With a sigh I come from behind the pillar and make my way down to the church door and open it. Once outside, I turn the corner and lower my head to lessen the chance that someone might recognize me. It means also that I can't see ahead and I come smack into someone.

'Sorry, sir,' says a soft voice.

I look up and recognize Alys. She's filled out more. Her breasts, once apple-shaped and firm, are now soft and full and make a deep curve in her dress. It's a fine dress she's wearing, too. Maybe one her mistress gave her, a deep blue that sets off her eyes. I take her by the arm. It's her eyes I notice now, as they stare up at me, large as saucers and holding a hint of fear.

'Alys.' I give her one of my old grins. 'It's me, Barnabas.'

'Barnabas?' She blinks a few times, furrows her brow. 'Is it really you?' She puts a hand briefly to my face and smiles slowly. 'It is you.'

The next thing I know she's hugging me tight, saying my name over and over. I'm not sure what to do. I put my arms around her waist and pull her in closer, taking in her musky scent and feeling her soft curves. The next thing I know I'm covering her mouth with mine, tasting her lips, sucking her tongue and realizing that it's the best thing in the world.

She pulls away and I try to pull her back again, take up where we left off, but all she wants to do is talk. Tell me all about her mistress' plight.

'I heard,' I say. 'That's why I came. It was said you were here with the Duchess, so I came now to see you. Are you going with her to Leeds Castle?'

Alys nodded. 'She hasn't come out and asked me, but I will go with her. She needs me. She has no one else on her side.'

'But is it safe for you? Will you be asked to answer questions in front of the ecclesiastical court, too?'

Alys paled and bit her lip. 'I don't know. But what else can I do? There's nowhere for me to go.'

'Don't you have any family you can go to?'

'My family are dead, except for my brother. I have no idea where he is. Gone off to sea somewhere, last I heard.'

I blink at her words. An old longing comes over me. 'Off to sea? Isn't that a fine thing.'

She snorts. 'Off to his death, more like. He was ever one for a brawl.'

'I'm sure he's fine. Enjoying himself in some ship bound for foreign lands.' I give her a feeble smile. 'That was my dream, once.'

Alys lays a hand on my doublet sleeve. 'But look at you now, Barnabas. You're so grand. And your speech. What has happened, where have you been?'

I give her a pained look. 'I can't tell you, Alys. I wish I could, but I'm risking everything just meeting you now. Especially with your connection to the Duchess. But I had to see you. To warn you to go. Things are much too dangerous for you, for me.' I untie the pouch at my side and hand it to Alys. 'Here, this isn't much, but it should be enough to get you away from here. Don't you have some cousin, someone in the country you can go and stay with for a time?'

She shoves my hand away. 'No, Barnabas. I can't take your money. Besides, my place is with the Duchess, no matter what.'

'But it's not safe, don't you see that?' My voice goes louder and squawks, I'm so worried she won't do as I ask. 'You must go,' I say in a loud whisper. 'I can't bear the thought of you risking your life like this.'

'What about you, Barnabas? What will you do?' She gives me a hard look and I know what she's thinking.

'I only wish I could take you with me, that we could go somewhere together that's safe. But I can't. I'm in no position and—'

'Save your breath. I wouldn't go with you in any case. I told you, I can't leave the Duchess to face this by herself. She's been good to me.' Alys steps away slightly, her expression closed.

I try to draw her into my arms again but she won't have it. She pulls away. 'Alys, please,' I say. 'Don't be mad. Can't you see the danger for me? I was the one who looked into the showstone. The Duchess isn't likely to forget that, nor will Mistress Jourdemayne. I have to go away, disappear for a while. Someone's helping me do that.'

'You have to go away?' Her voice is softer now and she steps closer again.

'Yes. I'm not sure where, or when, but I'll let you know if I can. But you must promise to tell no one.'

'I promise.' She tilts her head up and kisses me on the lips. It's a soft sweet kiss and I press for more and she opens her mouth to me. This time she lets me put my hand at the top of her dress where the curve of her breast begins to deepen and swell. I insert it further down, feel her softness and moan at the wonder of it. Her nipple goes firm under my touch and she sighs. I rub it more and her sigh deepens.

I'm hard as a rock and I start to ruck up her skirt, following the ways I'd seen so often behind *The Turk's Head*, or in the stables at Mistress Jourdemayne's. Alys pulls away and straightens her dress.

'I have to go, Barnabas. The Duchess is expecting me.'

There's no anger in her eyes, just a lingering trace of regret. I nod to her and catch up her arm. 'I will return, Alys. Don't ever forget that. I'll come and get you and we'll go away together, just the two of us.'

'Just the two of us.' She smiles at me then, but there are tears in her eyes. 'I will miss you, Barnabas.'

I stare at her a moment and pull out a small leather cord. I tie it around her wrist. 'There,' I say. 'Just so you don't forget me and my promise.'

She reaches up to me and plants a brief kiss on my lips. 'I won't forget you, Barnabas.'

⌘

'There's been nothing said in Chepeside, either?'

Master al Qali shakes his head. 'Giacomo, there are times when the world has other things to talk about beside the Duchess, Bolingbroke and Southwell. There are the matters of trade, high prices, drought and ruined crops. And plague.'

'The plague?'

'Rumours only. We have been fortunate to have escaped it.

I nod, reassured, though for a moment I wonder how much truth he hears in his travels around the city. Being such a figure of curiosity, people wouldn't forget he was near and would more likely guard their tongues.

The heat in the room seems unbearable at the moment. The sweat from my palms have dampened the parchment under them. Though it's mid September, the heat is still fierce to me. Master al Qali in his long robes and cloth cap seems cool and calm. There is never a trace of sweat on him. I go to the window and open it, knowing at the same time I'm inviting in dust and stench, rather than any cooling breeze.

Master al Qali wrinkles his nose. 'I will never get used to the odours of this city.'

I shut the window again and wipe my sleeve across my brow.

'It is not that hot,' he says. 'Relax, my good fellow. Put your mind to use instead of worrying about things you have no control over.'

I look down at the calculations in front of me and the numbers run together. Ordinarily, the beauty of their actions would hold my full attention, so that I would take little notice of time passing, but the last week with no word, not even a rumour of the investigation into the Duchess' activities, or the fate of Father Thomas, Bolingbroke, or even Hume, has kept eating away at me, until it was like a huge thorn stabbing my side.

'There is something more bothering you?' asks Master al Qali.

I look up and see the concern in his eyes. He's been so kind to me these past few months. Allowing me to stay with him, to sleep on a small cot with only a few fleas, and feeding me well. But more than those things, he has taught me so much, not just opened a world of literature, language, mathematics and astronomy to me, but also showed me vast opportunities. Now, I see so much more, not just through the books I've read, but also through the experiences he's shared with me. The last thing I want to do is to cause him problems.

I shake my head and mumble a few words in Italian about the heat. He comes over to me, puts a hand to my forehead and studies my face.

'I don't think there is anything physically wrong with you,' he says. 'I think it is your worries. They are becoming larger in your mind each day you hear nothing.' He gives a big sigh. 'I think we must do something about that.'

He goes to the chest at the end of the bed and withdraws the small wooden box containing the showstone. My eyes widen and my mouth opens to object, but catching the firm look on his face I shut it. I owe him too much to say no. And besides, he's doing it for me, to help me. Resigned to what was to come, I clear the papers away from the table and watch him place the showstone in front of me.

The showstone is cold to the touch and turns my fingers clammy. For a moment, I shut my eyes and try to calm my breathing. The exhalation and inhalation find their own rhythm and my heart slows enough that it seems safe to open my eyes and look into the showstone. For a moment it is only a cloudy stone that I see and the relief it gives me is almost palpable. But then it changes and images start to form. I see soldiers, armed ones, holding someone between them, marching the person through a stone archway. My breath catches. I can only see the back of her, but that's enough. I would recognize my former mistress anywhere. I pull away and throw the cloth cover over the showstone.

'You saw something?'

I nod. 'Mistress Jourdemayne. She's been arrested.'

Master al Qali sighs. 'Yes, I feared as much.'

I turn to him. 'You knew?'

'I said only that I feared as much. With the Duchess under investigation it is inevitable that they would bring Mistress Jourdemayne in for questioning.'

'Then it's only a matter of time before they come looking for me. She'll not hesitate to bring my name into it, if it gets her some advantage.'

'But you are Giacomo. Barnabas no longer exists.' He says these words with such a calm, assured voice that I believe him for a few moments.

Master al Qali nods to the showstone. 'Did you see anything else?'

I shake my head.

'Look again. See if there is anything more.'

I stare at the velvet cloth covering the showstone. Did I really want to know more? The image I'd just seen did nothing to reassure me. In fact it did the opposite.

'No,' I say. 'I can't.'

'Look again.'

There is iron in the voice this time and I glance at him. His expression is unreadable.

'Giacomo, I do this to help you. You must not be afraid of the showstone. It is what you make of the images you see that cause you fear.'

This time I nod and slowly remove the cloth. I take a deep breath and stare into the stone once more. It's cloudy again, with milky hues floating inside like a dense foggy day in London. An image forms. It's Mistress Jourdemayne's familiar shape, her face creased with panic, her hands bunching into fists. She sits alone in a small room, muttering to herself. A small beam of light filters through the narrow opening in the wall that is a poor excuse for a window. I can make out nothing more about the season, or anything else that might tell me whether this event has already happened, or if it is still to come.

'What do you see?'

I describe the scene before me and he nods. 'There's no sense whether it is now or in the future,' I say. 'Or if it has already happened.'

'Well, we can assume that if it has happened, it's been recent enough, since there is no news about it on the streets.'

I nod absentmindedly. I'm suddenly struck by the idea that I should warn my mistress. Perhaps if she escapes and hides until this is all over there would be no danger of my discovery. The idea fixes in my mind, but I say nothing to Master al Qali. I know he will think it a foolish notion and watch me to make sure I wouldn't act on it.

I peer back at the showstone, pretending to look for further images and eventually shake my head. 'There's nothing more to see,' I say finally.

Master al Qali pats my shoulder. 'You have done well, my friend. Extremely well.' With great care he covers up the showstone again and replaces it in its little box.

It's later, when I'm sure Master al Qali is asleep, that I slip out of my cot and creep out the door and find my way to the street. I know the direction like the back of my hand, and before long, I'm making my way down to the Queenshithe dock. Somehow though, I end up at the door of *The Turk's Head*. There are still some stragglers hanging around the doorway. A dark-haired drab rubs her hips against a gap-toothed sailor and three rowdies argue, spilling more ale down their fronts than in their mouths.

I squeeze through the doorway and find one of the dark corners, my heart hammering fiercely in my chest. I give Black Jack a nervous glance, but he's too caught up in a shouting conversation to notice me at this moment, and his missus is nowhere in sight. I breathe a sigh of relief.

'I'm tellin' you the woman's a witch,' says Black Jack. 'Didn't she rain hail and lightning down on the King?'

'Naw, that weren't her. That were the other one. The Cobham woman,' says a man with a huge mole on his cheek. Suddenly I remember him. I gave him some herbs for the clap. I shrink back into the corner.

'What will happen to her, I wonder?' asks the grey-bearded man beside him. 'Do you think they'll burn her?'

'She's got high connections, that one,' says Black Jack. He gives a shrug. 'But them connections may do her no good wiv Cardinal Beaufort.'

'You fink they'll burn a duchess?' says the mole-faced man.

'Naw, not her. Mistress Jourdemayne. They're sure to burn her.'

'But they've had her for a while now, and they've done nofink,' says the grey-bearded man.

'That don't mean a fing,' says Black Jack. 'They're just making sure they got all they can out of her. Beaufort's a canny man. He don't want the Duchess to get away wiv nofink.'

My heart sinks. I'm too late. Suddenly, all my fears come racing back and I start to struggle out of my corner, poised to run all the way back to *The Golden Lion*, until the next words freeze me in my seat.

'You think they'll burn Bolingbroke, too?'

'Well, he's in the Tower now. Stands to reason,' says Black Jack. 'Burn 'em all, I say.'

They continue arguing about whether to burn one or all of them and I use the time to sneak out of the tavern. By the time I'm on the street, I'm shaking so much I can hardly walk.

'Hey!' a woman calls out to me.

I turn and see one of the drabs. She's a regular I remember. I pull my hat down a little further, hoping she won't recognize me and turn away, muttering excuses. She grabs my arm and pulls me to face her. She puts her hand along my cheek and I pray the poor light will keep my identity safe.

'Where you off to in such a hurry, sweet one?' She drops a hand to my crotch and squeezes. 'I can give you something to make you stay a little longer.'

The odours of unwashed flesh and stale ale overwhelm me for a moment. I shake my head. 'I'm sorry I don't understand,' I say in Italian.

'Ah, it's a foreigner I've got here, is it?' She gives me a smile full of rotten teeth. 'I like foreigners.' She squeezes my crotch again and leers at me. There's no mistaking her meaning and my cock is more stupid than I think. It rises to the challenge just as I'm trying to pull away. She shrieks with laughter but lets me go.

I make my way down the street with quick strides as she calls after me. It's all I can do not to run. By the time I reach *The Golden Lion* I'm out of breath, but it's mostly because of the panic that's seized me since I left *The Turk's Head*. Before slipping inside, I try to calm myself. No one recognized me, I tell myself. Barnabas no longer exists. I am Giacomo Bonavillagio. Eventually, my breathing slows and my heart beats at a normal pace. I think how fortunate I am. And that tonight proved that I can move about the city with little fear of recognition. At least at night. I smile. For a moment there, it was almost as it used to be. Lurking in *The Turk's Head* to find out a bit of information. I was always good at that, picking up the gossip. I'm certainly still better at it than Master al Qali. Obviously, he doesn't know where to go to find out what's going on. Otherwise he would have learned days ago that Mistress Jourdemayne had been arrested and Bolingbroke was in the Tower.

CHAPTER TWENTY
Leeds Castle, Kent/Westminster, October 1441
ELEANOR

'Read something from my psalter, for me, Alys,' said Eleanor. She pointed to the book on the small table.

Alys went over, picked up the book and found a place on the stool near the fire.

'Not there. Take the chair. I'm fine here on the settle.'

Alys muttered an excuse and took the chair as instructed. She looked uncomfortable, as if the chair was much too big for her.

'Relax, child,' said Eleanor. 'Just read.'

She began slowly and stumbled over a few of the words. After a few sentences she stopped and traced her fingers over the illuminations at the side and top of the page, lost to the world of drawing images. Eleanor bit her tongue and tried to cultivate some patience. It was interesting and even amusing on occasion to help Alys over these many weeks of her confinement, but at times it was downright tedious. The girl was clever and had no problem learning her letters and grasping the new words Eleanor showed her, but still, it was situations like these when she wished Alys wasn't so caught up in the artwork that surrounded the books. If only she would focus on the words, they might progress faster.

Often she would try to steer Alys away from the images in the few books she was allowed and teach her other aspects of being a lady. Alys had a natural grace and gift for mimicry so she could curtsey and speak convincingly as a noble. On occasion, she'd even imitated the court ladies so closely she had Eleanor in fits of laughter. Eleanor's personal favourite was Anne Mowbray, the Duchess of Norfolk, whose squeaky high voice and pinched face Alys copied to perfection. Sometimes, when she was feeling really wretched, Alys' imitation of Alice Montecue, the Countess of Salisbury, cheered her to laughter. How perfectly she caught the lifted chin, the little sniff and studied disdain when sampling a make-believe pie.

Alys was a comely girl who was fast becoming a striking woman. Her long russet hair and deep blue eyes that were almost the colour of Eleanor's were only two of her many fine points. It seemed right to Eleanor that she should pass on her own skills and accomplishments to someone with so much promise. Didn't she rise on her looks and wits?

Her daughter and son seemed not to care whether she lived or died, though. Eleanor's letters to them at the homes where they were fostered had gone unanswered for the most part. Were they ashamed of her? The last message she'd had from Arthur was nearly a year ago and she could tell then that it was one his tutor had dictated. The most hurtful was Humphrey. Besides a brief note expressing the hope she fared well, she'd heard nothing from him, either. It might be that he was guarding his words and trying to be careful, but it truly seemed that Alys was the only one who cared about her now.

There was a knock on the door and the steward entered and bowed stiffly. .Eleanor sniffed. The man was such a bore, so proper, even pompous at times, as if his own father wasn't a butcher in Smithfield.

'What is it, Sir Alfred?' she said, allowing a note of impatience to creep into her voice.

'Your Grace, a letter has come. I'm to inform you that you are to proceed back to Westminster tomorrow for further questioning before the ecclesiastical court.'

There was something about the tone he used when he said, 'Your Grace', that rubbed her the wrong way. The man disliked her, she knew that much, but there was also something insolent about his manner. Now she could see he relished giving her such news and she wouldn't give him the satisfaction of seeing the fear that suddenly filled her.

'Thank you for the news, Sir Alfred,' she said in a cold tone. 'I'll be glad for the opportunity to see all this business put to rest, finally. Will you please see there is a horse made ready for me and one for Lady Alys?'

Sir Alfred glanced over at Alys. 'For your chambermaid?'

'For my waiting woman. Are you implying that a de Courcy cannot ride a horse? Or is it that you don't have two horses good enough in your stables, Sir Alfred?'

Alys gave him a cool look, shutting the book firmly and drawing his attention.

The steward turned back to Eleanor and gave a stiff nod. 'As you wish, Your Grace.'

He left quickly after that, shutting the door with a bang. Eleanor let out a peal of laughter, noting the slight hysterical edge to it. 'The man is such a buffoon,' she said.

'But Your Grace, I'm not a de Courcy. He'll know it's a lie.'

'Alys, dear girl, as I've told you before, the bigger the lie, delivered with firm authority, the more convincing it is.'

∽

She stared at the men in front of her and the words she spoke to Alys earlier echoed in her head. The lie they spoke loudly and with such authority made her shake so visibly it was all she could do to remain standing. The chill in St Stephen's chapel seemed worse than she had ever experienced, even in the depth of winter.

'You are charged with attempting to encompass the King's death by sorcery and witchcraft.' It was Robert Gilbert, Bishop of London, who delivered the charges this time. 'It is a most grievous and terrible charge that carries with it the stiffest penalty.'

She blinked at him. Had they some new evidence? Hadn't she strongly denied this charge and explained herself enough back in July? She took a deep breath and tried to steady herself. 'My lord bishops, I stand before you, as I stood over three months ago, innocent of that charge.'

Gilbert frowned at her. 'Your answers to all the charges were duly recorded on both occasions,' he said. 'And the record shows that on the first occasion that you appeared before this court you denied all charges, yet when confronted with further evidence and a witness, you admitted guilt on five charges.'

'Yes, and none of those five charges was conspiring to bring harm to the King.'

'But you admit that your story of innocence changed once further evidence was brought forth, so how are we to believe that you are innocent of this most serious charge we lay before you now?'

'Because it is the truth.'

Gilbert gave her a weak smile. 'Ah, the truth. Well, it appears your idea of the truth shifts, depending what evidence is put before you to contradict your version.'

Eleanor clasped her hands tightly in front of her, the sweat making her fingers slip a fraction. Alys sat in a chair over to the side, small and insignificant. What evidence did they have now? What lie was Bolingbroke, or worse, Jourdemayne, concocting to save their skins? Was Beaufort making them promises in return for a confession that suited him and permanently ousted Humphrey from favour?

'I stand behind all that I said in July,' she said, trying to keep the quiver from her voice. 'I sought out the Witch of Eye only to ask her help in my desire to have a child. Nothing I did was directed by the intention to harm the King in any way.'

'You may stand by that now, Madam, but will you stand by those words in four day's time, when we bring you before this court in the presence of this Witch of Eye?'

Eleanor fought off the stab of fear that seized her. She lifted her chin, kept her mouth firm and steady. 'I will answer any claim Mistress Jourdemayne may make, and remain firm in my statement of innocence.'

'Then, so be it. We will see you here before the court the twenty-third of October,' said Gilbert. He nodded over to the clerk who sat at his small scribe's table, his quill working busily across the sheet of parchment, his eyes down. Eleanor stared at his bald pate. For a brief moment he paused and looked across at her. His eyes were filled with pity.

～

Eleanor and Alys returned to the small apartment in Westminster Palace, where they now housed her. She dismissed her guard with a nod and shut the door behind him. She knew he wouldn't move from the position outside her door.

'Your Grace, shall I get you something? A cup of hippocras?'

'Hippocras? You think they will allow me expensive spiced wine?' Eleanor's voice held a shrill note and she took a deep breath to calm herself. It had taken all her restraint not to shout at Alys for being such a mouse while Eleanor fought for her life in front of the leading religious men of England and Beaufort plotted her downfall and that of her husband. Tears filled her eyes and poured down her cheeks.

Alys rushed to her side. 'Oh, Madam, please don't take on so. They have decided nothing, yet.'

Eleanor fought to control her tears. She dabbed her eyes with the edge of her sleeve. Alys went over to the small chest that held what remained of her clothes and retrieved a small clean square of linen. She offered it to Eleanor. Eleanor took a little comfort from Alys' show of concern and her breathing slowed and she was able to speak calmly.

'They have decided nothing except that they must ask me again and again the same questions. Only this time they've hinted that Mistress Jourdemayne has supplied them with fresh information under questioning.' She snorted. 'I can only imagine what form their questioning took.'

Alys paled visibly. 'You think she said something that will make them doubt your innocence?'

'They already have doubts over my innocence. In fact they are certain I'm guilty. They want me guilty, they just don't know how to bring it about for someone of my rank.' She gave a bitter laugh. 'In some ways you could say it is my rank that protects me, though it might be that it's my rank that got me here in the first place.'

'But what can Mistress Jourdemayne say that will be so terrible?' There was a note of pleading in Alys' voice, as if she desired above all that nothing of Jourdemayne's words would bring them ill.

'Are you afraid for yourself, Alys? You need not, you know. I'm certain that you are of no use to them whatsoever.'

Alys blushed. 'No, no. It's not me I'm worried about.'

Eleanor brightened and patted Alys' shoulder. 'I appreciate your concern, dear girl. It gives me no end of comfort to know at least someone is on my side.'

Alys lowered her eyes and nodded. 'I'm on your side of course, Your Grace. Always.'

A bit of parchment on the table caught Eleanor's eye. It was Alys', she knew, created sometime the day before, when Eleanor had no interest in it. She walked over to the table and turned over the sheet, ready for a distraction. She scanned the drawing. It was of a fashionably dressed young man whose fine face carried a mischievous twinkle. The girl was talented, there was no doubt. She'd captured a likeness so that it was not just any person, but an individual.

'This is very good,' said Eleanor. 'Is it someone you've seen at court? A young squire or soldier?'

Alys' face turned a vicious red. 'No—no. It's only someone I once knew. Well, yes. Someone I saw at court....' Her sentence trailed off unfinished.

Eleanor gave her a knowing look. 'Someone you took a fancy to, I think.' She studied the drawing again. There was something familiar about the face, but she couldn't place it. There were so many young men, though, that came and went at the court, it was difficult to place them all.

They were all there when the guards brought Eleanor into the chapel this time. The bishops, the Cardinal and all his toadies lined up in their seats, their faces solemn. Above them, the stained glass shone vividly from the sunlight that poured in the rose window. She thought of Alys and how much she would love the folds depicted in this cloth and the brilliant blues and reds the window contained. She glanced away and forced herself to remember where she was.

In a plain chair to her right was Mistress Jourdemayne. Bolingbroke was in a chair on her other side, and the fact that the two of them were seated in a world where no one would sit before a royal duchess and religious nobles told her volumes that their bruised faces and swollen fingers only confirmed. The rack, thumbscrews and hot tongs were only some of the various possibilities that might have been used to extract confessions from the two of them and make it impossible for them to stand. From their appearance, now, it looked as if no torture had been spared.

The chair provided for Eleanor was carved and padded, and gave some comfort from what she knew would be a gruelling morning. Margery turned her swollen and bloodshot eyes towards Eleanor. There was fear there and something else. The woman had every right to be afraid. Her own fate was sealed. There was no doubt she was more than a herbalist providing phials and tisanes and the like for ailments. Eleanor's own words had seen to that, and she was certain they wouldn't doubt that much of her testimony. Bolingbroke would certainly corroborate it. She glanced at him. His head was hanging and he was barely able to sit upright. She noticed then, at his feet were various objects including an astrolabe, some of his measuring tools, some vials filled with liquid, and a lumpy shape. Eleanor squinted against the light that shone through the chancel window and blurred her vision. It was a little larger than her hand, but she still couldn't make out what it was.

They had confronted her with Bolingbroke and his words of evidence before and she'd managed to defend herself well. What other facts could they have unearthed? Had Mistress Jourdemayne said something that made his words prove more than they had before?

'Eleanor, Duchess of Gloucester, you are reminded that you are still charged with the crime of attempting to encompass the King's death by sorcery.' As before, it was Robert Gilbert, the Bishop of London, who spoke to her, his voice ringing loudly in the chapel.

Eleanor drew herself up and tried to put as much iron in her voice as she could. 'I know the charge and my answer remains the same. I am not guilty.'

'Your words are noted, Madam, but we will see how you respond in the face of the statements of two of your co-conspirators and the physical evidence we have brought before you today.'

'There can be no true evidence in existence to prove my guilt.'

Cardinal Beaufort gave a grunt and glanced over at the Archbishop. 'We are the judges of that,' he said.

Eleanor allowed herself to cast him a brief venomous look. She knew such gestures did her little good, but at this moment she felt there was little that could harm her case more.

'Margery Jourdemayne, Mistress of Eye, and sometimes known locally as the Witch of Eye, you swore in a statement that Eleanor, the Duchess of Gloucester, came to you for help?' asked Gilbert.

Mistress Jourdemayne sat slumped, her head bowed. She nodded slightly.

'Speak up, woman. We need your word.'

Mistress Jourdemayne mumbled a few words, drool spilling from her mouth.

'Louder. Everyone must hear you.'

'Yeth,' said Mistress Jourdemayne in a strained voice.

'And is it true that this help took the form of potions and peering into a magic ball to predict the future, among other blasphemous things?'

Mistress Jourdemayne glanced over at Eleanor and nodded. 'Yeth,' she whispered.

'I told you to speak up, woman.'

Mistress Jourdemayne spoke the 'yes' loudly, her voice cracking with the effort.

Gilbert rose and made his way over to the chairs. He picked up the lumpy form at Bolingbroke's feet and stood over Mistress Jourdemayne, his eyes narrowed. 'And is it true, Madam, that you conspired with this man beside you and the Duchess to use those aforementioned tools and this'—he wielded the lumpy form over her head—'wax image made in the King's form to bring about his death by melting it in a fire?'

His voice was filled with threat and he hovered over her while she sat in terrified silence. 'Your answer, woman, what is your answer? You've already admitted to it, we now need you to confirm it here, to confront the Duchess of Gloucester with the horror of her deeds.'

Mistress Jourdemayne's body began to shake. Tears leaked out of her swollen eyes. 'Yeth,' she said and held up a bloated shaking finger to Bolingbroke. 'But he got the wax.' Spittle fell from her mouth with each word she tried to form with her fattened lips and split gums.

Beside her Bolingbroke moaned. 'N—no. That isn't so. I had no part in the wax figure.'

'But the figure is here, among the tools of your practice,' said Gilbert.

Bolingbroke shook his head repeatedly, moaning.

'My lords, it's clear that neither one of these two are able to know truth from falsehood,' said Eleanor. She'd watched with horror every word of confirmation that Margery Jourdemayne had spoken. It was only when Bolingbroke tried to contradict her that Eleanor had some hope of shifting the force of this trial and judgement.

'Their statements were clear enough before. They are only here to show you the folly of your own insistence that you're innocent,' said Beaufort.

Eleanor sniffed and looked at him. 'Nothing that has been said can make me change that statement. There is no doubt that these two are lying, and any information they gave you to the contrary was done so in an effort to save their own lives.'

'But Madam, their lives are already forfeit,' said Gilbert. They have nothing to lose by stating what they know to be the truth.'

At these words Mistress Jourdemayne wailed and fell off her chair to the ground in a crumpled heap.

Gilbert cleared his throat and spoke loudly over the wails. 'I must also tell you, Your Grace, that one Thomas Southwell, late Canon of this very chapel, Rector of St Stephen's Walbrook and Vicar of Ruislip, has also named you instigator of these said deeds.'

'He is lying, too. No doubt you had your men torturing him to give you the kind of answers you want.' Fear made it hard for her to swallow, to keep the tremor from her voice. 'As I said before, I went to Margery Jourdemayne solely for the purpose of assistance in conceiving a child. Everything I did was in aid of that, and only that. It was Mistress Jourdemayne who looked in the showstone. And that boy of hers, too. He looked in it. The wax image was a poppet for the son I was to have, it wasn't made in the King's likeness.'

'You admit that you made a wax image?' asked Beaufort, a triumphant note in his voice.

'The image wasn't made in the King's likeness,' she repeated. 'And it wasn't put in a fire. At least as far as I'm aware.' She nodded to Bolingbroke and Mistress Jourdemayne. 'They buried it in a cemetery.'

Gilbert moved toward her. 'You're lying now, to protect yourself. You state this image was buried in a cemetery and not melted in the fire so that it would be impossible to show it to us.'

She searched her mind desperately trying to recall the name of the place. 'They know which cemetery it's in.'

'But who would dare to dig up consecrated ground to bury a heretical object in it, but someone meaning harm?'

Eleanor bit her lip. How to explain what she didn't understand anyway? 'It is their practice and reasoning, not my own. I only watched and was assured that it would bring me a child.'

'Now you admit you conspired with these two and Southwell in heretical practices,' said Gilbert. 'How can we believe anything you say? The truth is, we cannot.'

Gilbert moved away from her, his mouth set in a prim line, and resumed his seat. Eleanor stared across at him, determined that she wouldn't flinch under his words.

'I maintain my innocence,' she said. 'I didn't conspire to harm the King. I did nothing that was not lawful.'

'This court will see fit to rule on that,' said Beaufort. 'In the meantime, we have heard the testimony of Mistress Jourdemayne and are ready to deliver our judgement.' He nodded to one of the armed escorts. 'Help the accused to stand.'

The man made his way over to Mistress Jourdemayne's crumpled form and lifted her with great difficulty, so that she faced the two bishops and the Cardinal. Her head lolled slightly to one side but her eyes were open and pleading.

'Margery Jourdemayne, we have heard the charges of witchcraft laid before you and the evidence given,' said Gilbert. 'Your past history has made us more conscious of the severity of your crime and so we hereby find you guilty of heresy and witchcraft. As such, you are to be sentenced to death by burning.'

Mistress Jourdemayne gave a great scream and then fainted. Eleanor looked on, speechless. Was she to be next? Would they sentence her to burning? Even now she could smell the acrid scent of roasting flesh and shuddered. She closed her eyes for a moment, until Gilbert's voice jolted them open.

'Master Bolingbroke, you will be removed to the Tower to await our judgement.' He gave a nod to the soldier near Bolingbroke. The man lifted him from the seat, and with the help of another, dragged him from the chapel to a barge that awaited to take both him and Mistress Jourdemayne back to the Tower. Two other men attempted to rouse Mistress Jourdemayne, but in the end she had to be carried from the chapel, the door shutting behind them with a resounding thud.

'And now, Madam, you have heard the statements of these two and seen the evidence before you, what do you say?'

Eleanor paused. Did they think by repeating the question numerous times they would weary her so much she would agree to anything? 'I am firm in my statement of innocence. I had no involvement in any evidence presented here.' She pointed at the lump of wax still clutched in Gilbert's hand. 'That's not the wax image made as part of my wish to conceive.'

Gilbert looked at the wax lump still in his hand and gave it to one of the servants nearby. 'That lump of wax, or any other tool of Master Bolingbroke's practice, doesn't take from the fact that you did indeed join the three in their heretical practices. And they have clearly practiced heresy and Jourdemayne most certainly witchcraft.'

'I am guilty only of asking Mistress Jourdemayne for help, nothing more.'

Gilbert frowned at her and glanced at Cardinal Beaufort. Beaufort nodded back, his face stern and his eyes glittering. Gilbert rose.

'We have heard enough testimony today. Eleanor, Duchess of Gloucester, you are to return to your apartment in the palace here and await our decision.'

Her guard moved forward and lifted her from her seat. She stood for a moment in a daze, the words still tumbling through her mind. The soldier urged her forward and she began her journey back to the apartment, taking in nothing of the cloistered courtyard, the flagged path, or the dark corridors that led to it. It was only when Alys took hold of her, sat her down in a chair and made her drink a cup of strong wine that she was able to bring her mind under some semblance of control.

'It is no good, Alys, they're determined to find me guilty.'

Alys crouched down beside her and stroked her arm. 'No, I'm sure you're wrong. They are trying to punish you, indeed, by putting you through all this.'

'You weren't there, Alys. They had Mistress Jourdemayne and Bolingbroke. They both admitted to everything that was put to them. And they said I was part of it. I tried to tell them that I only asked for Mistress Jourdemayne's help to have a child. She was the one who looked in the showstone, she and the boy. And it was not my idea to make that wax image.'

'You mentioned the boy as well?' Alys' voice rose.

Eleanor gave her a puzzled look. 'Of course I did. It was the truth, and better that they go after him than me. Why?'

Alys stood up and moved over to the chest, fidgeting with the clasp. 'No reason, only that it might not be wise to mention the boy, because if they bring him in, he might be tortured to say God only knows what.'

Eleanor chewed her lip for a moment, considering her words. 'Well, you could be right. It's too late now, though, to do anything about it. They didn't ask me anything more about the boy. They might forget about it. On the other hand, they might have heard about the boy from Mistress Jourdemayne and have already arrested him. Let's hope not.'

Alys' head was bent so Eleanor could hardly hear the words of agreement she uttered.

233

CHAPTER TWENTY-ONE
London, 27 October 1441
BARNABAS

I slip outside, sack in hand, checking the lanes before I move out of the shadow of the doorway. It's a habit I can't break, and it's a good one too, because I've still no idea if anyone is after me. I move along the lane, heading toward the crowds of Chepeside. I should take comfort from all these people, but I can't help but fear that I'll see a familiar face and there will be a light of recognition in their eyes. I keep my head down though it's hard to move like that among these throngs of people who bump and shove past you.

I manage to make it to Queenshithe and the shouts of men loading cargo is nearly deafening. Everyone wants to get their ships out and on their way now, before the winter storms come. It's this thought that makes me more jittery than ever. I know we need to be on our way soon, away from the dangers of London. Master al Qali is as calm as ever, doesn't seem to understand that we should waste no time and leave.

I move around the docks, avoiding anyone who looks remotely familiar, though I'm also desperate to know if there's any news of Captain Flores. Finally, I stop a Portugee-looking fellow.

'Do you know Captain Flores? Is his ship here?' I ask in English.

'I don't understand you, my friend. I'm sorry,' says the man in Italian.

I smile, delighted, and fall into Italian. 'Do you know Captain Flores?'

The man brightens and claps my back. 'Oho, my compatriot. My name is Pietro. And what brings you here?'

I cast wildly about for a story. 'I'm Giacomo. I arrived some months back, on Captain Flores' ship.' I curse myself, for is this the tale that Master al Qali would have me tell? I modify it back to the familiar one. 'I came with a friend of my father's. My father is a merchant.'

'I have worked on many merchant ships,' he says. 'Who is your father?'

I redden. 'He is only a minor merchant. I doubt if you have ever heard of him.'

'Ah you never know. I might have heard tell of him.'

'Bonavillagio. Carlo Bonavillagio. From Venice. I try to keep my voice firm and look him directly in the eye. The lie is bold and can be instantly undone.

Pietro shakes his head and smiles. 'No, I haven't heard of him, but then I am from Genoa. But no matter, what is it you asked me?'

I grin broadly, barely able to contain my relief. I'm near giddy with it. 'You must be thirsty, let me take you for a drink. I know a place that will quench any man's thirst.'

'Ah, you are more like a Genoan than a Venetian, I can see. And will there be any fair ladies to see to a man's other needs?'

'There will be indeed, my friend.' I put my arm around his shoulder and march him off in the direction of *The Turk's Head*, the weight of the sack reminding me of my other errand. It can wait for now. At the moment I am Giacomo, ready for a good time.

The tavern is crowded when we arrive. All the ships have spilled out their men for one last time to make merry and carouse among the drabs who are more than ready to take their last coin before they go to sea. The atmosphere is alive with singing and laughter, and it's not long before Pietro and I are sitting in a corner with a tankard in our hands and a drab in our lap.

My own drab is a woman of substantial parts that cover most of my body, and her lips and abundant greasy locks make for a wonderful screen against any eyes that might know me. Black Jack is in his usual corner with his cronies, rising only on occasion to help his missus serve the ale. Pietro called for our ales in his broken English, while his own piece of womanly flesh took her place in his lap.

Hey ho, but it's a wonderful feeling to be sharing a drink with a great companion and having my nether regions rubbed to aching by a woman whose dugs could fill the water trough outside. On the off chance, I put my hand inside her bodice and give her nipple a pinch and a tweak and she squeals in delight and rubs me down below with a free hand. I grin across at Pietro who is already halfway down his drab's bodice and halfway up her skirt. I take a large gulp of the ale, set the tankard down and try my own luck up the skirt across my lap. There are folds enough to make my progress slow, but I get there in the end, and am gratified to feel how wet it is.

''ere, me young lord. We can have a proper go at this outside, if you wants,' she says to me.

I can hardly contain my excitement and nod before I remember that she spoke in English and I've been pretending I don't understand. Still, in the heat of it all, who is she to remember what was said and what was just understood in a language common to most men and their doxies?

She tumbles off my lap and grabs my arm before I can say or do anything more and we're out the door in a trice. She leads me down the little lane beside *The Turk's Head* and pushes me up against the wall and starts to undo my ties. It's the middle of the day, but I've enough ale in me and a cock so eager to have its first real go that it's as tall as a pikestaff. We're still fumbling with my clothes when I feel a large hand grip my shoulder.

'Giacomo, aren't you forgetting something?' comes a familiar voice.

I look up. My hose is already sagging around my ankles, my cloak is twisted along my back and my arse and nethers are bare to the world. Master al Qali stares at me, a hint of amusement in his eyes, but behind that is something darker. He holds up my sack, still weighted with its contents. I dart another glance at his face, my own now drained of all its blood.

The drab stares at Master al Qali a moment. 'I ain't never done a blackamoor, she says. 'If you wait in the tavern, we won't be a minute.'

'N—no, no.' I stumble over the words, speaking in Italian as he'd spoken to me. 'I didn't forget the sack. My friend Pietro was inside watching it.' I push the drab away and start scrambling to draw up my hose and lace myself in place. There's no sign now of the proud pikestaff. I straighten the rest of my clothes and watch the drab retreat hastily.

'Your friend, Pietro? Who is this friend?'

'He's a sailor from Genoa. I met him on the docks,' I mutter.

Master al Qali nods. 'And you had no thought of the risk you took bringing him here, carrying this bag and then leaving it inside while you came out for a moment's satisfaction that might bring you any amount of disease, at the very least?'

I hang my head, giving no answer.

He held up the bag again. 'And what, may I ask, did you plan to do with this?'

My heart starts beating fast. I was afraid he would get around to that question and now that he has I am left with nothing to say. The silence lengthens.

'I hope you had no intention of selling it. That would be a foolish thing to do.'

I look up quickly and shake my head. 'Nothing like that. I'm not stupid.'

'The level of your stupidity is a question that is best not explored for now. If you weren't going to sell it, what were you going to do?'

I look at him, putting just a small amount of the defiance I feel into it.

'You weren't planning on getting rid of it, were you?'

I give him a straight stare, daring him to read the answer in my eyes. He grips my shoulder and squeezes hard.

'Giacomo, I must remind you of two things. One, this is an object that is worth a fortune, not only for its value as a large gem, but also for the power it has. Two, it is not yours to do with as you will.'

'I know it's powerful, Master al Qali,' I say in a wheedling voice from my past. 'It's too powerful. It's downright dangerous. You have to get rid of it. If they find it in our possession if they should come for us, we're lost.' I shake my head and try and clear the drink from it so I can put across all the reasoned arguments I can muster. 'It could have more power than we know, power we can't control. You don't want to have something like that in your possession, so that's why I was going to throw it into the river.'

Master al Qali frowns. 'I understand the fear you have, Giacomo. But, believe me, I am more than aware of the powers of this stone and the value it has.'

'But if they should catch us with it?'

'They will not find it in our possession. Not after today.'

'You're giving it to someone else.'

'This is not your concern, Giacomo. It will be looked after and that is all you need to know. In the meantime we will go back to our rooms. I need you to look into the stone one last time before I make other arrangements.'

⌣

I sit in the chair at the table, more sober than I've been in my life. The effects of the drink have long since passed and now I await Master al Qali's preparations with a thumping heart. It seems each time I look in the depths of the stone I feel more and more dread. Is it that I'm afraid of what I'll see, or is it what I don't see? I don't know. All I know is that my hands are sweating buckets and my mouth is dry.

Master al Qali sets the stone on a dark cloth in front of me. It's evening now, and with only the single candle lit that sits beside the stone, the room is filled with long flickering shadows that the meagre fire in the brazier does nothing to dispel. I close my eyes a moment and take a deep breath. I tell myself the images can't harm me and open my eyes to stare into the cloudy stone. The fog inside the showstone shifts and moves like a multitude of spirits at war. Suddenly, it clears and I hold my breath.

I can see Father Thomas in his prison cell. His pale, sweating face swims up out of the gloom, framed in a halo of candle-light. He sits on a stool, and beside him is a table with writing implements strewn across it. He must have bribed the jailor for these comforts.

Father Thomas sets down his quill, raises his right hand and stares at the ring on his middle finger. Licking his dry, cracked lips, he mutters a prayer. Then he flicks back the dull, pale stone in this ring and lifts it to his mouth. His gullet moves, swallowing hard. Beads of sweat pop up on his upper lip and brow, become a sheen across his skin, while his face twists into a hideous grimace. He brings his hands to his throat and then his belly and topples from the stool to writhe among the rushes. Finally, his body turns, face upward, still twitching, and he flings out a desperate hand, his fingers curled like a bird's claws.

Before I can lift my head, the image clears, and through my tears another one forms. I want to look away, but it's impossible, part of me can't help but want to know what's coming next. It takes a while for the image to form, there are pulses and fractured light from the candle that flickers and moves inside that obscure all else.

Eventually, I can make out a rush-strewn floor with a hunched figure crouching in a dark corner. The head lifts and reveals the bruised and haunted face of Mistress Jourdemayne. Her wild mane of tawny hair hangs limp over her shoulders and her broken and twisted fingers rest in her lap. She moves her lips as if she's muttering spells or prayers.

When this picture fades, a seething crowd appears. Coarse, leering faces pass before me, some of them stuffing food in their mouths, others showing broken, snarling teeth. Eyes roll with excitement and my head fills with their shrieks as they hurtle through the narrow streets towards Smithfield.

Smoke billows and clouds my view for a moment. Already the smell of burning wood wafts up my nose and catches in the back of my throat. Mistress Jourdemayne's soot-stained face appears next, her mouth open in a scream, her eyes rolling and searching—but finding no kindness. Flames leap and dance around her, crackle and snatch at her hair, melt her weeping eyes, devour her flesh and bone in a greedy roar that fills the air with the sour stench of roasting meat. I gag and choke, but I can't look away, until flakes of ash blow upward on the breeze and the hideous vision fades.

I turn to Master al Qali and the tears are streaming down my face. I don't know whether it's from the sting of the smoke, or the grief of witnessing the death of my mistress and Father Thomas. All I know is that it was too terrible to watch, and I'll be damned if I'm going to describe it to Master al Qali. I wipe my sleeve across my eyes.

'They're dead,' I say.

'Who is dead?'

'Me mistress and Father Thomas.' My mouth locks tight after those words. I'll say no more. I can't risk trembling lips and weeping eyes.

Master al Qali nods. 'I see. I thought as much. I did hear it mentioned that Mistress Jourdemayne was to be burnt as a witch today.'

'Today? It happened today?' I can hardly believe his words. How is it that she was burned and I knew nothing about it? 'I should have been there.'

'Now you know that is a foolish statement. The risk was too high.'

I know he's right, but still I set my jaw and give him a stubborn shake of the head. 'I should have been there,' I muttered again.

He pats my arm. 'We will speak no more of it, for now. There is much to plan and prepare.'

He's caught my interest and I focus on his words. He nods to me. 'Tomorrow I will go and arrange our passage for the continent.'

'We're going to the continent?'

'Yes, we can't afford to wait any longer. Except for the Duchess, they have fried most of the bigger fish and now they may go after the smaller fish.'

I flinch at his use of the word 'fried' but it's best to leave that aside and think on the rest of his statement. 'We're leaving? Going to the continent?'

'Yes. I have business there and it's time that I attended to it. We must hope that Captain Flores is well and that we can meet up with him another time.'

'But where in the continent will we go? Italy?' A small shiver of joy ran through me. I would be travelling, just what I'd always wanted to do.

'Not Italy, no. To Paris. There are scholars I must speak with. And it wouldn't do you any harm at all to broaden out your studies. There are some fine men that will instruct you.'

Paris. I have no idea at all about Paris, except that it's a fair size. Maybe not as large as this city, but big enough. 'Isn't our King at war with the Parisians?'

'You are a Venetian, Giacomo. It makes no difference to you what these kings of France and England are doing. As for me, I am a man of learning, from a place so far from these countries they will not consider me for one moment at war with them.'

I nod, his words echoing in my head. I am a Venetian, truly. Didn't my encounter with Pietro prove that? I think of the day and my almost coupling. Perhaps in Paris I will be able to go the full course. With a finer woman. A woman with russet hair and eyes as blue and deep as the sea. I think of Alys. I promised I'd let her know where I was going and when. Will I be able to do that in time? Master al Qali would no doubt be keeping a sharp eye on me now, after my exploits today. I sigh. I will have to try.

CHAPTER TWENTY-TWO
Westminster Palace, 1 November 1441
ELEANOR

Eleanor frowned over the letter she clutched in her hand. She tugged up her bodice in an unconscious effort to protect her chest and her heart. A moment later she crumpled the parchment fiercely. The message told her little, yet that didn't stop her from being afraid.

She turned to Alys, who stared out of the small window of the stuffy apartment. In her hand Alys held a small piece of charcoal and she was working it absentmindedly on a piece of parchment.

'Do you remember the name of the boy that Mistress Jourdemayne had at her house?' Eleanor's voice was querulous and uncertain.

Alys turned to look at her. 'Which boy is that?'

'You know who I mean. The one who looked in the showstone.'

Alys pursed her lips and then shook her head vigorously. 'No, I don't remember.'

'You don't remember him, or you don't remember the name?'

'I have some recollection of him, but I don't remember the name.'

'Wouldn't the household know him?'

'I think that much of the household has either been dismissed or left.'

Eleanor nodded. It made sense that those who had anything to do with Margery Jourdemayne would have left at the first whiff of trouble.

Eleanor tapped her finger on the table. She knew if she thought hard enough she would recall the name, but part of her wondered if it was just as well she didn't know. She looked at the crumpled parchment. If they wanted to know they should find it out themselves. After further thought, she decided it was best to answer their request for the name with ignorance.

'Let them ask Margery Jourdemayne for his name, if they're so keen in knowing it now,' Eleanor said.

'Margery Jourdemayne was burnt at Smithfield a few days ago,' Alys said quietly.

Eleanor's eyes widened. 'Why didn't you tell me?'

'I only heard of it yesterday and I didn't want to upset you.'

Eleanor could tell by Alys' face it was a bold-faced lie. She'd known of it longer and had kept it from her. Eleanor forced a smile. 'Thank you, child. You were thinking of me, I know. But I would have heard sooner or later. Best to know what I'm up against.'

She looked down once more at the crumpled paper. She would feign ignorance of the boy's name. Let them unearth the household if they wanted to discover his name and whereabouts. She'd write a brief note, and after that she must do what she should have done long ago.

She would write to the Duke of York and every other noble who disliked Beaufort's influence. They might not like her, but she knew they disliked Beaufort more and wouldn't want him to bring down her husband, the highest noble in the land.

There was a tap at the door. Alys made her way over and opened it. The guard at the door handed her a folded parchment. She took the parchment, nodded and shut the door on him. Eleanor rushed to her side and snatched the parchment from her. She saw her husband's familiar seal fixed to it. Her hands trembled as she fought to open it. Would this be the end to her troubles? Had Humphrey found a way to secure her release? She scanned the words impatiently. The colour drained from her face as the words started to sink in.

My Dear Wife,

I have spoken at length on your behalf to all who support me. There is little to be done, for my influence is small enough now. The King will hear no words from me on any subject since he is increasingly giving his attention to Cardinal Beaufort and all of his supporters. The situation is now that I cannot risk coming to you in person in fear of endangering what little influence I now have. It is in God's hands.

Your husband,

H.

Eleanor sank to the floor under the shock of the words. Alys rushed to her side and struggled to lift her to a chair. Tears rolled down her face.

'Humphrey,' she said. 'He can do nothing to help me.' She held out the letter to Alys. Tentatively, Alys took the parchment and scanned it.

'Perhaps one of his supporters might have words with the King. Maybe they have done so already.'

'Who? Who would take that risk? It's clear that anyone who mentions me earns nothing but anger from the King.'

'Young Warwick? Or maybe the Bishop of Salisbury?'

Eleanor sniffed and considered Alys' words. Alys had free reign of the palace and was more than familiar with the various court alliances and intrigues by now. She had proved she was quick and careful and was able to elicit information from many an unwitting servant.

'Do you really think so?' asked Eleanor.

Alys nodded, her face bright and determined. Eleanor sighed and allowed herself to be convinced.

⌒

Alys walked slowly at Eleanor's side. Behind the two of them, a soldier followed at a discreet distance, a pike in his hand. The small walled garden they strolled in was past its peak. The pear tree had lost its leaves and those on the ash and oak were brown and curling.

Eleanor pulled her thin cloak around her, wishing she had her fur-lined one at hand. She'd no idea where it might be, or where her jewels and other precious possessions were. They had taken them off her long ago.

'You went to mass this morning before I was out of bed, Alys. Did you hear any other news that you've thought to keep from me?'

Alys shook her head. 'No, I've heard nothing more, Your Grace.'

Eleanor sighed. She needed something to take her mind off the bit of news she did know now. The thought of Margery Jourdemayne's burning flesh had haunted her constantly since Alys had told her the day before.

'Can you remember any of the poems we read this morning?' she asked Alys.

'The troubadour's poems?'

Eleanor nodded, but before she could respond, women's laughter echoed from the other side of the wall.

'The Duke of Norfolk was there, too,' said one of the voices.

'She be guilty, make no mistake. You've only to look at her to know that.'

'But guilty of treason? We do know she's a witch. She learned everything from that Witch of Eye.'

'Aye, well she's burnt to a crisp, that one. And this one is sure to follow.'

'No, no, they're wanting to have her convicted of treason, not witchcraft. She wanted the throne for herself and those men at the Guildhall are certain they have enough proof to convict. I saw them come out the day the witch was burnt. Saw it wiv me own eyes. Duke of Norfolk, four earls and noble judges. And the Mayor of London.'

'Then she ain't long for this world, I'll be bound.' There was more laughter, this time raucous and mocking.

Eleanor froze in her place and grabbed Alys' arm for support. She could feel her legs give under her, until she sank into blackness and knew nothing more.

∽

Eleanor looked down at the plain gown that hung across her frame. Her breasts no longer strained against the fabric in a becoming fashion, but drooped low and tired like some old sow. In place of cleavage she could see wrinkles, wrinkles that were repeated across her belly and most horrific of all, along her eyes and mouth. The reflection in the peer glass she held in front of her did nothing but mock the image she'd carried in her mind since the first day she'd noticed her blossoming beauty.

She handed the glass to Alys, bemoaning the fact that she had thought to ask for it so she could prepare herself better and look well for her appearance before the ecclesiastical court. They'd made their decision and she was determined to see it through with as much dignity as she could muster. There were no jewels to improve the lustre of her hair and disguise the travesty that was her breasts. No fine hennin to give her height, or silk gown to mark her rank. She was grateful that Alys had been able to secure the gown she had. The blue was faded, but at least it deepened her eyes to something near the colour that they had been.

She sighed. She'd still had no letter or note from any of the nobles she'd written to, only a few indirect words from some of them saying they had received her missive and understood her need. It was the best she could hope for.

There was a tap on the door and Alys went to answer it. The guard that always stood outside her door spoke. 'They are ready for you now, Your Grace.'

She nodded and rose. Alys offered her arm and led her to the waiting guard. Though Alys was pale, Eleanor couldn't help but notice how fine she looked in the old green gown she wore. It complimented her sleek hair, which she now had caught up in a simple net. Her skin was peachy smooth and her eyes were bright. Eleanor saw the guard give her an appreciative look as Alys moved gracefully into the corridor. The guard bowed to them both, his pike gripped in one hand.

Eleanor felt like an old woman hobbling to her corner of the hearth after a day gathering kindling in a damp wood. Her steps were slow, acknowledging her aching knees and swollen ankles. It was this incessant confinement, she told herself. She was young still. She made her step fall firmer and faster.

When she entered the chapel she found the same horrid faces waiting for her. She could see no sign of the Mayor of London, four earls or the Duke of Norfolk. Had that been a terrible rumour? Bigger ones had been spoken. London loved a scandal and she was the latest one.

Alys helped her to the chair and stood behind her. It was significant that they'd let Alys accompany her today. Eleanor knew that it wasn't a good sign when the people who are out to persecute you allow you a comfort they hadn't done before. It meant they had bested you. That they felt they could concede on little things, because they had won the big thing. She could have the comfort of her waiting woman because she would need the comfort of her waiting woman.

Eleanor stifled a sob and took a deep breath, remembering her resolve to meet whatever they had to say to her with as much dignity as possible. She took her seat and faced the men in front of her. Her hands were folded on her lap, a semblance of calm.

'We have reviewed carefully all the evidence brought forth for each charge levelled against you, Eleanor of Cobham.' It was the Bishop of London, Robert Gilbert, speaking again. It seemed they had settled on his grating voice to deliver their words. He rose from the chair and stood in front of the others seated behind him. The man was like a troubadour who must be the focus of attention.

'We hope you are aware of the gravity of your situation. Because it is serious indeed.'

There was something in his tone that started to give her hope. Something about his words that led her to believe this might not be the death knell she had feared. Such hope gave her courage. She lifted her chin.

'I am aware of my situation all too well. These past months of confinement have told me much, as did your probing and extensive investigation to unearth the poor evidence that you laid before me.'

'We ask you to remain silent, Madam. Your time for statements is over. You are here only to receive the court's judgement.'

She folded her mouth in a tight line and gave a condescending nod. The impudent puppy. Let him strut then.

Gilbert cleared his throat. 'It is the judgement of your peers that there is insufficient evidence for the charge of heresy and treason. But we do find you guilty of sorcery and witchcraft.'

Eleanor's heart stopped. Margery Jourdemayne was found guilty of these same charges. Was her fate to be the same as Jourdemayne's? She clasped her hands tightly.

'You are therefore sentenced to undertake a great penance by walking barefoot around Westminster and the city of London in front of whatever crowd may gather. After your penance is complete, you will remain imprisoned for the rest of your life at a location yet to be determined.

'And further to the evidence we heard from one Margery Jourdemayne that you used her services to provide you with such drinks and potions to force the Duke of Gloucester to love you and wed you, we declare your marriage to him null and void.'

Eleanor stared at Gilbert in shock, his final words echoing in her head. Humphrey not her husband? They couldn't do that. They were lawfully married. He loved her. She gave a little moan.

'Your guard will now lead you back to your apartment where you will prepare for your penance that will begin tomorrow.'

Penance. She would do penance. The words slowly sank into her mind. She was not to be burnt as a witch. She released her breath, not realizing until that moment she'd been holding it. The guard stood before her and Alys came around and took her arm to guide her up from the chair. She must go and prepare, she thought. Tomorrow she must walk Westminster, and the day after, and the day after that until her circuit was complete. Then she would do London. It would take many painstaking days, but she was alive. And by God's grace she would be alive when it was finished.

⌇⌇

The morning dawned grey and wet. Eleanor sat up in bed when Alys came to her and pulled back the curtains. From a small tray on the table Alys picked up a steaming goblet and brought it over to Eleanor.

'Drink this, my lady, it will give you strength for the day to come.'

Eleanor took the goblet from her and looked down into the heated liquid. 'What is it?' she asked.

'Strong mead. It will help keep the chill out as you walk.'

Eleanor nodded and forced herself to take a sip. Suddenly her hands started to tremble and it was all she could do not to spill the liquid on herself. The penance would begin soon. When she was up they would lead her out to the street with her hair unbound and nothing on her but a plain gown. Even her feet were to be bare. All the resolve and courage she'd had yesterday had vanished in the night. Now she fought back sobs of fear and loathing at what she was about to undergo.

'Oh, Alys,' she wailed. 'I don't think I can do this.' She inhaled a ragged breath.

Alys put her arm around her and stroked her hair. 'You can do this, Your Grace. You're strong, always full of courage to face down those who feel they're better than you are. You're someone to be reckoned with and I know you'll never let them forget it. Now drink this up and you'll soon be ready for them.'

Eleanor took a deep drink and hiccupped. 'But all of London will be out, shouting insults and ready to pelt me with any bit of rotted vegetable or mud they can put their hand to, I know it.'

'And you'll greet them with the disdain of the duchess you are.' Alys rubbed her shoulder. 'And I will be there, behind you, ready at hand should you need my help.'

Eleanor nodded, taking comfort from the words. She looked down into the cup and drank the rest of the contents. Already she could feel it going to her head, making her almost giddy. Perhaps with a few more cups of this she might be able to last through the day.

She handed the empty goblet back to Alys. 'Pour me some more. And make sure that there is mead ready for me at the end of the day, too.'

CHAPTER TWENTY-THREE
London, November 1441
BARNABAS

'Traitorous whore!' someone shouts and the crowd roars in agreement. A small wet cabbage flies through the air and hits the Duchess' back. Ordinarily I'd laugh at a sight like that, the high and mighty brought low, but with Alys trailing not far behind her I can't bring myself to feel any joy. There is only worry in my guts. Worry that Alys might get hit, or worse, the mob that is gathering fast may become violent and trample Alys in their eagerness to do the Duchess harm. I take no comfort from the few puny guards that surround the Duchess and Alys. It's more of an invitation than a serious message that the crowds should mind themselves.

I've been following the procession for a good while now, conscious that every moment I'm away from my rooms I'm increasingly in danger of Master al Qali returning and finding me gone. He has been away much these last few days since he's told me we're off to Paris. Arranging our passage, I suppose and so I've stayed well clear of the docks. No trips to bid Tom farewell. I dare not do that.

I watch the crowd continue to throw whatever they can find and listen to the shouted insults and comments. The Duchess looks terrible, her hair is straggly and her dress is stained worse than a drunken alewife's. Her pace has slowed since I first saw her and she winces occasionally when she steps with her right foot. I know it won't be long before she's limping, because these roads are rutted and full of stones that will carve out your foot. I have scars on my own feet to prove that.

I tell myself again that I should go back to the rooms. But I can't. I know there is nothing I could do to protect Alys should anyone get out of hand, but I can't help myself. I'm looking for a chance. Just a few moments alone, that's all I need.

The sun is way past its highest point when they finally allow the procession to stop so that the Duchess can rest a little and have something to eat. It's at a small church, just outside Cripplegate. I slip inside the back door of the church while the crowd surrounds the place, waiting for the Duchess to emerge again. The guard takes my coin without a second glance, unconcerned about my intentions. This is the kind of duty he would rather have ended abruptly, anyway, and seemingly those in charge of him wouldn't care if I do her harm either.

I watch Alys from the cover of the narrow doorway. She's kneeling at the Duchess' feet, bathing them with a cloth. The Duchess is drinking deep from a goblet and I can only hope it's something strong. She'll need it if she's to walk on her feet for the rest of the day.

Alys looks up and I'm certain she sees me, but she only looks back down at the Duchess' feet and continues to gently dry them with a cloth. I pull back into the entrance and wait, hoping that she'll find a way to come to me.

A few minutes later she appears by my side. I take in her rounded breasts peeking out of a rumpled dress and the russet hair that has nearly come loose from its braid and wish we had more time for a proper greeting.

'Bar—' she says and halts a minute. 'What are you doing here?' she finally adds in a whisper. She glances around wildly at the guard just outside the door and narrows her brow. 'Go. It's too dangerous for you to be here.'

I take her hand. 'How are you? No one's hit you with anything, have they? I couldn't make it to the Tower to see the beginning of your procession, but I was there soon after.'

'You've followed the procession?' Tears glittered in her eyes. 'Why? So you could gawk at a good woman brought low by wicked, unscrupulous men?'

'Good woman?' I can't help myself. I didn't think anyone could call the Duchess 'a good woman' and be sincere. Vain, ambitious, yes. But good? I shake my head.

Alys lifts her chin. 'She is good to me. If you knew her like I do you would see what a good heart she has really.'

I nod to her and make some reassuring noises. The last thing I want is to fight with Alys.

'I didn't come to gawk. I came because I was worried you might be harmed.'

Alys' face softens and I take up her hand to kiss it. I see she is wearing the bit of leather I gave her around her wrist. For some reason I am so pleased it makes me silly. I give her my lopsided grin.

'Ah, Alys, if only we could have more time alone. I'd give you something better to remember me than that bit of leather.' I squeeze her backside and she jumps and gives a small yelp.

'Stop it,' she says with whisper. 'Do you want to get caught?'

'It'd be worth it.' I lean in to kiss her.

She pulls away. 'How can you think of kissing at a time like this?' she says with a hiss.

I hang my head to look suitably repentant. 'I'm sorry. It's just that you're so tempting, there.'

She blushes, which makes her look even more comely and I can feel my reaction. I shift my thoughts to the real reason I'm here with her.

'I need to speak with you alone.' I take up her hand again. 'Can I meet with you tonight?'

'What? What is it you need to tell me?'

'I'm leaving soon. In a few days' time.'

'What?' Her face pales in the dim light.

I nod. 'We're heading off for Paris.'

'Paris?'

Eleanor calls Alys' name and she starts to pull away.

'Meet me tonight?'

She shakes her head. 'Tomorrow night. At Eye. At the manor. We'll be staying there. I'll meet you outside after nightfall.'

Before I can say anything she whisks away and I'm left standing there holding onto empty air and hoping that she will be there at the manor.

I follow the procession a little more, watching out for Alys until she catches sight of me and shakes her head and frowns. I know it's dangerous, the Duchess might recognize me and call out, but I can't make myself turn away until I see Alys frown at me again and there's fear in her eyes this time. It's then that I slip away and make my way back to my rooms.

I hardly have time to sit in my chair and arrange my books around me when Master al Qali returns, and his expression tells me he's not had a good day.

'Those ignorant fools,' he says in an angry voice. 'No matter who I tried to see to complete the travel arrangements, they were all gone. All of them. Off to watch that fool of a woman make her procession around the city.' He shakes his head. 'What do they gain by watching such a sight? What they find amusing is fit only for fools. I don't know what I expect from those of lesser rank.' He eyes me. 'Those with no ability whatsoever.'

'You mean the Duchess? Everyone was watching her perform her penance?' I try to pretend I knew nothing about what had happened that day.

Master al Qali nods. 'It would hardly have been an edifying sight and most certainly it would bring out the worst in people.'

'Oh, but this is something that hasn't ever happened before,' I tell him. I make myself forget about the worry I felt the whole day while I watched it. 'A Duchess accused of witchcraft and then made to walk barefoot around the city as penance, for everyone to see.'

'Yes, but do they not understand the message behind it? Do not dare to raise yourself above your rank—is that a message you in particular would like?'

'It's because she was a witch they tried her,' I say weakly.

Master al Qali raises a brow. 'That is your reasoning? Come now, I thought I taught you more than that.'

I know he's trying to get at me, but at the same time he still can't resist trying to make me, his protégé, think. 'Her husband. It was to get at her husband. He will be tainted by her conviction. But why Hume? And Father Thomas and the others?'

'Hume, he was just someone caught up in the rush to pull in those connected with the Duke. He has allies powerful enough so that he will be punished only in a minor way. The others did not and were key in discrediting the Duke. They were part of the Duke's intellectual circle and their interest reflected his own. You prove they are guilty of serious misdeeds and by inference he is guilty, too, without the disgrace and problem of bringing a royal Duke to trial.'

'But Mistress Jourdemayne? What of her? She had no direct connection with the Duke.'

'Ah, but she was such a key player in bringing the Duchess to trial. A tool. She was a female whose practices could easily be used to convict the Duchess of heresy and witchcraft at the very least. Your people fear what they do not understand. You, my friend, should know that.'

I thought about his words for a moment. 'So, would they still be looking for me? The Duchess is convicted and the Duke is discredited, why would they still be interested in me?'

'We don't know what Mistress Jourdemayne told them. Any hint of witchcraft beyond the person of Margery Jourdemayne might cause them unease. Something that lingers, rising up when they least desire it. What she was accused of was more than just a few herbs given to a woman wanting a child, or even a love spell. It was treason and heresy. We don't know if she or the Duchess mentioned you in any way. Or the purchase of the showstone. A remarkable showstone from a foreign place through which your talents revealed visions about the King. No, it is still a risk. A risk for both of us.'

I nod at his explanation. It is reasonable and part of me is relieved because I was looking forward to the journey to Paris and to Paris itself.

CHAPTER TWENTY-FOUR
The Manor At Eye, November 1441
ELEANOR

Eleanor's hair hung wet with mouldy vegetables and the contents of night waste pots. Any lustre that it might have had left had disappeared under all the refuse flung at her over the past two days. Residue dripped from her shoulders, down her back and her chest. The acrid smell of the dung and piss left her dress steaming in the late autumn air and burned her nose. She had tried to shut out the smell while she was walking by breathing through her mouth, but that proved a foolish action when the contents of another stew pot was thrown at her and it entered her mouth. She'd spat out the piss as much as she could, but the sour taste of it lingered on her tongue.

It was her second day of penance, and at this point she wasn't certain she'd be able to manage the rest. Her feet were sore with cuts and blisters from her walk on the rough tracks and paths that she'd been made to tread, and her back and knees were aching. The first evening, when she'd finished her trek and was led by Alys inside the stone chapel that was to provide her night's shelter, she collapsed as soon as she was inside the door. Alys had helped her up and led her to a small bench in the little sacristy and went off to find water to bathe her feet and clean up the rest of her.

And now she neared the manor of Eye, so close to where so much of the cause of her troubles had taken place. It was an irony not missed when she was told they would stop there for the night. Now, it made no difference to her, she just wanted to lie down.

Once inside the manor, there were servants to bring her hot water and linen cloths. They gawked and snickered at her appearance and visibly held their noses while they offered cloths to Alys and brought in a tray of simple bread and water. Bread and water, that was all she was allowed, and these people who hosted her were delighted to comply.

'Thank you, Alys,' she said when Alys bent down before her and placed her feet in the wooden bowl filled with water. Taking another bowl of water, she set to work on Eleanor's face, hands and hair, scrubbing away as best she could the filth that clung to them. It was a thankless task, but Alys did it without blinking.

'Oh, your feet, Your Grace,' Alys said when she took them from the bowl to dry in a cloth. 'If you don't get some salve on these tonight you will do serious damage to them.'

Tears pricked Eleanor's eyes and she forced them away. 'There is no need to call me "Your Grace". I'm not a duchess anymore.'

'You will always be so to me,' Alys said softly. 'You are my duchess. You've done so much for me.'

'And I won't forget how you've stood by me. You won't leave me, will you, Alys?'

'Of course not. I will remain with you as long as you need me.' Alys' eyes flickered but her smile was sincere.

Eleanor relaxed back on the bench and allowed Alys to continue her ministrations. When she'd completed them, Alys helped Eleanor into a fresh shift and then over to the cot that was in the corner of the small room. Alys' cot was on the opposite wall and contained only a straw pallet and a coarse blanket. The moon was out and cast strong light across Eleanor's cot through the window above it. The ill-fitting glass panes were pocked with bubbles, but they kept out most of the night air at least. Eleanor was certain she would sleep soundly in any case. She sighed and laid her head back against the rough linen.

Sometime in the night she awoke with a start and looked around. The moon's position had shifted higher in the sky and it illuminated the whole room. What had awoken her? She glanced over at Alys' bed and saw that it was empty. Panicked, she got up from the cot and paced around the room, as if she might uncover Alys from the bare boards beneath her. She tried the door. It was open. For some reason she couldn't bring herself to leave the relative safety of the room, until she was certain what it was that had woken her. Where had Alys gone?

She made her way over to the window and looked out. Below her was a small patch of grass in the area where the two gables of the house met. She could see a man and a woman there embracing. It was difficult to tell much through the mullioned and bubbled glass, so she eased open the window casement. The woman pulled away from the young man and Eleanor gasped. It was Alys. What was she doing with that young man?

'I only wish it was possible for you to come with me.'

'Even if it was possible I wouldn't come. I've told you that.'

'I will miss you, though. And I promise I'll return. When it's safe.'

Alys nodded. 'When it's safe.' She pulled out something from her bodice and gave it to him. 'Take this with you and remember me when you look at it.'

He took it from her. 'What is it?'

'It's a drawing I made. It's not very good, but it's the best I could do.'

'A drawing?'

'A likeness. Of you.'

'You drew a likeness of me?'

'Yes, I thought you'd like it.'

The man leaned over and kissed Alys hard on the lips. 'You are lovely, Alys.' He ran his hand along her bodice and started to tug at her bodice. Alys pulled away.

'No, none of that.'

'Aw, Alys. Please. Who knows how long it will be before we see each other? I might be killed, or you might die of the plague.'

'Don't say that,' Alys said in a fierce whisper. 'Don't tempt fate.'

'But there are sure to be others who'll come along to turn your head.'

Alys put her finger to his lips and shook her head. 'No. I will wait for you. I promise.'

Alys rose on her toes, put her arms around the man, hugged him tightly and allowed him to kiss her once again, this time, deeper and longer.

Eleanor pulled the casement shut, her mind awhirl with questions. She thought she knew all about Alys. What was this about? Who was that young man?

She was waiting for Alys when she returned, her mind a hum of accusations and questions. Was it so unreasonable to assume that Alys was chaste and completely dependent on Eleanor for help and guidance? She put the question to her the moment Alys walked in the door. Alys gave a little shriek of fright when she saw Eleanor standing there in the moonlight clad only in her white shift.

'I d—don't know what you mean, Your Grace.'

'Of course you do. I saw you just now, kissing and cuddling with that young man, making all sorts of promises that no young girl of virtue would.'

'But I didn't, Your Grace. I made no such promises.'

'He asked you to go away with him. You told me you would remain at my side.' Eleanor cringed at the whine in her voice but she couldn't help herself. Alys was her comfort. She relied on her.

'And so I shall, Your Grace. I told him no. I'm not going away.' She moved toward Eleanor and took her hand. 'I made a promise to you and I shall keep it.'

'But you want to stay with me, don't you, Alys? I can still teach you much.'

Alys gave her a wan smile. 'Of course I want to stay with you, no matter what you may or may not teach me. Haven't I told you that often?'

'Yes, but who was that man that he should make such a bold request of you?'

Alys bit her lip and looked down. 'My brother. It was my brother. He's off to sea, to the continent to try his fortunes there. He wanted me to come with him and look after him.'

Eleanor snorted. 'That was an awfully passionate kiss from a brother.'

'Well he isn't exactly my real brother, he's a step brother.'

Eleanor gave her a disbelieving look. 'Well, we'll do no more for now. It's late and I need my rest. Come to my cot for the night. It comforts me. I know I'll fall asleep quickly if you're beside me.'

'Of course, Your Grace. You can rely on me.'

Eleanor nodded and crawled into bed, satisfied. Though she knew the girl had lied about the relationship, Eleanor was certain now that Alys meant it when she said she wouldn't leave her. She allowed her mind to drift and form plans for the months to come. She would get through the next few days. She must. If only she knew where she was to go when the penance was complete.

CHAPTER TWENTY-FIVE
London, November 1441
BARNABAS

I watch the rows of figures on the dock pass me slowly. Men heaving crates onto carts, tying off heavy sisal ropes on thick iron rings. The river's stench is pungent and it fills my head and I love it. Shouts ring in the air and men scramble to unfurl and position sails. The water is alive with wherries, cogs, crayers, barges and even a few caravels. And I'm on one of them.

I can hardly believe it. It's a crayer that's carrying me down river and out to sea. Though it has only one mast and is slow as a rheumy old lady, it's a ship and I'm on it, headed to foreign parts. It's all I can do to stand quietly by Master al Qali's side and watch the seamen heave to when I really want to go down and coil the ropes, tie off the sails and help in a hundred and one other things I've watched them do through the years.

I catch sight of a familiar face on the deck and, on impulse, give him a great wave. Pietro. I'm surprised to see him working here on such a merchant vessel that is only crossing the channel.

'You know that man?' asks Master al Qali.

'He was with me at *The Turk's Head*,' I say and nearly clap my hand over my mouth after. I really don't want to remind him of that folly, but it slipped out before I knew it. 'He's a jolly sort. From Genoa.'

We're speaking Italian all the time now. Ever since we returned from the tavern those days past. Master al Qali says it's important that I think, dream and be Venetian. I am Venetian to all who meet me, now. The captain of this ship believes it, and his First Mate. They gave me a suspicious looks as I came on board, like any true Englishman, but they reserved all their curiosity for Master al Qali. They'd seen enough Venetians in their time, but a Blackamoor was something else again.

The captain comes up beside us. 'Can you tell your charge that once we are at sea it is best that you both go below? There will be a meal waiting for you in the cabin.'

'Of course,' says Master al Qali.

His English is doubly precise, just as he's been doubly clever in his story to the captain. My English is poor after my few months in London, much to Master al Qali's dismay, and I will be the despair of my merchant father who has sent me to London and now on to Paris to learn the languages as well as the cloth trade. Still, he has hopes for my success in France, since the language is not too different from my native Italian.

My eyes find the captain's and I give him a suitably blank look before he nods sourly and leaves us. Once his back is turned I grin widely, enjoying the charade. Nothing can stop my good humour. I turn my attention to the shoreline. We've passed Blackfriar's Stairs and Temple Bridge. Ahead, and closer to shore, I'm sure is

Tom's wherry and for a moment my eyes fill at the thought of leaving him. What larks we had together. Would I ever have such a truer friend than him? I think back on my life when I would take off to be with Tom. It seemed so long ago and so much had happened. I sniff away these thoughts. I'm best here now, heading to adventure.

Even now, I know they are dragging Bolingbroke to Tyburn gallows to be hung, drawn and quartered. If I was still here tomorrow I would see his head set on London Bridge and witness his four quarters being dispatched to Cambridge, Hereford, Bristol and York. That was the last word we had before we left the docks, catching the early morning tide. That and the fact that Eleanor Cobham, as she's known now, is headed to Chester Castle.

My thoughts turn to Alys. I pat the folded parchment of the drawing she gave me that's tucked inside my doublet and remember the sweet kiss we exchanged those few nights ago. It had been tricky going to see her there. I'd gone on foot and watched the Duchess make her penance with Alys trailing a little distance behind her. It had been hard to watch and not rush and grab Alys safely away, but I bided my time. When they arrived at the manor, I shoved myself forward, so she could see my face. Her eyes lit up and I knew she recognized me and would find her way to the grounds when she could. It was a long wait, but worth it. The kiss alone had been payment enough, though it was sad to make our parting.

I know Alys'll be there now, alongside the old duchess as they journey to Chester Castle. It is for the good, I tell myself. She'll be safe enough there, out of sight of those troublemakers in London who want to pull down everyone connected with Duke Humphrey. And Master al Qali would never have agreed to take Alys, I know deep down. I still can't believe how lucky I am that Master al Qali has been persuaded to take me. I resolve to study harder so that Master al Qali won't regret his decision. I'll ask him if I can begin studying Arabic and the other languages that Master al Qali knew, so that I can help him in his work.

'You are not homesick, are you?' Master al Qali asks. He's been watching me for the last few moments and I can only hope that I haven't shown too much of my thoughts.

I give him one of my old grins. 'Not a bit. How could I be? I'm on a ship, travelling to foreign parts. It's what I've always wanted and I have you to thank for it. I'll always be grateful to you.'

He smiles back at me and pats my arm. 'I'm glad to hear it. I am certain I have made the right decision in bringing you with me. You are a deeply talented boy, a precious jewel, a treasure, some might say.'

I feel a little embarrassed by his words. A treasure. I've never been called that before. A precious jewel. I turn my face away, not knowing what to say. Master al Qali has never flattered me like this before and I'm not certain how to take it. I know he cares for me. Hasn't he looked after my wellbeing so meticulously? He's never been angry at me, not really. The only time he's shown any kind of disapproval was when he caught me with the showstone in the sack. He'd called the showstone precious too.

'Did you own the showstone yourself before you sold it to Mistress Jourdemayne, or were you acting on someone else's behalf?' The words had been in my mind only seconds before they popped from my mouth.

I give Master al Qali a nervous glance. Would he be annoyed for bringing up the showstone? But his face is calm as ever and his eyes hold a trace of amusement.

'No one owns the showstone, Giacomo,' he says. 'Its powers are beyond ownership. But you will learn that in good time.'

My surprise is written on my face, I know. 'How will I learn that? I thought you got rid of the showstone.'

'Got rid of the showstone? No, I never did that. I merely put it in safekeeping.'

'But I thought we were done with the showstone. Why would we need it anymore? We won't need it for translation work.'

'You are correct that it isn't necessary for translation work. But its worth is too great to set aside completely. There may come a time when we will find that it is the key to our future.'

'Master al Qali, I beg you, please don't make me use the showstone again. It's not right. I can feel it. There's something evil in it, I know it.'

Master al Qali puts a hand on my shoulder. 'Calm yourself. You are just anxious after your experience these past few months. That was not the doing of the showstone, but the inept people involved. There is time enough to recover from this feeling. There is much to do before we even turn our thoughts back to the showstone.'

I nod and try to take comfort from his words. Turn my thoughts to the sea crossing. The tang of salt in the air has grown stronger and it settles on my tongue. It's a taste I love and I lift my face up to catch more of the breeze that's blowing stronger now. It's a breeze that will become a wind and that wind will take me to France and a new life.

HISTORICAL NOTE

This novel is based on actual events in English history. Margery Jourdemayne, 'the witch of Eye next Westminster', Eleanor, Duchess of Gloucester, Thomas Southwell, Roger Bolingbroke and John Home (Hume) were all accused of witchcraft in 1441. The Duchess of Gloucester's trial was one of the most sensational events of the mid-fifteenth century. Not only did Eleanor move in the highest circles of the realm, she was married to King Henry VI heir and uncle, Humphrey Duke of Gloucester. The events of the novel including the trial, Humphrey's previous marriage and Eleanor's history are all based on the historic accounts of the time.

Eleanor's trial and conviction were more reflections of the politics of the time then any determined effort to get rid of a witch. Beaufort and his faction wanted Humphrey of Gloucester disgraced and powerless, something they ultimately accomplished. It was also a ground breaking event in that the wife of a royal noble was put on trial. In some ways you could say this paved the way for Henry VIII to put his wives on trial some eighty years later.

On my behalf and Moon's I would also like to take the time to thank the efforts of our writing group for their tireless support and readings of drafts of this novel, especially both Karens, Jane and Claire and also Jessica Knauss for her wonderful editing and Jane Dixon Smith for the terrific cover.

ABOUT THE AUTHOR

Originally from Philadelphia, Kristin Gleeson lives in Ireland, in the West Cork Gaeltacht, where she teaches art classes, plays harp, sings in a choir and runs two book clubs for the village library. She holds a Masters in Library Science and a Ph.D. in history and for a time was an administrator of a national denominational archives, library and museum in America. She also served as a public librarian in America and in Ireland.

Kristin Gleeson has also published a literary novel, *Selkie Dreams*, *Along the Far Shores*, and *Raven Brought the Light*, all of which are part the Celtic Knot Series and are available through Amazon. She has also published a commercial biography on a First Nations Canadian woman, *Anahareo, A Wilderness Spirit*, published with Fireship Press and available on Amazon.

Moonyeen Blakey, a native of Cleethorpes, Lincolnshire, was an English and drama teacher who wrote and produced plays for the community theatre. In 2012 she published *The Assassin's Wife* with Fireship Press. She passed away in 2013.

This novel was a collaboration between the two and it will live on in this series about Barnabas, 'The Renaissance Sojourner Series'.

If you have enjoyed this book please post a review on Amazon. It helps so much towards getting the book noticed.

If you go to the author website and join the mailing list to receive news of forthcoming releases, special offers and events you'll receive a FREE prequel novella to *Along the Far Shores.*

www.kristingleeson.com.

Look out for the next novel in the series coming early 2016.